DEATH SCENT

S.V. WOLF

DEATH SCENT

S. V. WOLF

Prologue

Grandmother Spirit hummed a tune low in her throat while rubbing the Shepherd puppy's belly. Titan was spread out in her lap on his back, basking in the sleepy feel of her hand. "Amazing," she murmured with a soft hum. "Amazing that you are so big, amazing what you're born to do!"

Nine week old Titan jumped from Grandmother Spirit's lap, and darted toward the sound of the doorbell. The door opened slowly, a tan face with fair green eyes appearing in the crack. "Shawnee, my dear, how are you?" Grandmother Spirit pulled the door open wider, allowing the petite young woman to step into the living room. Titan watched the strange woman move through the door like the wind was at her bidding.

"Is this him?" Shawnee asked her grandmother.

Beaming, Grandmother Spirit scooped Titan up with wrinkled hands; his big belly sloshed from side to side as oversized paws flopped wildly in the air. She cradled him like an infant. "Yes," she said with confidence, "he is the one. There's no doubt." The leathered old woman smiled. "He has the mark of Weshimaneto, look." She was referring to the Great Mystery. Opening Titan's small mouth with the tip of one bony finger, she pressed down lightly on his tongue. Shawnee looked to the back of the little red muscle where the mark was revealed; a black ink-like birthmark in the crude shape of a cross, just like her own.

DEATH SCENT

Dance with what life has to hand you, and you will always walk your intended path.

1

"My feet are pawed, and my coat is thick. Muscles sway as my claws churn the surface of the Earth and swallow lengths of ground with my stone limbs. My eyes see glimmer of shadow that should not be, and my ears catch sounds that have been and gone. My nose, an instrument of perfection, seeks those who have been hidden away and those who have been forgotten. On the backside of an angel's wings comes the sweet smell of death, undesired by others but welcomed by those special ones who serve. This is my destiny, this trail I follow; this path to the lost, this Death Scent that I seek. I am Titan, and I am a Makujay Death Dog!"

Two days after Christmas, a police car pulled into the driveway of Titan's rural home. The Police Chief reached a burly leg out the driver side door, and pulled his thick sturdy frame upright. Two year old Titan watched through the window as the man adjusted the straw cowboy hat on his wide head, and then hitched his pants up over one hip. His name was Norm Wiley. Titan knew the Police Chief would have a dog biscuit in his left front pants pocket, like he always did when visiting. That, however, was only going to get the man so far; after all, he was not pack.

Moments later, the expected knock sounded, and Titan pulled the rope tied to the door knob, swinging the front door open. He stretched a slow-moving head out towards the Police Chief's left knee, a growl rolling out a warning from deep within his chest.

Norm expelled lungs full of air. "Are we gonna have to go through this every time, Titan?" the Police Chief asked with a long southern drawl, eying Titan dutifully. "I know you could remove my knee from my leg faster than I could turn to run off this porch, but we both know you only want one thing."

Norm stood still as Titan pulled his tight body onto the porch, circling the Chief's legs, sniffing his pants pockets. He stopped suddenly and barked. Norm reached slowly into his left pocket, and extracted the price of admission. Titan grabbed it quickly, running back into the house through the open door. Norm let out a busty laugh as he removed his hat and stepped substantial legs through the doorway, ducking as he went, pulling the door shut behind him.

Hearing the commotion, Shawnee entered the living room from the kitchen. "Norm, welcome, what brings you over?" She set down the towel she was drying her hands with, and hugged Norm warmly.

"You know Patrice, right?" the Chief inquired, getting right to the point.

"Yea," she replied. "She sings over at the nursing home on the weekends." The town she and Titan lived in was rural and so small that last names were not often needed.

"Patrice is missing," the Police Chief said flatly.

"Tell me what you know," she implored as she got situated in a living room chair. She motioned for Norm to have a seat.

Norm shifted and squeezed himself uncomfortably into a plush but average width recliner. "She and her husband Jeran have been separated for some months now," he began. "Well, according to Patrice's Aunt Jenny, Patrice was going to tell Jeran on Christmas night that she wanted a divorce. I asked Jenny why she would choose that night to tell him such a thing. Jenny said 'cause they'd been living apart and never saw each other 'cept to pass the kids back and forth. But they would be together sharing the kids that particular night. Patrice told Jenny that she didn't want to tell him over the phone, but she wanted it over with."

Titan listened intently as the Chief went on to explain. "Jeran admits he was the last person to probably see her that night; says they were arguing, and in the middle of it all he decided to take the two kids off to a relative's house for the duration. He says he went back to Patrice's afterwards, in time to see her driving off in her SUV. Says that's the last time he'd seen her."

Shawnee posed a question, "Jenny has not heard from her since?"

"No, 'fraid not," he sighed with weariness. "Jenny doesn't have a good feeling 'bout this, and neither do I."

Titan felt the swell of suspicion ooze from the Police Chief's tone. The Chief raked sausage-like fingers through his tight red curls. "Jenny says yesterday morning she called Jeran at his place to see if he had seen Patrice, and he told her what I just told you. I went over there yesterday afternoon, and got the same story from him. Jenny filed a missing' person's report, so I took an official statement from the both of 'em."

"What is it that you think Titan can do, you don't have much to go on?"

Norm dropped his chin ever so slightly.

"Is there something you are not telling me?"

"Yea," he blew through gritted teeth, "we just found her SUV parked on the side of the road about twenty miles from here. She ain't in it, Shawnee," his eyes met hers, "and…the driver seat is pulled way too far back for her to have drove it. From what I can tell, there is blood on the carpet behind the passenger seat. I just came from there; I haven't even let the evidence techs process it yet. I want you to take Titan out there first, let him see if he can pick anything up from the SUV that will help him search that area out there… see if he can maybe find her. There's a large wooded area within carrying distance from the vehicle." The Police Chief cast a facial expression toward Titan that all but conveyed his thoughts. He reached a meaty hand to the short black-and-tan fur on the dog's forehead, and rested it there gently. Solemnly he said, "I want him to smell the age of the blood there in the vehicle, and see if he can find the likes of it elsewhere."

When they arrived, Shawnee could see the evidence technician airing up a flat tire on the back of the burgundy SUV. "Find it that way?" she called, as she strode average length legs up next to the man bent over the tire. Her shoulder length black hair swayed slightly in the breeze, its particularly straight nature giving away her lineage. She revealed even white teeth in a sincere smile, looking down on the man at work.

"Oh hey, Shawnee," the man said, looking up with a tobacco stained grin. "Yea, it doesn't appear to be flat a'tall, actually. In fact, the valve cap is missing, and none of the others are, might'a been let out purpose like."

Titan padded up next to her; he was trained to protect her, so he was free to be where he wished. The small-structured man suddenly caught sight of him out the corner of his eye, and yipped in fear.

Like I would ever have need of worrying about you, Titan mused to himself.

"He's not going to eat you, Melvin," Shawnee chided for what seemed the 100th time since she had met the man two years earlier.

Really Melvin, get a grip.

"Don't matter how many times you tell me that, Shawnee, having that dog unhandled 'round me is no comfort."

"I'll leave you to it then, Melvin," she said, twisting her face in mock of his paranoia. Melvin returned the friendly mock with a chiding facial expression of his own. Titan played along, trying in vain to twist his lips, but only succeeded in producing a snarl that caused Melvin to inhale a ragged breath.

Oh good heavens, Titan expelled in thought as he turned away. *Next thing you know, he will be peeing on himself.*

The Police Chief opened the back passenger door, the congealed odor of two day old blood swarming out the portal and into Titan's nostrils. He threaded the few paces to the open door, reached his head in the opening, and placed his nose delicately over the dark stain. Closing his eyes, he processed the information that fed his nose through his keenly developed brain. *Female, still alive when she bled; not for long, though...*

"What is it, Titan?" he heard his mistress ask. Regaining his normal senses, he turned to face her, dropping firmly to the ground on his stomach. This was his trained alert, the behavior that told her he had found the smell of human remains or the human fluids that once sustained life.

Without taking her eyes off Titan, she said, "I don't need to explain that to you, do I Norm?"

"No," he said with malice not meant for Titan. "I have seen him do it enough times. It's just what I suspected, unfortunately."

Titan, losing his patience with the chatting pair, barked in discontent at waiting for his reward. This was his work, and he expected to get paid!

"Sorry big guy," Shawnee blew. She threw him his blue rubber ball; he caught it clenching long white fangs around its orb, and then trotted off to be by himself.

"The carpet inside the vehicle is wet, seats are damp too," Melvin offered, peering around the Police Chief's back, making sure Titan was well away. "Almost looks like someone pulled it into one of those open stall car washes and let'er have it, inside and out."

"You think it's Jeran, don't you?" Shawnee implied, looking directly at the Police Chief.

His brimmed head was bent in thought, and he didn't lift it to answer. "Innocent until proven guilty, but informally that would be my guess. Statistics would certainly support it being the husband in a case like this, but let's see what the evidence will say, shall we? Melvin!" he yelled.

"I'm right here," Melvin voiced in annoyance.

"Well, get from behind me, man, what's your problem anyway?"

He's a wuss, that's what his problem is, Titan projected to no one but himself. He had found a mound of winter puff dragons to lounge in, and was trying to enjoy being alone with his reward.

Seeing Melvin's despair, Shawnee snickered behind the back of her hand, trying not to let him see her.

"Get this vehicle outta here and get it processed ASAP! I want no delays, you hear me?"

"Yes sir, yes sir," Melvin acknowledged with a bobbing head. Still eying the dog, he made no attempt to move.

The Chief swung back around. "Get yer hands out yer pockets and Get going Melvin!"

Melvin's eyes flew wide, and he nearly fell over himself scrambling to get to his tow truck.

"You know, Norm," Shawnee grinned, "your southern gets worse when you're mad."

"Yea, well, folks should not provoke me." His fury shaped features turned to worry. "Let's you and me talk about a search pattern here."

They walked with purpose towards the wooded expanse. Shawnee pondered at how huge the coat was that the man wore to cover his massive form. He wasn't overweight really, just a big, big, man. Even her father could not compare to this man's mass. She had known Norm ever since she was relocated here by the tribal elders in support of law enforcement in the region. The ability to work with these specialized dogs is a craft that her family had been born into for centuries past; the Spirit family had been chosen and committed to this work from birth. Part of that commitment entailed breeding a special line of Shepherds and recognizing the dogs born to various special causes. Shawnee's grandmother's talent was manifest in that particular skill, while Shawnee's was to guide, handle, and communicate to the marked ones. Along with this distinguished calling, the clan of the Makujay Shawnee (of which the Spirit family is part) were all dedicated to certain talents and skills. Along with that service came private and personal funding that allowed them to devote all their time to these causes.

Norm broke into her thoughts. "It's about five acres of wooded property," he explained.

She smiled. "No problem, it's a cool day," she voiced.

In south central Texas, December temperatures are mild, like fall to people in the north. Reaching down, she gripped the portion of ball protruding from Titan's mouth with her fingertips. He tried to suck it behind his teeth, but alas she had been faster than him. Having no prize to occupy his time, he sauntered off toward the trees. *No problem, she says; it's a cool day, she says.... maybe I should follow her around the woods and see what that gets us.*

With its coolness, the air retained a certain amount of moisture, which mingled with the dead foliage and the fungus in the soil. It rousted Titan's nasal passages as he entered the uneven grounds of the woods. He could smell the algae off the pond nearby and the odor of the ducks that had migrated from much colder climates. He marched with purpose through the brush, not giving care to how much he disturbed the compost, as he needed the odors to shift, giving him the ability to decipher the elements around him. He didn't need Shawnee to direct his path, he knew how to pattern the search parameter in order to cover it efficiently. He had spent the last two years training and working to learn things just like that. He was good at his job. The Great Mystery – his father – often told him so. Titan reached his nose upward to catch the scents on the air. He was an air-scenter after all, not a ground trailer like the dogs that look for live humans. The death odors he used came to him in puffs and whiffs of particles on the wind or from within disturbed matter.

In less than an hour, he had nearly covered two of the five acres. Trotting along, he felt a familiar stirring at his chin; the tiny little winged creature the Great Mystery sometimes sent to warn him of danger – or as when he was a puppy, to keep him out of mischief. He flicked his head, pushing the little being gently away from him. *I think I can smell what is out here*, he puffed out mentally at the Seraph. The Seraph needed no mind link to communicate; it could understand Titan's thoughts. He resumed his endeavor as Shawnee took up her usual place behind him.

He stepped steadfastly over a medium size tree that had fallen from a summer lightning strike. "Chhhhhhhh…," he froze. How had he missed it, he scolded himself.

"I got it, Titan, don't move."

I wasn't planning on it, he scoffed to himself.

"Chief," she called behind her.

"Yea," he yelled as he ran to move up beside her; scattering leaves, limbs and one tiny unseen Seraph.

"We….," Shawnee stopped at the repeated reverberation.

"Chhhhhhhh."

"You want me to get it or you?" she asked him.

"You got snake shot in that .38, right?" pointing at the weapon strapped to her right thigh.

"Yea, but Titan is too close to it," she offered with a grimace.

Whisking his radio from its holder, he called to his deputy stationed near the crime scene. "Riley, come in."…squelch…

"Riley here, Chief."

"Riley, get that shovel outta the back of my pickup, and bring it down here."…squelch….

"The Techs are still processing the grounds up here, Chief. You want me to leave them to it?" Riley asked with trepidation.

"Aw hells bells," the Police Chief mumbled to himself. "I need him to keep the looky-lous away, Shawnee," he explained, "I gotta go get it myself." She watched as he jogged his bear-like shape out of the woods.

It took no more than ten minutes for the Police Chief to get there and back, but Titan felt like it was forever. *About blasted time, he complained to himself. My back muscles are burning from being frozen in this spot*!

"What's he whining about?" the Police Chief puffed out, pulling up abruptly from a brisk jaunt.

"I think he is complaining, if I had to guess," she answered.

"Well, I got here fast as an old man can. Whew," he said, letting out a long breath. "OK, let's see where Mr. Rattler is hiding." He moved around the other side of the decomposing tree trunk. "There ya' are," he exclaimed. "Come to daddy." Reaching the shovel out at length, he poked the coiled Rattle Snake. In response, the irritated reptile struck out at the shovel head, eerily grating projected fangs across the metal of the blade. The snake promptly coiled back into position, refusing to leave the rare spot of sunshine it had found.

"OK, Titan," the Police Chief advised. "When I hit this rattler again, you move out quick, you hear me, I mean quick!"

Titan rolled one unfrozen eye toward the man.

Straightening, he rebuked, "Why am I talking to a dog?"

"He understands you," Shawnee voiced with a nod toward Titan.

"Yea," the Chief laughed, "if any dog could it would be him alright. OK Titan, ready?"

Titan whined.

"Here we go." The Chief extended the shovel to its full length with force, giving the snake no other option than to abandon Titan completely and go on full defense against the invading tool. The reptile struck out, and Titan fled as fast as taut burning muscles would allow. Disaster avoided and nature intact, the Chief and Shawnee sighed in relief. Titan kept running.

2

Slowing after a short burst of speed, Titan caught his breath. After only a few moments, he was back to normal and resuming his search. Treading one great paw after another, he dipped his wet nose to the currents of wind stirring in the deeper center of the forest. The damp underbrush attempted to conceal some of the associated smells, yet he collected and analyzed each odor that drifted to his nose as he padded along. Dipping his head through an opening in a section of thick shrubbery, he tested the lingering odors. Although he caught no trace of human remains, he felt the familiar sense of foreboding that often accompanied the nearness of a murder victim who had so recently met their demise.

Shimmying through the tight opening, he ceased to move when he felt the tremor of shadow approaching. Eerily, he felt the trickle of the presence of the dead and the essence of evil. Tuning out the birds still singing and the squirrels that chattered overhead, he concentrated like his father had taught him in his dreams since he was little. Moist microbial specks of blood glided ever so softly to make contact with the fine sensors within the tissues of his olfactory system. Titan processed the information in his mind: *Very, very faint… but I know it is human blood* …He thought about the vision he experienced in his dreams the night before, where a dark noiseless flash had exploded around him and he was suddenly surrounded by subtle hues of soft gray wispy light. It crept around him like a fog that might consume him if he did not maintain control of where he really was… What world he walked in at that time he wasn't sure, but he knew even in his dream that he would have to remind himself to breathe.

He lay still among the shrubbery while he immersed himself in the memory of the dream, losing all sense of space and time. He watched as the milky image of a man in his early 40's dragged the still and near dead body of a woman through the winter cactus, thick oaks and thinly populated ash trees. He recognized the pretty face; he had not known her name, but he had seen her several times before, and she had always been nice to him. Titan watched as the images drifted in and out of clarity and then crystallized to a picture as clear as life. In his dream, he was there with them, but a bystander only, observing what was taking place. It was rare that such visions came to him, for the Great Mystery to help him in such a way had to mean the woman was destined for a special purpose, which had been abruptly cut short.

Titan's ears popped as the pressure in the cloudy sphere of his dream adjusted. He heard the woman moan softly, her head bobbing across the compost of the forest floor as her husband gripped tightly to her ankles, pulling her body with a fury born of pure rage. He had already lost her shoes somewhere between the SUV and the woods; now he was angry that he would have to take the time to locate them. He cursed her for causing him so many complications. "Had you just listened to me, Patrice," he bolstered with a venomous sneer, "I would have given you the chance to come back to me!"

Patrice moaned again, but her eyes never opened, Titan observed; she was almost gone even then. Patrice's husband exerted himself in one last effort, pulling her body close to a grave that was obviously dug many months before. Grass had claimed the bottom of it, even though it was now brown and dry from the off-and-on cold snaps. It appeared to the untrained eye as no more than a large natural expulsion of earth, possibly the result of flood waters at some point in time; known to occur in this area. "Bitch, you should have listened to me," Patrice's husband announced. With a kick, he shoved Patrice's still living body into the prepared grave, and then spat on her.

Patrice rolled unevenly into the bottom. Her face lolled upward toward the canopy of trees above. Titan moved in closer, standing nearly at the edge of the grave to be. He could see the smeared blood on the left side of her face and how it matted thickly in her long brown hair, clotting wetly against her scalp. Titan growled low in his throat. He knew there was nothing he could do to change the course of events, what he was witnessing in his dream had already happened; what was, was. It was his job now to recover the victim and any evidence that remained; that was what his father had born him to do, that was his destiny.

Static electricity rolled across Titan's spine as he came back to the present, leaving the memory of the dream behind him. The hair on his back stood on end, he shivered.

"Titan, you OK?"

His mistress was beside him, her hand pressed gently across his broad shoulders. He whined, then promptly pushed himself up on wobbly legs and proceeded on his journey to locate where Patrice had been abandoned.

Even though he had seen the image of her burial in the vision, he still had to locate exactly where it was. He lifted his nose skyward once again, and invested his brain in assimilating the various smells. Turning left then right, he stopped… The wind drifted delicately past his face, rustling his cheek whiskers and telling him a story of deceit and death. He took off at a steady pace with his mistress running alongside and the big Sheriff dropping heavy boots close behind.

Titan stopped suddenly, and studied the earth before him. *She is close, very close.* He took one step, and stood solid as if met headlong by a blustering northern gust. He breathed in deeply…. *she is here,* he judged. Descending his head to the forest floor, he again breathed in the wet soft soil. Weathered but freshly broken tree limbs were in disarray before him; leaves were strategically heaped, but there was no hiding it from Titan. Freshly disturbed dirt lay beneath it all, and the smell of human decomposition lay below that. Titan dragged dark black claws ever so slightly across the surface to release more of the pungent smell; *yes, she is here, there is no question.* He dropped to his belly and barked at his mistress; promptly, she threw him his blue rubber ball, and he caught it before it could bounce off a nearby tree and flitter away. Contentedly, he rolled it in his mouth, enjoying the luxury of sinking his teeth into the soft thick substance. He lay down beneath a scrub oak to chew to his delight and to wait for the work of others to begin.

Back at the police station, Melvin jumped with a start as the radio on his hip blared. "Melvin, get all them evidence boys back over here but fast! I want this whole area cleared and processed ASAP, hear me!" ....squelch.

"Yes Sir, Chief Wiley, loud-n-clear!"

Hitting the radio microphone button again, the Chief yelled, "Riley!"

"Yes Sir, Chief, Riley here."

"You stay up there, but send them Techs down here, and I don't care if they say they are finished up there or not." ....squelch.

"Yes Sir, Chief!" ....squelch.

The excavation began its usual way. Flags were placed around the area to cordon off the parameter to be searched, and the evidence teams began the slow process of removing layer after layer of dirt from where Titan had alerted. As three technicians removed the dirt, two others dumped the full buckets into wheel barrows where screeners waited to shift the soil back and forth on wood frames covered with wire.

Every once in a while, Shawnee would ask Titan to come back and check the hole being unearthed, and each time Titan confirmed the location was accurate. Beginning to bore of the process, he wandered off from the malady and sought out quieter refuge to take a nap. He had almost finished circling a spot in the winter sun with his usual three turns when he felt a warm and friendly hand upon his head. He looked up to see the wavering image of Patrice in a silhouette of delicate green. Patrice looked down upon him with eyes graced in adoration and a smile that all but voiced a thank you. Titan whined in recognition. Her thin image vanished as quickly as she had appeared. He often had to help the spirits make their journey, and rarely were they able to appear in recognizable form. Strangely, Patrice seemed to know her way; she was already walking the wind.

Deciding to forgo the nap, Titan returned in time to watch as Shawnee assisted with the excavation. Patrice's body lay lifeless except for the boldness of the purple sweater that spoke of bright days and pleasant recount. She seemed untouched in death. Even though Titan's senses could detect it, there was little evidence of corruption of her once living tissues. The cold earth had kept her remains well intact. Shawnee helped the Sergeant in charge of the Evidence Team pull a white sheet beneath the still body; all those holding the corners pulled in unison until the lifeless Patrice was released from her undignified tomb.

"What's that?" the Police Chief asked, pointing fiercely at Patrice's furled hand.

The Sergeant leaned down with gloved hands. Uncurling Patrice's tightly cupped fingers he retrieved a rectangular piece of shiny plastic with two prongs sticking out of the backside. "Jeran," the Sergeant read aloud.

"Go get him," the Police Chief shouted to whoever was there to obey his command.

Several uniformed officers having been abruptly roused from their comfortable posts holding up nearby trees, made haste to get out of the woods and to their waiting squad cars. The sirens began wailing immediately. "I ain't waiting for confirmation of her DNA," Norm growled at those left behind. "I'm getting him locked up before he heads for Mexico."

Later that day at the police station. Holding up the plastic bag containing the name plate, Chief Wiley asked, "Missing something from your work shirt?"

Handcuffed and sitting uncomfortably in a bare metal chair scooted under a low table, Jeran Lonney sneered at Chief Wiley without making eye contact.

"See Jeran, I kinda think you had yourself a little digging party up in the woods there near Kayle Pond. You know where that is, don't-cha, Jeran? That's where you left Patrice's vehicle and let the air outta the tire, so it would look like she had a flat and just walked off." Jeran pursed his lips but said nothing. The door to the interrogation room swung open, and a baleful eyed young officer poked his head in. "Chief Wiley, Sir, we got the labs back from them boys at the FBI. They was needing to run some tests for a study, so they agreed to make our samples their personal project. Don't hurt that them boys at the FBI in San Antonio don't like wife murdering husbands," the youth turned his grin toward Jeran.

"Hear that, Jeran," the Chief said with a fake look of amazement on his features. "We got us some lab tests back, that was quick I'd say seeing how we just sent them over. See them boys in San Antonio; they got a whole bunch of new equipment so they don't have to send their stuff off no more. You know who else has contacts over there, Jeran? No? Why, the dog handler that worked this case. Kinda helps when you're needing things done in a real hurry."

Jeran made no attempt to answer, only looked up and glared at the Police Chief.

"Speaking of which, have you ever met the dog who located your lovely wife's body today?"

Jeran's eyes opened wide in the knowledge that Patrice had indeed been found. He pressed his lips tighter together in defiance.

"Oh, so we have your attention now, do we?" the Chief smirked.

"I don't know nothing 'bout no body, Chief Wiley," Jeran blurted, "I told you I ain't seen Patrice sense she drove off Christmas."

"He speaks," the Chief scoffed.

The officer still in the doorway opened his mouth to respond, but a shout from the hallway pulled him up short. His legs quickly disappeared out from under him as Titan burst through the doorway and into the interrogation room. As quick as he had turned the corner, he had Jeran on his back with bent legs in the air, his frame still fixed in the chair.

With cuffed hands pinned in his lap, Jeran screamed, "Get this beast offa me!"

"Uh Jeran," the Chief introduced, "this here is Titan. Say hello to Titan, Jeran, he's just making friendly, he's kind of a mascot round here; makes folks feel welcome and all."

Titan pulled back the flesh from around his teeth, showing Jeran how long his white fangs were; spittle dribbled onto Jeran's chin. As if to make his point, Titan further pressed big front paws into Jeran's chest, curling his claws into his skin.

"I think he likes you, Jeran," the Chief laughed. "If not, you know, I think you could be in a bit of trouble there."

"Titan," Shawnee breathed in a whisper, entering the room at last. "Titan, let Norm do his job now, let him go boy." Titan felt the tension ease from his limbs, something in the gentleness of his mistress's voice was always able to do that. He growled hotly as he backed slowly away from the sprawled man. Stopping, he sniffed. Then he smiled inside, *and I always thought that Melvin would be the first one to do that.*

Jeran tried desperately to cover the wet spot in the crotch of his pants with his cuffed hands, but it was too late; laughter broke out loudly in the room.

Two months later, sitting at her kitchen table, Shawnee read the paper aloud while drinking a cup of Vanilla Biscotti coffee. "Prosecuted in record time, husband convicted in Wife's murder – small town east of San Antonio." She scratched the little groove behind Titan's ear that he enjoyed so much. "Evidence Technicians dutifully sprayed the carpet with luminal, and discovered Patrice's blood behind the front passenger seat. DNA beneath the victim's fingernails was confirmed as the husband's. Concurrent work accomplished at the residence also discovered smeared blood along the bedroom wall and the bloody impression of the husband's right thumb print on the door knob...a local K-9 hero discovered the body....that's you they are talking about, you know," she said while smiling down at him. Titan looked up and whined. Resuming, she read, "It took the jury only 2 hours to reach the verdict; guilty of second degree murder."

3

The Rain came down in rivulets so thick it further mottled the already hampered visibility on the dark rural road. Corin Wester eyed the taillights of the Toyota Corolla in front of him, keeping his distance but staying close enough to keep the girl driving the car in his sights. He suspected the pretty young brunette was having a hard time judging the roadway in this down-pour; after all, she was creeping along at no more than forty mph. Suddenly, the car's brake lights lit up; it was the moment he had been waiting for. He did nothing to avoid the collision; after all, the front of his Ford F150 was reinforced with a heavy steel grate for just such occasions. He gunned it, and was rewarded when the red trunk lid flew up as his truck's front grate impacted the car's rear fender. He eyed his rear-view mirror, no one was behind him; the road was miles from anything or anyone. Immediately, he pushed the button for the emergency lights. He had to act fast just in case some lost city-goer came along and stopped to help. He felt inside his center console for his Taser.

Tap-tap-tap. Elisa jumped in her seat at the wrap on her driver's side window. The exploding air bag had rattled her nerves and bruised her face. Rubbing the fog from the inside of the window, she eyed a man with mopish hair hunched over in the cold rain. She eased down the window a couple of inches, the rain pouring down the interior of the car door. Despite the scare she had just endured, she could not help noticing the rain soaked shirt he wore clung tightly to his upper torso, revealing a body builder's stature.

"You alright?" the wet guy asked.

"Yea, I think so. I took a beating from this dang airbag, that's all. A dog or something ran right out in front of me, so I had to hit the brakes fast."

"I understand," said the man. "You know your back bumper is bent up against your tire, you're not going to be able to drive this thing anywhere. Why don't you pull completely off the road and come take a look?"

"Yea, OK, just let me call my mom first."

"You really should move off the road first. Your flashers don't appear to be working, and it could be dangerous just sitting here like this."

"I don't really know where the flashers are," admitted Elisa.

"That's OK, pull off the road and I can show you."

Elisa put the car back in drive and pressed the gas pedal gently. The car felt a little awkward, but nothing seemed to impede the wheels. She wondered if she might be able to drive it, after all.

"Come on out, and let me show you the damage," the wet guy insisted.

"Uh, I really think I can drive it," Elisa implored – half scared of driving and half scared of the muscled up wet guy. He wasn't that much older than her, she surmised, and seemed harmless enough, but still she was wary.

"Is this your car?"

"No," Elisa offered "it's my mom's."

"Well, believe me, you don't want to damage your mom's car any more than it is already," insisted the man, rain running down his cheeks. He looked pitiful standing there in the downpour, his hands stuffed deep in his jean pockets for warmth.

"Come on out to the back of the car, and let me show you the damage, then you can decide."

Elisa hesitated, not just because of the stranger but also because she didn't want to get soaked. But she unlocked and opened the door anyway, thinking the whole time her mom was going to kill her. Leaving her jacket, she ran to the back of the car, the cold rain pelting her bare arms like pea sized hale.

"See that," the wet guy pointed.

Elisa leaned down to look closer at the left rear tire in the near darkness. The man leaned down too; but what was in his hand she wondered? She felt a sudden shock burst through the back of her skull and into her body – like, she thought, if lightning had struck her. She fell to the ground, utterly paralyzed. The wet guy easily lifted her, and slid her face first across a cloth seat…of her own car? No, not mine, she considered in a daze. It smells of an overabundance of pine-tree air freshener and men's cologne. Brutally, she felt another jolt at the base of her head, and darkness consumed her.

Elisa opened hazy eyes and blinked. The light was too bright, it hurt her pupils. She turned her head. Sitting in a recliner, watching the animated show Family Guy and laughing, was the body builder who rear-ended her car, now dry and groomed. He was handsome enough, she thought oddly, clean shaven with a tan complexion. She moved her eyes around the room, where she was surrounded by bare concrete walls. It looked like a basement, she concluded. She tried to move, but her hands were bound – and so were her feet, she soon discovered. She tried to sit up, but had been tied down to the metal table she was lying on. It was cold against her back, and she was still soaked from the rain storm.

"Ah, so you are awake, how nice." His tone was even, strong yet serene.

She attempted to scream at him, but found her voice muffled and her lips unable to form words; her mouth was covered with some kind of tape. Her head cleared as she struggled at her bindings... She was in a car crash, the man insisted she look at the damage, he pressed something against her head, and then lightning struck her. No, it wasn't lightning, it was a Taser! She started cussing the stranger even though she was gagged.

"Now, now," he said as if correcting a naughty child. "You don't want to hurt yourself; just lie still, and everything will be just fine." He reached over her to a counter on the other side of the gurney she was strapped to. She flinched as his torso rubbed across hers.

"Now then," he smiled with nearly perfect teeth, "let's begin." The stranger pressed a button on the piece of handheld equipment he had retrieved. It began to buzz right away.

Elisa pressed herself into the gurney, what was he going to do with that? Quite gently, he stroked her full head of dark hair, then roughly pressed the dog shaver with a brand new Oster blade into her scalp, and began shearing her head.

"Who found her?" asked the tall, red haired detective.

The patrolman flipped open his note pad, and recited from the notes he had taken. "Emma and Garrison; a couple of kids from A&M University, they were visiting relatives in San Antonio for the weekend."

"What were they doing in the dry creek bed?"

"Said they were just out exploring, ran into her hanging in the tree there, scared them pretty bad, the girl was awful shook up."

Shawn McClough slid his lanky body down the slope, plummeting several feet into the dry creek bed known as Skull Creek. The woman he observed was no more than 20 years old at best, and probably pretty once. Her face was bruised, her eyes bulged, but that could be expected when you are hung upside down by your feet from a tree branch. The tree she hung in was the only tree growing in the creek, a lone survivor of the many torrential floods that had passed this way over the years.

Her wrists and ankles were bound with braided hay twine; her neck wrapped tight in the stuff. Shawn observed a long section of the twine hung down and gathered on the rocks below her head....her bald head. A scuffling sounded audibly behind him, he turned to see his partner Lizzey tripping over rocks in her high heeled shoes.

"Why don't you get some real detective's shoes?"

"Shawn, we have been over this and over this; a woman needs her heels that is all I am going to say about it, so get over it!"

Lizzey was as tall as Shawn at six foot two and about his age, in her early thirties. In contrast to his freckled light features, Lizzey sported olive skin and dyed her naturally brunette hair a bleach-like blonde. Both had gone through the police academy at the same time and graduated at the top of their classes more than 12 years earlier. They had both been in homicide for the past 2 years, and had become partners only a few months prior. "Besides," she added, "they aren't really even heels, they are only two-inchers."

Shawn tilted his head down to look, his hands remaining poised in his pockets. "Whatever, luv; rocks are still rocks."

"Whatever, Irishman," she scorned. "What do we have here?" she asked in an attempt to get Shawn off his favorite subject; her inappropriate choice of shoes. Stumbling around the body she squatted down, then leaned in to get a closer view of the woman's face. "She really took a beating."

Shawn squatted next to her. "I would say so," he grimaced.

"Her head has been shaved just recently; you think the perp did it?"

"I don't think the hair is here," Shawn surmised, looking around for confirmation. "That doesn't mean it didn't happen elsewhere, though, little weird isn't it?"

Lizzey nodded in agreement.

"It's starting to get dark, let's get her to the Coroner's office and see what he can tell us." Shawn stood and stepped off to hale the patrolman he had spoken to earlier.

"Shawn, wait," she whispered. Stretching out her hand slowly toward him, she wagged her fingers, beckoning him to come back.

"What is it?" he asked excitedly.

"Look," she said, pointing with her chin, keeping her eyes fixed on the woman's naked stomach.

Shawn looked. "I don't see anything, Lizzey, what?"

"Wait for it…wait for it."

Shawn stared. The clustered evening clouds above them created a deeper, more forlorn shadow of the coming night; but as they drifted apart and the quiet moonlight dipped mixing with the last of the sun's rays, Shawn saw it begin to form. The letters were random at first, then words appeared, then sentences. "For every one you find," he read out loud, "I will reward you with clues to the next one!" Jumping up, he yelled, "Patrolman! Get me an Evidence Technician with a night focus camera ASAP!"

"Glow in the dark paint," the Coroner dictated. Steve Harroway was a well past middle aged Medical Examiner. Medical Examiner, was the new age term he preferred to be called over a Coroner, but there were many who just couldn't seem to make the switch; he tried not to hold it against them. His belly had long since gotten in the way of his bending over fluidly, and his eyes were not what they use to be; but still, he had seen a lot of murder victims, no one came close to knowing what he knew about the dead. This girl, he thought to himself, she is a different kind of victim. This was no ordinary homicide; he calculated, there was thought in this, no blitzkrieg of an assault; this was more planned, more precise. He was quite sure she would not be this killer's last victim.

He pressed the button again on the recording device. "Head has been shaven, slight scrape marks appear on the scalp from the pressure applied during the procedure." Moving to the naked upper torso, he examined the girl's chest, then her throat. "The ligatures around the throat appear to be braided hay twine, I will unwrap the cords now." He set the recorder down. With nimble experienced fingers, he grasped the end of the long cord that extended from the tightened twine around her neck. Finding the place where it crossed through the wraps around the throat, he snaked it through until he could begin to unwrap it. Loop after loop, he slid one hand under and then over the girl's neck until at last it was free.

"Let the record show I have completely removed the twine from the victim's throat. The twine was wrapped around the victim's neck twenty times. I am now going to bag the twine and examine the throat."

He retrieved a paper bag from under the shiny metal examination table, marked it as neck twine and dropped the twine inside. He placed the bag back under the table, and then leaned in to examine the girl's neck. An obvious burn mark presented itself; a mark he knew to be from a Taser. He pressed down lightly on the side of her esophagus, dark bruising canvassed the flesh. Reaching up, he swung a magnifying lens in front of his eyes. He adjusted the monocular to focus inside the grooves within the flesh where the twine had bitten deep into the skin.

The ligatures marks were deep…very deep, he mused. Too deep, he decided, to be caused by strangulation with just using the hands to pull it tight.

He pressed the buzzer next to the examination table the girl was lying on.

"Yes Sir," a voice responded.

"Ernest, get that detective over here that's working this girls case."

"Will do, right away."

An hour later. "Did you happen to look around the area where you found this girl, detective?"

"Well, of course we did, Doc, but it got dark on us; we won't be able to see anything more till the morning," Shawn stated defiantly in a slight Irish accent. He had lost most of his Irish-ness living in Texas for so many years; but the more frustrated he got, the thicker the accent became.

"Well, morning is only three hours away, detective. I suggest you do the following: Go back out there and look for something that is just far enough away for the length of cord that was hanging down from her neck to have been attached to. I measured it, it was twenty feet long before I unwrapped the rest of it from around her neck, which – I might add – was wrapped twenty times."

"What are you thinking?" asked Shawn suspiciously.

"I am thinking, son, that this girl was strangled right out there where you found her; and not by somebody pulling on that cord by hand, but by somebody tying it off to something, then using her own body weight and gravity against her."

"But it wasn't tied to anything when we got there," Shawn blurted in frustration.

Steve cocked his head and eyed Shawn with a look of simplicity, waiting.

"He stayed and watched her die," Shawn voiced in realization. "He untied or cut the twine after he was sure she was dead." Fatigue, then anger washed over Shawn's face.

"That would be my guess, son," replied the robust Medical Examiner. "By the way," he said, turning back to his work, "he used a

Taser to subdue her."

Shawn flipped open his phone on his way out the door. "Lizzey, meet me back at Skull Creek - just do it, and no heels!"

Meeting Shawn back at the creek, Lizzey swatted another mosquito. "How can there be mosquitoes in February for heaven's sake," she cried sarcastically.

"Because," Shawn said, sitting on his rump on the hillside, "it just doesn't get cold enough here to kill them. Go back to Wisconsin if it's so bad."

"I am from Michigan, you freckle-faced string bean; and no thank you, it gets too damn cold there. Besides, like you Irishman, I have been living here too long now to live anywhere else. Texas kind of grows on you."

Bounding to his feet, he said, "Let's go, the light is coming in."

Shawn slid down the rise in the same suit he had been wearing the evening before, now soiled from too many trips up and down the hillside; it was probably beyond saving, he sighed. Brushing off his rump as he reached the bottom, he began banging his shoes together to dislodge the clods packed in front of his heels. Looking up, he saw Lizzey making her way down one foothold at a time. "Today Lizzey," he grumped.

"One of these days, Shawn, you're going to find you a pretty little wife to make miserable and leave me alone."

"Don't bet on it." He turned away, leaving her to her fate.

Shawn took out a tape measure. "Hold that end against the tree." Placing the end of the tape measure in her hand, he stretched the tape out walking backwards, measuring off twenty feet. Nothing, he noted. The nearest tree line from the lone sapling the woman was hung in was another fifteen feet up the opposite embankment. *Look closer!* He told himself. Reaching down, he turned over rock after rock, still nothing.

"What's that?" remarked Lizzey, who was still standing under the hanging tree holding the reverse end of the tape measure.

"What?"

"There." Pointing to his right, she marked the spot. He walked the short distance, scuffing once polished black shoes on white jagged rock.

Catching a glimpse of a metal object, he bent over to get a closer look, discovering a shiny aluminum handle. Tied to the handle was a piece of hay twine. Following the twine with his eyes, he saw that it led under a rock.

Lizzey appeared at his side. "What do you have there?"

Shawn lifted the rock, placing it next to his left foot. At the end of the twine was a piece of notebook paper in a clear plastic zip-loc bag. They both rotated bent over bodies in a circular motion to the other end of the notebook paper.

"It sounds like holler, but holler's not the road. Find the right one and find an old abode. That's not where she is, but use it as a flag. 200 yards past there you'll find a stag. Follow the deer trail west, and then turn sharply south; there she will be hanging. Oh, she had a pretty mouth." Bolting erect, she exclaimed, "I'll call it in."

Turning the police radio dial to channel B, she spoke to the dispatcher on duty. "I need an E.T. at Skull, pronto!"

4

Twenty-four hours went by, and no word had yet come back from the forensics lab. If they could get a fingerprint or any DNA evidence, we would have someplace to start, Lizzey thought. None of their attempts at finding a road like Holler had come to any positive end. They were growing tired and running out of ideas.

"OK," she offered, "let's do yet another Internet search for all roads in San Antonio that sound like Holler, but without the H. You know replace it with something else."

"Try using a different search engine this time and replace the H with a wild card," Shawn replied.

Lizzey began tapping away at the keyboard. After two hours, they were even more tired, more frustrated, and no closer to finding anything tangible. "Wait," she exclaimed, "what if it is not within city limits, but out in the county?"

"Brilliant," he agreed, "let's try it."

She changed the search criteria from San Antonio to Bexar County. Instantly, she got a hit. "Foller road," she read out loud. Shawn jumped up from his chair beside her.

"Where are you going?" she called.

"Just get the coordinates," he yelled as he ran down the hall to his office.

He flicked one business card after another out of his desk drawer, until finally he saw what he was looking for. Chandler Fox, FBI Emergency Response Team profiler. He dialed the number, a man answered on the fourth ring.

"Fox."

"Yes, Mr. Fox, this is Shawn McClough over at SAPD Homicide. Do you have a minute?"

"Sure Shawn. I remember you from that blood splatter class I gave last year; how are you?"

"Good, good, but I need some information. You told me about a Cadaver Dog that you have worked with on past cases that you believe to be quite credible; do you still have contact with that handler?"

"Yes I do, her name is Shawnee Spirit, and the dog's name is Titan. He's a big beautiful Shepherd. They live southeast of here, about forty miles or so."

"Excellent, I am in real need of them like yesterday. Not sure what it costs, but I am sure the Deputy Chief will sign the check – within reason, of course."

"No need," said Chandler. "Though she doesn't flaunt it, Shawnee is well enough off on her own that she doesn't accept any payment from law enforcement."

"Exceptional," beamed Shawn, "when can you get her to me?"

"That depends, Shawn-me-boy. Are you sharing info with your local FBI?"

Shawn hesitated a moment, then began to relate the details of the case he was working on and the clues they had recovered at the scene.

"I heard about the body being found," Chandler commented. "After hearing what was written in the note, it sounds to me that you may have a serial killer on your hands; that won't be confirmed, of course, until you actually locate a second body, if there is one. You could just be dealing with a quack. A murderous one, but just because he says so doesn't mean he killed anybody else. However, if he did, you are going to need a profiler, and a profiler is what I am."

"You're absolutely right, can you get it cleared?"

"I already have," smiled Chandler through the phone. "I emailed my boss on my Blackberry the minute you asked for Titan."

"Washicatwelo," Shawnee greeted Chandler, meaning "may we always do good."

"Washicatwelo," Chandler returned.

"How are you?" she asked, pulling him into a hug.

Returning the embrace, he remarked, "I am well indeed, young lady. How are you getting along these days?"

"Right as rain," she declared. She had not seen Chandler for several months. He appeared thinner than she remembered; something about his face and shoulders spoke to weakness. He never was a big man, not much taller than her 5'5, but he had seemed stouter only a short time ago. His dark hair; nearly the deep black of her own, was in its usual messy state, but his naturally matching clear green eyes sported a cloudy hue.

Titan romped up next to Chandler. "How are you, mutt?"

Titan bumped Chandler's knee with his forehead, looked up, and barked. Chandler peered over to Shawnee, who was twisting a smile. "He doesn't forget anything, does he?"

She laughed.

"I didn't bring you anything, Titan. Besides, I am family, I am supposed to get a pass."

Titan, not fooled by the charade, bumped Chandler harder and growled. "OK, here, before you take my leg off." Pulling a piece of beef jerky out of his shirt pocket, he dropped it to the ground in front of the big dog.

"He is such a garbage gut," Shawnee replied embarrassed.

Garbage to you maybe!

Shawn approached the pair, reaching a hand out to Shawnee. "I'm Shawn...." Snap! "Hey!" Shawn cried, jerking his hand away, stepping back in retreat.

Titan, having seen the stranger approach, gobbled down the last of his jerky and flew toward his hand as the man stretched it toward his mistress. *Sorry, freckled man; no stranger not introduced to me first, gets near her.* Titan stood stiff legged between the man and Shawnee.

"It's OK, Titan," she explained, "he is here to work with us."

Titan growled softly, and then sat, still maintaining a barrier between the man and Shawnee.

"Here," Chandler offered.

"What's this?" asked Shawn, taking the piece of jerky from Chandler's hand.

"We in law enforcement call it the price of admission. Once properly introduced, he won't take your hand off anymore, but he does expect homage to be paid before he will allow any real discussion to begin."

"You've got to be kidding me," remarked Shawn, looking from Chandler to Shawnee, then to Titan.

"I wish he was," Shawnee shrugged. "Titan seems to have a mind of his own, nothing I can do with him. His training taught him to protect me, but he seems to have his own rules about how that applies."

"Did you train him for protection yourself?" asked Lizzey, having joined the group.

"No," replied Shawnee. "He attended private training for his security work, I have no idea what goes on there."

"Oh," came the surprised response.

"Titan," said Chandler, taking Shawn by a lengthy bicep and pulling him forward, "this is Shawn, and this is Lizzey." Chandler turned with an outstretched arm indicating for Lizzey to come forward, too. Lizzey hesitated, but took two steps closer. "Now Shawn, you may pay homage." Chandler swung an open palm toward Titan and bowed, pressing his lips together trying not to laugh.

Smirk all you want brain-prober, Titan looked Chandler in the eye, *I at least get snacks.*

Shawn stretched a wary hand outward toward Titan's muzzle. Quickly, Titan snapped the jerky from his hand, trotted away, leaving the humans to their babble.

Shawn stood staring at his left fingers curled in a fist before him, as if taking count of the appendages. "Will we have to go through this again?" he asked with a suffering look.

"Always," Chandler smiled, showing white but slightly crooked front teeth. "He won't give you so much trouble next time, but he will expect you pay the…"

Shawn cut him off, "Yea I know, the price of admission." Everyone laughed, except Shawn.

Inside the homicide department, the group settled into a conference room with a projector flashing images of the crime scene on the wall. A fair haired older woman walked into the room carrying a cardboard box; she sat it on the table and left without a word. Titan saw the haze that surrounded her body as she moved across the room in her swaying ankle length skirt. The haze was thinly protruding into the space around her. Her light was leaving her soul, he concluded; she would not be on this Earth another year.

Lizzey reached in with gloved hands, pulling out the note they had found under the rock, the spiral metal stake with the handle on the end, and the hay twine that had bound and strangled their victim.

"Who is she?" Shawnee indicated the dead woman in the images with a flick of her head.

"Elisa Bowles," replied Lizzey. "She was 20, living at home with her mother, just started community college here in S.A," referring to San Antonio. "Borrowed her mother's car the night she went missing, was due home about eight pm. Her mother was worried when she did not show up at ten, and called the police when she was not home by midnight. Patrolmen found her car on the side of the road off Hwy 151. It had some rear-end damage, and the air bag was blown, but it was drivable."

"There was no paint scarring from the vehicle that hit her," added Shawn, "and no sign of foul play at the scene."

Rain washed away any footprints that we might have been able to recover," Lizzey provided. "The car was about a mile from the only business around for ten miles, a convenience store. The kid working that night is a bit of a jug-head or a junk-head, truth be known, and isn't sure if she is the girl he saw come in late that night or not. There were no cameras at the store. It's an area that's off the beaten path."

"Forensics just got back to us," Shawn said, scrolling through a message on his Blackberry. "The note at the crime scene bore no fingerprints, the body was washed in alcohol; no sign of any traceable evidence was found on the girl, and nothing about the hay twine tells us anything other than the bad guy likes hay twine. Then there's this." He held up the metal spiraled stake. "We have no idea what this is, but we think it was used to tie off the long twine that was hanging down past her neck; he used her own body weight to strangle her."

"You don't know what that is?" asked Shawnee.

"No," said Lizzey, "do you?"

"Yea, that's a dog stake, you use the handle to twist the spiral body into the ground, then clip the dog's leash to the handle to keep them from running off. Anybody who has shopped for a dog has seen one before"

Titan picked his chin up from his front paws. *You're not hooking me up to that thing,* he mused.

"You are certain?" Shawn asked, excited to have a possible clue, and feeling a bit embarrassed that something so simple had eluded him. But then again, he had never owned a dog. He had never even owned a hamster.

"Of course she is," supplied Chandler. "If something has to do with dogs, she knows about it, trust me."

"I am sure. I have seen them lots of times at PetSmart and on-line pet stores."

Lizzey reached in her front pants pocket and pulled out her purple Lotus cell phone, punched in a speed dial number, and asked for Mel. "Mel, I need you to run down every PetSmart and PETCO in S.A., and see if any of them keep video footage of their sales. Then get on the Internet, and start tracking down all of the on-line pet supply stores that carry a spiraled metal stakeout kind of twisted looking thingy for dogs; see who you can get to cooperate without a search warrant to supply us names of any San Antonio customers who bought them in the last month. We will start there anyway. No I don't have a better description, I don't own a dog! I will have someone send you a picture." She hung up.

The following day at noon, the group met where Foller road jutted off at a jug handle from FM 1234 at the southern end of the county. "Here comes our Bexar County liaison." Shawn tipped his chin toward the plainclothes man approaching.

Chandler turned around. The man reached a long arm out, handing

Chandler a length of paper rolled up like a tube. "Hi, I am Detective Backster, the Sheriff asked me to deliver this map to you." Shawn took the map from Chandler, spreading the topographical parchment on the hood of his car. Pointing, he showed Chandler how the road snaked around the back country and dead ended at no place worth mentioning.

"Read it to me again," asked Chandler.

Shawn tossed open his notepad and recited the message. "It sounds like Holler, but Holler's not the road. Find the right one and find an old abode. That's not where she is, but use it as a flag. 200 yards past, and there you'll find a stag. Follow the deer trail west, and then turn sharply south, and there she will be hanging; she had a pretty mouth."

"He fancies the game," Chandler supplied. In a familiar ritual that helped him think he scratched the thin bit of stubble he managed to grow on his chin. "He wants to be engaged with law enforcement, thinks he is helping us earn our keep. If there really is a body at the end of this elusive trail, this guy – and I'm sure it is a guy – could be a real problem and really, really dangerous."

"Well, happy hunting," quipped the county detective. Turning away and reaching an arm back to wave, he replied, "I have to get back to my solitaire game."

"I guess we are on our own," Chandler said sardonically, watching the man retreat.

Shawn looked at Chandler intensely. "Do you think our offender might be setting a trap for us?"

Chandler looked over at the light skinned detective. "No, I highly doubt it. He wants to play chess, and we are his pawns. He is moving us where he wants us to be, but not to eliminate us, rather to keep the game going. It's exciting to him. I imagine that by choice, he keeps pretty much to himself. Socially though, he is probably charming enough to fit in when he is in the company of others. Our guy is bored, I think."

"So nice to be some psycho's personal entertainment," scoffed Shawn.

"Ah, you get used to it chap." Grinning, Chandler slapped Shawn on the back.

Passing out the radios and giving instructions to everyone on how to use them, Shawn schooled the group – consisting of ten police academy cadets, Shawnee, Chandler, Lizzey, Steve the Medical Examiner, and two Evidence Technicians – on the specifics of what everyone was to look for. "Now when we get to the old house," he continued, "I want everyone to spread out in a straight line. We need to be no more than five feet apart and stay even with each other. We will sweep the property surrounding the house, while the E.T. searches the interior of the house. Just like on the road here; if you spot something, stop and yell for an E.T. – don't touch anything. After it has been cataloged and photographed, it will get bagged then tagged, and we will be on our way again. Any questions?" No one spoke. Forming up as instructed, they all marched down the winding dirt road toward the old house.

Titan watched as the people formed a single line of orange vests and walked purposely from one side of the property to the other. No one stopped or requested assistance with any discovered bobble or trinket, so he figured there was nothing to be found. The interior search of the crumbling old farmhouse had yielded nothing of value either. Titan searched it himself, but he was only searching for the death scent, the rest was up to the others to find. Having yielded no results at the shack, the crowd formed up in two groups. Lizzey sectioned off parameters of the woods on the topographical map, and assigned her group and the other group (made up of the cadets and one E.T.) their own area to search. She, Shawn, Chandler, Shawnee, Titan, and the remaining E.T. would search the primary area of interest based on the note they recovered near Elisa Bowles' body. Steve, out of breath from the march, decided to stay at the shack and wait for someone to call him if he was needed. "Call on the radio," Lizzey instructed sternly to the cadets, "if you locate anything you think is suspect."

5

Titan took the lead; he wasn't following any map, notes or instructions other than those he was born with. He pricked his ears and lifted his nose to the wind, testing it for those recognizable odors that would tell him what was ahead and if what he sought was out there. He sifted the fine dust of the day through soft tissue sensors; *rabbit, deer, mankind – not here now but within weeks, and yes....death scent.* He took off at a brisk pace, head high, nose searching. Shawnee knew the signs as did Chandler; they both stepped out behind him without a word.

"Hey, where are you guys going?" shouted Lizzey.

Chandler turned his head just slightly, and shouted back without slowing his pace or changing direction, "To find our victim."

With everyone running to keep up, Titan pressed ahead. Despite what he had been taught, he weaved through brush and cactus, bending and crawling through places he knew the humans could not easily follow. But he was following the death scent, and could not concern himself with their inability to keep up. They would find their way eventually, he decided. He was not concerned about his mistress, knowing that she would proceed through every port that he himself pursued. Like an able pack member, she was as nimble as any dog could be. Quickly enough, Titan located a deer head jammed harshly atop a metal fence post. Shawnee soon appeared at his rear followed by Chandler.

She approached the deer or what was left of it, walked around the cranium with her nose twisted to inspect it further. "It reeks," she puffed, "and it doesn't have any lips."

Titan sniffed it from a few feet away. *It smells of death, yes, but something more too....fear....it died in pure fear.*

Chandler pulled a latex glove from a pants pocket. Reaching under the bloody head at the base, he extracted a small zip-loc bag with a white paper in it. Shawn and Lizzey joined them out of breath, donning scratches on their arms and wearing fragments of leaves and branches in their tussled hair. All peered over Chandler's shoulder to read the note.

"You have done well, congratulations are in store. Now you are only steps away from my prize you must adore. In the meantime, enjoy my animal art work, lovely is it not!"

Chandler blew out a breath. "They," he observed meaning serial killers, "almost always start with animals before graduating to killing humans; but it looks like this guy is killing both at the same time, very unusual."

"Let's go," Shawn stated flatly, brushing debris from his short hair, "and keep an eye out. Who knows what this weirdo is up to."

They continued on their way; Chandler and Shawnee following close behind Titan. Shawn and Lizzey following close behind them. The Evidence Technician remained with the deer head and note to catalog and photograph them. Titan sneezed from the hackberry that grew so prevalent in the vicinity even in the cool winter; it always irritated the sensitive lining of his nostrils. But that is not why he had lost the faint air trail of the death scent: The wind no longer drifted through the fairly leafless trees to carry the odor to him. Ahead, he spied a deer trail, and decided to use it to wind through the shrubs with less effort. As soon as he completed the first meandering bend in the trail, he distinguished the just noticeable odor of stage-two death scent: a bloated body. He whined loudly breaking into a run.

"He's gone," Chandler yelled back at the stragglers, "you better keep up!"

Just joining them, Shawn and Lizzey grabbed the Evidence Technician's equipment and pushed the man on.

Titan was close, so close that the odor overwhelmed him and made it difficult to know which way to turn in the thick set of trees. The trees tended to collect and confound the odor, but then he broke free of the shrubbery, entering a clearing. It was not a natural setting; stumps of trees raggedly cut, lay all about. The property had been dismally cleared but only by a small margin; perhaps a fifty foot circumference at best. There in the middle was an old and leaning telephone pole. Hanging upside down from a hook on the pole was the dead, naked, and just slightly bloated body of a female. Reaching him soon afterward, the crowd of onlookers gathered around the dog, they stood staring at the ghastly scene.

"Good boy," Shawn said softly, still staring at the dead woman in a bit of shock.

Titan did not bother performing his alert to tell his mistress he had found the victim who produced the death scent, it was obvious. He barked at Shawnee, who reached in the canvas bag at her hip and produced the reward he always received for finding the dead; his blessed blue rubber ball.

Shawn snapped out of his reverie, swung around to the Evidence Technician, and instructed, "Wade, make sure you photograph every inch of this place, we don't want to miss anything."

Wade stood fixed to the Earth like a newly spawned tree that had just taken root. Shawn gripped his shoulder. "Wade."

"Huh?" Wade blinked at him.

"Wade, snap everything, don't miss a spot, OK?"

"Of course, yes, I will take care of it, Shawn."

"Let me know if you need any help," he offered, not entirely confident Wade was out of his stupor.

Titan padded around the dell, rolling the blue bliss in his mouth. He heard the minuscule flutter even before he saw the Seraph. *What do you want now?* He complained in thought, exasperated he had to endure this interference from the beyond. The little Seraph flittered across his muzzle, coming to a stop directly in front of his big wet nose. Titan crossed his eyes to focus on the blurry figure. Straightening them again, he leaned forward, but the Seraph pressed itself against his nose with firmness in strength such a creature should not possess. He made to walk past it, but the Seraph moved to the left and positioned itself in front of his nose again. Its minute wing movement pushed slight currents of air across the short hairs of his black muzzle. Growling in discontent, he initiated: *You realize I could just eat you, right?*

The Seraph was not intimidated and did not move. It continued to flutter microscopic wings as fast as a hummingbird might. If it were larger, Titan thought it would look like a distant cousin without the long beak and with a solid white body.

He dropped his head in frustration. *OK, you obviously feel the need to nag me, so I will listen, but then you will go away, yes?*

In answer, the tiny creature darted to the right, looked back, and waited for him to follow. Reluctantly, Titan did so. The Seraph turned sharply left, then turned to face Titan, still fluttering in mid-air. Titan stopped, looked over to where he had previously intended to walk, and saw the rusted mountain lion trap hidden beneath the tall dried grass. The trap was poised for engagement; he would have lost a leg. He eyed the Seraph, whose finer features were almost indistinguishable except for two miniature diamond colored eyes that shown bright as stars. It blinked, creating a flash of light and dissolved into thin air.

Titan stood grounded where he was, looking to the humans hard at work, some inspecting the victim, some the glade, he barked furiously to draw their attention. Not dropping the ball from his mouth, his barks were muffled; he had earned the ball, he decided, and wasn't letting it go. His antics finally drew notice from the populace; everyone that is except Lizzey, who kept working diligently searching through the tall waving grass for evidence.

Shawnee came running, but when she got close enough, Titan moved between her and the trap, barring her progress. She bent down to peer in his face. Folding soft tan jowls in her hands, she kissed his head. "What is it T?" she asked, using one of her affectionate names for him. Titan exhaled a long low whine, and swung his muzzle toward the trap.

Standing, she looked over him into the grass. "Chandler," she called.

Chandler, already heading her way to see what the commotion was, answered her by appearing at her side.

"Pesalo (beware)….look over there," she pointed.

Chandler eyed the trap and whistled. "Shawn, Lizzey, better get over here and see this," he called.

In answer, a scream cut through the air. Lizzey was bent over, grasping her left ankle, blood streaming down her foot and over her bright blue two inch high heeled shoe. Wade reached her first; using a small crow bar he kept in his kit, he pried the trap open. Lizzey screamed again, then blacked out, falling face first into the dirt. Shawn pulled the police radio off his hip, and hit the emergency channel.

"She will be alright, the medics said its deep and the bone is fractured, but it missed cutting any major arteries. Biggest worry will be from bone infection. It appears our boy may want to eliminate us, after all," Shawn speculated, running freckled fingers through blondish-red hair.

Chandler rubbed his chin. "Perhaps he just wants to make it more interesting; but if he starts getting us hurt, his game won't be able to continue, it doesn't make sense to me."

Shawn bent close to Chandler and whispered, "Do you think he meant it for the dog?"

Chandler paused in thought, pulled thoughtfully on his stubble, and replied, "He better hope not, he will be asking for more than he bargained for."

Shawn's lips pursed to ask what Chandler meant, but Chandler was already walking away, to speak privately with Shawnee.

"We found three traps around the outer parameter," remarked Wade to Shawn.

"So it's cleared to go back in then, right?"

"Yes sir, it is. Also, we found your dog stake twenty feet in front of the telephone pole. It's twisted down into the ground just like the other one was at Skull Creek; here is the note that was attached to it. Don't worry, I already cataloged everything."

Shawn pulled on a pair of latex gloves, and took the Ziploc bag from Wade's equally gloved hand. Wade turned on his heel and left Shawn to read it.

"Here," Shawn handed a glove and the bag with the note in it to Chandler.

Steve had arrived a few minutes earlier, and was busy examining the dead woman on the pole. They had not pulled her down yet, because he wanted to perform his inspection where she was before going any further.

"Another note?" asked Chandler. Shawn nodded.

Chandler read the note aloud, "She was killed before the first, but I guess that you can tell. She is not in such good shape, but oh thee well.

The next one will be fresher, but will be marked by a hog, I hope you got my message and eliminate the dog. So, Chandler breathed, "he does know about Titan."

"Looks like it," Shawn acknowledged. The pair eyed each other with alarm.

"I have already talked to Shawnee, she is making some phone calls. Don't ask me to explain any further, Shawn, I can't. I can say only that there is more to Shawnee and Titan than can be spoken about outside of a very elite and private circle. Secrecy is the only way the organization can work."

"I take it you are in that elite circle?"

Chandler considered how he was going to respond. "Yes," he admitted reluctantly. Examining Shawn, he made a professional assessment and added, "I was born into it, just like Shawnee was."

"I should have guessed at the last name and the color of your skin; it's so hard to tell a Native American from a Hispanic in this town, though," Shawn admitted. An unspoken understanding was reached between the pair of lawmen; together they strode to the body, where Steve stood poised with a tape recorder pressed to his lips.

"The face is battered…. hay twine is strung around the neck with extra cord on the ground. The body is slightly bloated, has probably been here a couple of weeks. Temperatures have been cool to cold over that time period, but warmer during the day. The head has been shaved." Steve hit the pause button, made eye contact with Chandler and Shawn, and remarked, "She is not much older than the last one, I'd guess, though it's hard to tell with her face so bruised."

Any identification anywhere?" asked Shawn.

"No," replied Wade, hearing the question. "She is naked as a jay-bird, nothing at all at the dump site to indicate who she is…was."

Chandler contemplated Wade's words. He was correct in referring to the location as a dump site. The victim may actually have died at the location, but there was no evidence to indicate she had been attacked there. There was no evidence the beating she received was perpetrated there either; no blood-splatter. This perp had probably encountered these women in one place, attacked them in another, tortured them elsewhere, and strangled them where he intended to dump their bodies. The depth of the planning involved in this killer's mind articulated a man who planned his violence in a very intimate way. Chandler chewed on his lip.

"One more thing," Steve added, breaking Chandler's train of thought. "The missing Deer lips, they are sewn to the victim's mouth."

Shawn dropped his lower jaw involuntarily.

Chandler swallowed hard. "He keeps changing his pattern, almost like he is unstable."

Shawn looked at Chandler incredulously. "You are kidding, right? You didn't think him mad already before that tidbit of news?"

The team of Evidence Technicians gathered around the telephone pole to see this queer development. No one was amused. The technicians extracted the dead woman from her internment with care. Titan searched the clearing with his eyes, still rolling the blue ball around with his teeth and tongue. He wondered if the girl's light would come out to visit with him. Sliding her into the body bag, Wade zipped it closed. The team grasped the handles on the sides of the bag, and lifted her body onto the back of a four wheeler.

"Shawn, come see me at my office tomorrow, I will work on this young lady tonight and tell you what I can when you get there," Steve directed.

"Will do, give me something I can go on, Doc."

Steve waved a hand in the air and pulled himself onto the bench seat of the four wheel vehicle.

Wade slid in beside him, started the red Kawasaki Mule and with a nod to Shawn, accelerated the vehicle, slowly driving it out to the road where Steve's attendant waited in the morgue transport vehicle and an already growing throng of reporters. Forty-five minutes later, the rest of the team exited the woods and were met by the clamoring voices of the news crews. Secured behind caution tape stretched between and attached to the side-view mirrors of two police cruisers, the reporters' cameras flashed, trying to catch that one special photo. Several stretched out long-poled microphones, trying to catch anything spoken in supposed secret. Titan trotted past with deference as the cameras swung his way.

"Who's the dog?"

"Who is the dog?" they all yelled.

"No comment," Chandler yelled back, and left it at that.

6

Several weeks had passed since Corin Wester had an opportunity to scope out another participant in his game of life and somebody else's death. He had been assigned a big story to write at the newspaper where he freelanced as a crime journalist. He had spent more time than usual at the gym wearing off the frustration of not being able to get out of town to prowl. He chuckled out loud, remembering how his editor had told him another young woman had been found slain in the San Antonio area. The police, of course, were less than forthcoming; same as the first time he questioned them at Skull Creek. Corin chuckled again. How clever he was, he thought to himself, hiding how much he already knew from them all: He knew more than they ever would.

He watched the girl. He liked to station himself near rural convenience stores in the late night hours. It was a good way to find young women making a last minute dash for snacks, milk, or sodas, and these older stores never bothered with surveillance equipment. Most of the young women he stalked were likely still living at home and borrowing their parents' vehicles. He didn't care about their living arrangements; once he chose a target, they would never make it home again, anyway.

The girl he was eying now was alone, dark haired, and no older than twenty or twenty-two. Just the way he liked them. It was close to midnight. He was well hidden in his dark green truck across the street from the country store in a vacant lot. His vehicle tags were stolen; he always switched them before he went out on an escapade. Tonight, he was prepared to take a target back to his farmhouse in the county if he found the right girl. As he looked through his binoculars at the girl paying for a can of Dr. Pepper, he felt he had indeed found the right participant. A tingle ran up his spine as he thought about the task at hand. The rush he got from the abduction was nothing compared to the exhilaration of the torture and then the climax of the eventual ceremonious strangulation.

To add to the pinnacle was the ultimate game he played with law enforcement. He enjoyed dealing with proficient people, he loathed stupidity. If the detectives playing his game turned out to be incompetent, he would have to find a way to get new players. He was worthy of talented opponents, nothing else would do. The dog, however, had to go. It was an unfair advantage, not part of his game rules, not allowed. He had learned about the dog when a man in a small town southeast of San Antonio had been convicted of his wife's death. Corin had covered that story, too. It was easy to figure out the dog would be brought in to help with this case as well. You could not fool someone as smart as he was, he would always be a step ahead.

The girl he had been watching emerged from the store, opened the door of her cranberry 2002 P.T. Cruiser, took a swig of her soda, and flopped into the driver's seat. She cranked up the volume on her radio, while turning the car onto Onion Creek road in Austin, Texas. Corin pulled onto the rural road long after the girl's car was out of sight. As soon as he was past the weak exterior lights of the store, he gunned the engine and turned his headlights to bright. Seeing her taillights in the distance, he gained on her rapidly.

Twenty-three year old Barbara Ekle was tapping her toes and fingers to the rhythm of Melissa Lawson singing "What if it all goes right." A bright blinding splash of light suddenly enveloped her, and she looked in her rear-view mirror. Headlights were approaching her too fast for her personal comfort.

"What is this guy doing?" she voiced aloud. Reaching up, she adjusted her mirror as the headlights overtook her field of vision. The impact was hostile; her car was spinning out of control. She screamed as it went airborne. Landing with several bouncing thuds off the roadway, the nose of the car perched in a ditch as the rear became elevated against a burn.

She was shaking when the man approached. Reaching through the broken glass of the driver's window, he shook her shoulder and asked, "Are you OK young lady?"

"I, I don't know," she said shakily.

"Here," he said, "let me help you." Pressing something cold against the back of her neck, he said, "This will make it all better."

Fire exploded in her brain.

Corin drove the two hours back to his farmhouse in Bexar County, far south of where his apartment was in San Antonio, and completely out of touch with the city of Austin. He had laid the girl in the usual place in the basement, bound and gagged, waiting for him to begin his work. She stirred and tried to scream, but only a squeal made it past the tape across her mouth. She struggled against the bindings and against the gurney she was strapped to.

"I see you have joined me once again, how sweet of you." Her brown eyes shot to his face. He smiled and turned on the shaver. Pressing it against her follicles, he applied enough pressure to remove the soft brown hair and a few layers of scalp. It felt good to humiliate them before he made them feel real pain.

She twisted herself as much as she could to fight him. He ignored her attempts, but used it as a reason to be even harsher with the procedure than he had planned. She was bringing this on herself, he reasoned with a grin. Not that he needed an excuse, but he liked the thought and logic that went into his actions. The hair fell softly to the concrete. Corin scooped up the pile of hair with his hands, not wanting any blood to drip onto his latest trophy.

He raised the fistfuls of hair to his nose, and drew in a deep breath. "Uhm," he brightened, "smells like Herbal Essence!" He dropped the shiny dark hair into a white pillow case that already contained the other hair he had collected. He zipped the pillow-less case closed with one fluid motion, like he had practiced the effect many times.

Barbara screamed at him through the tape. Blood was dribbling down her scalp, her skin burned.

"You have something to say?" he asked. Gripping the edge of the tape between an index finger and thumb, he ripped the tape from her swollen lips.

She yelped. "What do you want, you son-of-a-bitch?" she blurted. She stared at the skin from her lips hanging off the inside of the tape in his hand.

"Well, you are right there," he said, flicking the tape aside. "But I did away with that problem a long time ago. In fact, it was my mother who started me on this glorious road."

Barbara stared at him, trying to decipher what he was talking about. She was confused, scared, and completely unsure of what was happening.

"Nothing more to say?"

"I, what is it you want with me? I have a credit card; my father has some money in oil stocks, he can pay you!"

"Oh, he will pay, my dear, I assure you he will pay, but the price is nothing monetary."

"Then what, what do you want with me?" she asked almost inaudibly.

"Why your fear, your life of course, what else would do?" Corin cocked his head to show her she was silly for not knowing the answer.

He placed tender fingers on her cheek grinning mildly, then swiftly brought up his free hand containing the rubber mallet, and swung it powerfully downward, hitting her squarely in the stomach. The muscles bulged in his thick neck as he completed the action. Air whooshed from her lungs, then her lungs tried feebly to suck the air back in. She felt instant suffocation. Her eyelids stretched upward, widening the whites of her orbs to huge egg-like spheres. He breathed in as if tasting a fine wine. Then the muscle structure of his face shifted. His calm features turned ominous. "That's just really the start," he bellowed between clenched teeth.

She struggled to regain any ounce of air she could. When at last she drew in a ragged breath, she witnessed his fist wrap tightly around the handle of the mallet once again. It impacted her left cheek this time, then her nose; the noise made by bone being crushed always made him salivate. A crack resounded throughout the small concrete room each time the hard rubber head of the mallet met the swollen flesh of her face and body. Barbara lost consciousness.

When next she came to, she could barely open her bloated eyes. Unable to draw air through a badly broken nose, she parted split and bleeding lips, sucking in a wretched breath; it hurt her lungs. She tasted tininess on her tongue as the blood oozed from her lips into her mouth. Using her tongue, she swabbed the inside of painful jaws; her teeth were broken, her jaw too.

"Are you ready, my dear?" she heard the insane man ask. She jerked her head toward the voice, her neck and head screeching in her brain from the pain it caused. Her confused mind pondered how odd it was that he could be so cruel and have looked so normal, like any body-building guy she might have met at the gym, even dated. Through the slits of her barely open eyes, she saw the mallet glide through the air. She screamed, but her voice was strained and did not match the shearing pain she felt in her head. And so it continued.

7

"**S**ame glow in the dark paint, see here?" Steve flicked the switch on the black fluorescent light, and dimmed the white lights with a remote control. He moved the wand across the woman's stomach slowly.

Shawn read out the message. "Trailwater. What does that mean?" he asked rhetorically, although Steve responded.

"Probably another road, be my guess."

Shawn looked at the older man. "You sure you weren't a detective in a former life?"

"Me?" Steve mocked shock. "I just call it like I see it, young man; up to you to do something with the genius information I provide you."

Steve handed Shawn the file he had compiled on the young woman overnight. "I ran her against the missing person's database here in San Antonio for age eighteen to twenty-five; I came up empty. She may not be from here."

"Thanks," Shawn responded in thought. I will ask Laura to start running checks in the county and cities outside of San Antonio, based on what you have here," waving the file in his hand.

"How's Lizzey, by the way?"

"Oh, she is on enough morphine to keep a cow down and still yelling at the doctors," Shawn laughed. "She is going to be in the hospital for some time yet, they are worried about infection setting in the bone. She will lose the leg if that happens."

"Give her my best when you see her," Steve insisted.

"Will do, Doc, and thanks for this." Holding the file up in salute, he left Steve to his speechless clients.

Driving back to the Police Department, Shawn spoke with Detective Laura Collen on the phone.

"No, no fingerprints again," she responded. "Body was washed, there were traces of alcohol like the last time. She appears to be approximately the same age as Elisa Bowles, same basic hair color – from what we can tell, height and stature look to be similar as well. And forensics came up empty on the search for those tie-out stakes the perp is using."

Shawn sighed at the news. "Can you run the databases for Austin, Boerne, Bulverde, Johnson City, and Floresville? Steve says San Antonio came up zilch, but run it again, too."

"What are you going to do?" asked Lizzey's replacement on the other end of the phone.

"I am headed back to the office."

Titan's feet twitched in rapid succession, keeping cadence with his equally twitching eyelids. It was not a dream of chasing balls or those ever elusive rabbits that he was having, but a talking dream where the Great Mystery spoke to him about the purpose of his life, about things to come, people to avoid, dangers to beware. He never saw the Great Spirit; he only heard the soft gentle tone of his voice. Sometimes, there was reproach or admonishment; for Titan was stubborn, yes, but his extraordinary father always told him how special he was and how much he loved him no matter what.

Loping along a leaf strewn path on a high mountain trail, he absently sent pebbles over the edge with heavily plodding paws. It was a fine warm day, but still snow trickled from the expansive sky, landing on the tip of his nose, tickling the pores of the gifted instrument. How funny, he thought, that it could snow in his dreams. How not funny, he thought, that humans could do such terrible things to each other.

"It is in their nature, young one." The voice boomed in the crevices of the mountain peaks so loudly that it shook them, yet Titan heard it as

softly as the snowflakes that passed his ears on their way to melt on the warmed rocks beneath his paws.

"But you have told me many times that you created them, created me; how is it that you made them this way?"

"I made them to make their own decisions, like I made you to make yours. You do not follow me because I tell you to; in fact, you often do the opposite of what I tell you to, do you not?"

Titan thought about this, darting his tongue out to catch a falling snow drop. *"I suppose, father,"* he admitted. *"It's just that I know how smart I am, and I don't think I need you to send the Seraphs to show me how to do my job."*

"There is little you or your humans can accomplish that is done by one alone; this is an abundant lesson you must learn."

Titan eyed the tree at the top of the mountain he had just climbed, pleased with himself for reaching the top so quickly and with so little effort.

"Your ego is beyond reprimand even in your dreams, young one."

Titan bowed his head in humility, sorrowful for his pride always getting the better of him.

"I leave you with this, my charge; beware of the evil-doer. There is great wickedness around you now, among you, near you; watch your mistress for she is in danger, as are you. In trials to come, you will be challenged and strained to the depth of your talents. You are, as always, close to my heart."

Silence followed; Titan knew there would be no further explanation. *Always so cryptic,* he fussed to himself, *never exact about anything.* He reached out his tongue to catch another falling snow drop. He awoke with his tongue stuck to the roof of his mouth.

Three and a half weeks after finding the dead girl in the woods, Chandler hurried into Shawn's office, plunked down a picture on his desk, and remarked, "I think we have a match on your second girl."

"Who?" Shawn stood instantly, pushing his chair back so hard it hit the thin wall behind him. An indignant reprimand came through the wall of the accosted office resident on the other side.

Chandler tapped the photo with his index finger. "This is Norma Herrera, age twenty-three, went missing just a little over two weeks ago from Marble Falls."

"Marble Falls? If this is our girl, our perp is expanding his territory."

"He may just have given us another clue to his personality, though. See, he is what we profilers refer to as a geographically transient killer, meaning he is not stabilized to one location. He is more confident in his ability to move about, and arrogant enough that he is not too worried that he can actually get caught. But we have an advantage there."

Shawn eyed the shorter man. "Please do tell me what this advantage is, I could use a positive lift about now."

Chandler grinned, picked up the picture from atop the desk, and eyed it once more. "So far," he said, shifting his eyes back to Shawn, "he seems to feel a need to bring his victims back home, to us. We know he doesn't torture them or kill them where he abducts them. I suspect he has one place and one place only where the torture occurs, and it is likely here in the San Antonio area. The farther he travels with them alive to get them back here, the more chance there is that he will slip up and get stopped for something. There is a better chance of one of them surviving since he doesn't commit the act where he abducts them. We at least still know he is going to bring them back here; that means we will always have jurisdiction; which means no break in the evidence chain, no arguments with other departments; we will maintain the best chance to solve this and catch this son-of-a- bitch."

Shawn scrubbed tired eyes with his fingertips. Sliding fingers down his cheeks and pulling his lower lids downward, he looked up to the ceiling and sighed. "I am not sure that was the advantage I would have chosen, but I see what you mean, it's better than nothing."

"It also means something else."

Shawn dropped his hands to his sides. "Why do I sense you are going to tell me something I don't want to hear?"

"He wants us as the players in his little plot, not some other town or city department."

Shawn let out a deep breath. "You make it almost sound like he is keeping tabs on us."

"Who's keeping tabs on us?" asked the broad shouldered blonde entering the room.

Shawn's spirits rose. "Chandler, this is Laura Collen, she is working with me on the case....cases with Lizzey out."

Chandler reached a hand out in greeting. Laura took it readily, and remarked with a confident voice, "Chandler, Chandler Fox?"

"The one and only," he answered, displaying rarely seen dimples.

"You profiled that child killer in Austin ten years back, that was great work."

"A fan!" Chandler winked at Shawn, releasing Laura's grip with a pat.

"Wonderful," Shawn derided, tossing a hand over his head, "now you have his head swelling, way to go."

Chandler bowed. "I am glad to be at your service. In fact, as of today, I have been assigned to the Upside Down Killer full time till we solve it."

"Upside down what....?" Shawn waited for Chandler to fill in the blanks for him.

"Oh yea, sorry, we FBI profiler geeks have a way of dubbing our serial killers with names that denote something about their kills. Don't look at me," he said, pressing palms outward at shoulder height. "I didn't come up with it, but it got started around the office, and well, it's in cement now."

"Just don't let the press get hold of it," Laura said, rolling her eyes.

Shawn thumped the picture now back on his desk. "So where are we on this, girl?"

"The parents are on their way over to the San Antonio morgue. Steve said there is no way to make identification from her face, it's too badly ruined. But he plans to take their DNA to compare it to the girl's. I thought you could take their statement while I walk the DNA through our FBI lab on a fast-track. My boss has given the thumbs up on putting all evidence in this case at the head of the line. Everybody wants this guy caught."

"Good," Laura announced. "My Internet searches have come up empty on finding a Trailwater road in the city, county, or any of the surrounding towns or cities."

Chandler scratched his chin with the tip of his thumb. "Have you tried looking at them as separate roads?"

Shawn clasped his own temples. "Chandler Fox, you are a genius!" Palming Chandler's ears in Irish fashion, he kissed him on the forehead. Chandler stood dumb. "Laura…," Shawn started.

But Laura was already pivoting on her heels and trotting down the hall. She yelled back, "I am on it!"

"So, you say she was last seen at the Marble Ice House?"

The older woman dabbed wet eyes with a small white embroidered handkerchief. "Jes," she answered in broken English. "My granddaughter, she wuz to stop at the convenience store on her way home to bring me some Pepo Beezmal, ju know the pink medeecin?" she asked Shawn with a tilt of her small gray-haired head.

"Yes ma'am, Pepto Bismal," he repeated correctly with an Irish flare as he took notes.

"My daughter," the grandmother squeezed her daughter's hand seated beside her. "She works very hard, like her husband Rodolpho, they were both working, but I had a stomach ache; too much jalapeño, you know."

Shawn nodded in sympathy, but wishing the older woman would concentrate.

"I called Norma on her pocket phone and ask her to pick up the medeecin," the grandmother finished.

"Ma'am, you are Norma's mother?" Shawn pointed to the younger woman.

"Jes, I yam."

Shawn jotted a note. "And where is the father….Rodolpho, is it?"

The mother dropped her face in her hands, sobbing uncontrollably.

The older woman spoke up, "He eez in the back with the muerto….the dead girl." The grandmother pulled her daughter close, placing a hand over her already covered face.

"I am sorry you are going through all of this," he added genuinely, seeing the real pain in their faces. Both of the women looked at him and nodded earnestly.

"Can you tell me who saw her at the store?" He looked from one woman to the other, willing either to answer.

The mother sat up. Through choking sobs, she managed to explain to Shawn that her cousin worked the night shift at the store, and that is why Norma had stopped at that particular store so late. She thought it safer.

Shawn listened on, continuing to write the story down as the mother tearfully provided him with the details. The cousin who worked till midnight said Norma stopped at the store at 10:00 P.M., chatted for a while, leaving about 11:30. He saw her pull out of the parking lot and turn right on a dirt road, heading home. He saw no other cars, and there were no security cameras. When the cousin locked up and left the store, he headed out the same way Norma had, and soon came upon her old beat-up Chevy Impala precariously off the side of the road.

Shawn sparked at the promise of a positive identification from a credible witness – a relative. "How far past the store did he find the car ma'am?"

She thought a minute. "Dose miles," she held up two fingers, making sure he understood.

Scribbling again, "My partner is acquiring the Marble Falls Missing Persons report, but I wanted to interview you myself. Sometimes, it helps to put things into perspective."

A thick, middle-aged man turned the hallway corner. His eyes were watching his feet, as if removing his gaze would surely make him falter and fall. His features told Shawn he was looking at the father, Rodolpho. Based on the man's disposition, Shawn speculated what was coming. The women caught sight of the man, and ran to his side. His knees buckled when they reached him, and only sheer will kept him from dropping to the floor. Shawn hurried to help them. Holding Rodolpho around the shoulders, he escorted him to the seats where the ladies had been sitting in the hall.

"It eez our baby," he sobbed. He made no eye contact with the women or Shawn, just kept looking at his feet and repeating, "It eez our baby."

Shawn saw the Medical Examiner talking to an assistant at the end of the hall. "Excuse me, please," Shawn addressed the grieving family.

They were so enveloped in their grief that no one heard him, so he moved on quickly. Steve pulled him into the examination room by an elbow. Shawn faced him. "How does he know for sure? Her face cannot be recognizable."

"He said Norma had an imperfect left ear. She had no left ear drum. She was born without it," Steve told him.

Shawn stared at him, confused. "How does that help us identify her? You said nothing about a missing ear drum on our girl."

"That's because I missed it," he confessed. "Well, not exactly missed it, I wasn't sure until now; at least, that's why I didn't say anything before. The damage to her skull was so severe that it was not easy to discern. I suspected it, but wasn't sure I could prove it. I still can't, not without the lab putting Humpty Dumpty back together again. With us processing the DNA, it doesn't seem like an expense worth taking on." Shawn started to argue, but Steve held up a hand. "Peace, I only mean the DNA will be back long before we could accomplish it."

Shawn relaxed. "So again, why is Rodolpho so sure it is Norma?"

Steve regarded the tall Irishmen. "Don't laugh," the rounder man insisted.

Shawn thought him crazy. "Laugh, at a time like this?"

"He looked at her feet," Steve said quietly.

"Excuse me?" Shawn's words were flat, hoping he had heard incorrectly.

"He looked at her feet," Steve maintained, louder this time. "He said her feet were the spitting image of his own dead sweet mother's, and he would know those feet anywhere in any condition."

Shawn dropped his chin to his chest, his arms falling loosely to the seams of his smartly pressed trousers. Lifting his head, he looked the M.E. in the face. "That's what we are going on, your suspicions about her ear and his belief that he has seen the image of his once living mother's feet on his dead *potential* daughter?" Shawn, grimacing, turned abruptly for the door. Mumbling, he said, "Call me when you get the DNA results from the lab."

Back at his office, he gripped the arms of his desk chair, pulling long legs up he rested his heels on the top of the metal desk. Leaning back, he closed his eyes. He was exhausted; having slept little and eaten less, he was beginning to wear down. He should go see Lizzey, but just didn't have the time, he needed something substantial to catch this guy. In moments, auburn eyelashes were nictitate in deep sleep.

The phone sprang him out of his much needed nap. "McClough," he answered, trying to clear the cobwebs from his head.

"Shawn-me-boy, we have a match, it is the Herrera girl."

"Chandler?"

"Yes, it's Chandler, who did you think it was your fairy godmother? The DNA is a match; we know who the girl is, positive I.D."

"His mother's feet," Shawn muttered.

"Whose feet, what?"

"Nothing, I was just remembering something," Shawn answered distantly. "OK," Shawn started, still trying to clear his groggy mind, "So we have a name. What now?"

"Let's see what we can glean from the Marble Falls report. Did you get anything tasty from the interviews?"

Shawn excitedly sat upright. "I did," he admitted. "She was seen last at a convenience store, and her car was found off the road about two miles away from the store."

Chandler was silent for a moment.

"You there?"

"What time was our second girl….Norma, last seen at the store?"

Shawn paused, trying to recall the details. "It was about 10 pm, I think."

"And Elisa?"

"Uh, it was also late, but the cashier was never able to say for sure that it actually was Elisa who came in that night."

"I think we can surmise now that it was in fact Elisa," Chandler espoused. "So, he stalks them after dark at out-of-the way pit stops, and then runs them off the road. We have established part of his pattern, my leprechaun friend."

"That's positive news, it is!" Shawn was ecstatic. "We should put out something to the public on this right away."

"Hold on, I am not sure it's in our best interest or the public's to do that right now."

"We have to! If another girl gets killed because we didn't share this information, then we are at fault."

"What's worse, Shawn, to put the info out there and tip our guy off that we are on to him and save a local girl, or don't tip him off and we get another day of having the upper hand? It's harsh, I know, but we can't reveal what we have on him, not yet."

"We have to tell the public something, I don't feel right not telling them anything."

"Tell them to avoid being out alone late at night, travel in pairs, be in before dark, and make sure they keep tabs on each other by cell phone. That's the best advice you can give them, anyway," Chandler offered.

"I can stomach that, I guess, for now," Shawn agreed grudgingly.

Laura stepped into his office. "Hold on, Chandler, Laura may have some news for us."

"Afraid not," she offered. "The Marble Falls report is fairly minuscule and lacks sufficient detail. I don't think they expected it to turn into much. I hope you got more from interviewing the family than I got from this." She plopped the report on his desk.

Shawn put the phone back to his ear. "Sorry, nothing new."

"Well, I wouldn't go that far," she said with a smirk, tossing an 8x11 piece of printer paper in front of him.

He picked it up, still holding the phone to his left ear. Hitting the speaker button he replaced the handset in the holder. "Chandler, I have you on speaker. Laura just handed me a printout from MapQuest, and it looks like you were right: There is a Trail road that intersects with Water road in west Bexar County."

"Good work, lady, what time do we meet up?"

"The day is already three quarters worn," she stated, looking at her watch.

Shawn nodded in agreement. "Are Shawnee and Titan available tomorrow?" he asked.

"They just wrapped up a case in Boerne today; false lead. They will be tired, but I know you couldn't make her stay home if you tried, not when this guy is still floating around out there somewhere."

"You always know where those two are?" Laura asked, peering at the speakerphone with upraised brows.

"Uh, they use them a lot," Shawn explained.

"Exactly," Chandler filled in cautiously.

Laura glowered at Shawn and then the speakerphone. With an air of suspicion, she responded, "Uh-huh," not at all buying the guilt laden answers. "What's the plan, boys?" she asked, blandly crossing her arms over her chest, accepting the hustle for now.

"Tomorrow at Trail and Water eight o'clock sharp. Come stacked and packed for terrain and walking, it looks like this is another rural area."

Chandler and Laura acknowledged Shawn's instructions. Chandler disconnected. The pair of detectives briefed their lieutenant about the new developments, then left to get their affairs in order for the next day's efforts.

8

Shawn and Laura pulled up to the countryside intersection of Trail and Water at six o'clock in the morning. Already parked along the roadside was a dark brown and white 30ft long RV.

"What the heck is this?" Shawn put the city car in park, cut the engine, and exited the car simultaneously with Laura. They reached the cab door at the same time, puffing white cold air out of their lungs. They both reached up to knock, hesitating when the door creaked open.

"Come on in, neighbors," Chandler stepped aside so they could access the steps. Neither of them moved. "What's the matter, have you never seen an evidence van before?"

"Chandler, this isn't a van, it's a house. Is that bacon I smell?" Shawn's nose flared as he took a step up inside the RV. Laura followed him inside.

"Unbelievable," she remarked. "You guys have absolutely got it made in the FBI."

"Not really," Chandler offered, a little embarrassed. "This RV was paid for out of the budget allotted to Shawnee and Titan for their annual expenses. It's kind of considered support for her and Titan." The pair stared back in awe. "You are welcome to it, though. We have a fully equipped kitchen, beds, toilet, and shower. And in the back there, we have a basic lab for logging and storing evidence."

Shawn whistled.

"I was thinking you two would show up early, so I made breakfast, hope you are hungry."

Laura looked at Shawn. "Might as well eat," she shrugged, "it's too dark to get started yet."

Seating themselves at the table, the three of them passed the platters among themselves, filling their plates. A rap on the door startled the detectives.

"No worries, it's just our hairy friend and his pretty handler coming to join us." He stood to open the door for the duo.

Shawn's eyebrows drew upward.

"What's wrong?" Laura asked, noticing the change in expression.

"You'll see," he gasped.

She eyed him, curious about what was to come.

Titan sauntered up the steps of the RV, smelling the enticement of bacon and eggs. Catching the familiar smell of the tall detective he met recently, he slowed his gate. He stopped intently, however, when inhaling the odor of a total stranger. He bent his neck back to see where his mistress was. Stepping steadily to the table full of food he found two very still people.

"Oh, look how pretty he is," Laura purred, a pleasant smile turning her lips.

Seeing she was about to reach a hand out to the dog, Shawn grasped her wrist and held it. "No, no!" he said, almost holding his breath.

Titan's eyes never left the woman. He growled to let her know her smile was no deterrent from him taking a bite out of her if she made one wrong move. His hackles stood slightly upright as he neared her, breathing in deeply, assessing her intentions. Finally satisfied there was nothing in her character that he needed to be concerned with, he promptly sat back on his haunches and stared at her.

Shawn released his grip on her wrist. "Now you can pay him the price of admission." He straightened in his chair finally taking a steady breath.

"Pay him a price of what?"

Shawn, trying to explain, said, "Pay him the….give him something, a piece of bacon, I guess."

Laura examined his face for any sign he was losing his faculties, or at least playing a joke on her. "You are serious?"

Titan barked, tired of waiting.

Laura jumped in her seat, grabbed a piece of bacon, and threw it at him. He leapt sideways on his back legs, caught the bacon, and scarfed it down. He drew his attention to Shawn.

"I didn't forget," Shawn said, quickly tossing the dog three pieces of bacon in rapid succession. Titan caught each one, swallowing them down nearly whole.

Chandler and Shawnee slid back chairs from the table and took their seats, as if nothing unusual was going on. Titan walked around the table, and bumped Chandler on the hip with his head. Chandler reached a hand over to the counter, and slid a plate onto the floor. "Here you go, your own bacon and eggs."

Titan launched into the food. Chandler returned his gaze to the people at the table. Laura was astonished, Shawn was almost paralyzed. "Ah, don't worry kids, it gets easier with every meeting," Chandler laughed with amusement. Shawn relaxed his shoulders, releasing the pent-up tension. Laura looked from one person to the next, watching them dig into their food as if a mad dog had not just entered their midst and demanded breakfast.

Shawn saw her bewilderment. Holding his fork in one hand and a piece of toast in the other, he said, "I will tell you later. Eat. We may not get another chance today!" He was glad he sounded much more composed than he felt.

The sun rose enough to bring in the daylight, but it did little to subdue the crispness in the air. Laura, being a true Texas native, bundled herself in a thick coat, gloves and cap. Winter didn't last long in San Antonio, but Texans found it bitter bearing anything under 60 degrees. It was at least 35 degrees, with the high not expected to reach beyond 50.

"Not sure how you are going to maneuver in all of that garb," Shawn remarked.

"It's freezing out here," she responded, noticing that all Shawn was wearing was a knit cap and a lightly lined jacket. "Aren't you cold?" she asked.

"Some, but I will warm up once we get moving."

"Brrrrr, not me," she quipped.

Having already examined the topographical maps Chandler had brought with him, they were ready to get started. Chandler, Shawnee, and Titan ambled up to meet them. Shawnee spoke first. "This is a flood-plain like most rural areas in this part of Texas, but it doesn't look to have flooded out here recently. The terrain will be varied due to the push and pull of past flood waters, though."

"We stick together on this," Chandler instructed. Everyone nodded. Continuing, he said, "This section of woods is not as big as those we had to search the last time, so it shouldn't be a problem with us five."

Laura looked around, counting to see if she had miscalculated their number. Resting her eyes on Titan, she realized who number five was. He stared back at her, creasing his eyebrows. She drew in a breath, and fumbled with her cap as if not noticing the dog at all.

"I thought it would be better to keep it small and hopefully unnoticed for a while."

"You should have thought about that before you drove that mobile home out here," Shawn remarked humorously. Laura laughed, though a bit nervously. Shawnee snickered.

"I see there is no appreciation for the finer things. Are we ready to go, you clowns?" Chandler rotated at the hips, proceeding down the slight shoulder and around the end of the culvert sticking out of the side of a mound. Stepping over a collapsing and rusted fence, he peeked over his shoulder to make sure his entourage was following. Titan jumped the barely upright portion of fence and trotted up next to Chandler. Chandler looked down at him and smiled, happy to have the big dog at his side.

Several feet into the woods, Chandler stopped to pull his Garmin GPS out of his pocket. He checked the pre-set coordinates with the figures he had jotted down on the back of his hand, making sure they would be able to find their way back to the RV. Confirming they were accurate, he held the device up at eye level, pointing the rubber antenna at the sky. The others gathered around. "We need to crisscross the property from edge to parameter edge as best as we can, until we complete a search of the coordinates," Chandler specified with a fingertip pressed to the screen.

"Titan, that means you keep close so we can all stay together," Shawnee insisted.

Titan searched her face for any flexibility in the demand. Finding it firmly convicted, he accepted the rules, but was not at all happy to be restricted. Swinging his black and tan face toward her, he barked in loud exhortation.

Speaking to him in the tribal tongue, she said, "Enee, Nepwa," meaning "yes, dead."

Taking his cue, Titan lifted powerful legs and swung them into action. He had been released to find the dead if dead were there to be found. As his legs flowed fluidly through the mixture of live and winter-dead forest, he sucked in long drawls of oxygen, allowing his brain to process all the particles that flew past the tissues of his nostrils before entering his expanded lungs. He identified the usual musty scents of dead winter vegetation, dormant wood, and woodland creatures waiting patiently in hidden dens for the sun to warm the earth. His ears twisted back, hearing the soft footfalls of the two pairs of feet behind him; his mistress and Chandler.

Chandler was not full-blooded Maykujay Shawnee; he was born to a Kishpoko mother and Maykujay father. His exceptional intelligence is why the Makujay placed him in a position to become a renowned FBI profiler. Titan knew these things from the conversations he had in his dreams with his father, whom the Makujay referred to as the Great Mystery. Ahead of him, a thin twig snapped, breaking into his thoughts. He stood transfixed, with one large paw hanging suspended in the air as still as a statue.

Seeing Titan take up a sentry stance, Chandler and Shawnee reciprocated the act. The two non-Natives continued to walk and talk, running into the back of the stationary duo. Recovering, they noticed the quiet disposition of the pair, and took up a more alert posture, scanning their surroundings.

"What's...."

"Shhh!" came the simultaneous response from Shawnee and

Chandler.

Titan descended his suspended paw, lightly pressing it down upon the dried leaves beneath it. Turning a wary head left, then slowly right, he focused his eyes. Squinting, he commanded binocular vision to center on every tree, shrub, hovel, and creature within his range. Nothing was out of the ordinary. He closed his eyes, commanding every brain cell and sense to combine in an effort to process the minutest presence. His nostrils expanded with the recognition of a familiar smell – no, not just familiar but pack, family! Titan sat, lifted his muzzle high, and wailed loudly the greeting song of the Makujay Death Dogs. In answer came a more human version, but recognizable nonetheless. Titan bounded over the trunk of a crooked tree, landing atop a medium-sized man with dark green eyes, shoulder-blade length black hair, and a thin jagged scar running from the corner of his left ear to the bridge of his nose. Titan swathed his face with long wet swipes.

"Oh you big brute, get off of me! I never can fool you, can I, no matter how long it's been?"

Titan allowed the man to stand, but lolled a tongue out as if laughing at him. Five foot ten inch Sky Spirit stood brushing dirt off the walnut skin on his face and hands. He made a swipe or two across his denim jacket to remove the dead leaves. Noticing Laura and Shawn had their nine millimeters drawn and pointed at the stranger, Shawnee and Chandler chuckled. Realizing they'd been had, they scowled and re-holstered their weapons. Titan grabbed Sky by the end of his jacket sleeve, tugging it as he walked backwards, pulling him impatiently toward the group.

Shawnee reached out with open arms to embrace her older cousin. "Washicatwelo."

"Washicatwelo, cousin," he returned.

Chandler approached, reaching out a forearm, pressing it into the one offered by Sky. Both men laughed, embracing each other vigorously. Chandler asked Sky when he had arrived.

"I have been in town a few days. I have been watching from afar, keeping an eye on things around Shawnee's place. I followed her out here, and guessed where you planned to search. I thought I would see if I could finally get an upper hand on this one." Sky ruffled Titan's forehead and laughed; a deep warm sound.

Like that will ever happen, man tracker.

"That's a good way to get shot," Shawn scoffed.

Sky exchanged looks with Chandler and Shawnee. All three broke their composure at the same time.

"What's so funny?" Shawn demanded, astonished at the mockery.

"Nothing," Chandler retorted, trying not to laugh again. "Let's just get going."

"Sky here is a scout, he will work side by side with Titan, following Titan's every move, making sure the way ahead is safe," Shawnee subtly explained.

Sky bent down to look deep into Titan's eyes. "You remember the way of this right Nepoowe Wisi (death dog)? We stay together, no taking off if you catch odor, we have to go slow and careful."

Titan whined. He remembered, but it meant more restrictions and rules. He hated rules.

"OK then," said Sky. "Let me grab my bag over there and we will saddle up." Sky trotted over to the tree where his bag was hidden.

"Did he bring a horse?" asked Shawn.

"It's a saying, Shawn," replied Laura, bumping his shoulder as she walked past.

Hooking a thumb toward Sky, "I know the saying, I just didn't know if it meant the same thing coming from him."

Shawnee and Chandler stifled another laugh.

"Let's go," castigated Laura, "before we embarrass ourselves any more than we already have."

Sky swung a canvas backpack over his shoulders, then clipped on a web belt with a variety of sheathed knives and daggers hanging from it. "Ready?" he asked Titan.

Titan answered by pivoting on his hind legs to take the lead. Remembering the rule, he slowed for Sky to catch up; then they settled into a familiar pace. This was the Death Dance as it was called by the Makujay; the Nepoowe Menyelwa. Titan, a Death Dog, would pit his senses against the elements to find the missing dead, while the scout (Sky) would pit his skills against the human enemy who might lie ahead. It would be Titan's job to establish the course, Sky's job to seek out any dangers along the way and eliminate them while looking for any human tracks. Shawnee would take up her normal position to Titan's rear, following his body language for signs of recognition, communicating with him when needed.

Titan stopped at the intersection of an animal trail where the wind was cutting a course through it. He bent his head into the waft. Finding it a useful tool, he turned his course onto the path. It was not wide enough for Sky to walk beside him, so he waited for the feel of his hand on his haunches that he knew would come. He felt the fingers slide into his fur and rest gently on his hip. Sky would keep pace with him this way, looking over Titan's head at the trail as best he could.

A tree branch stirred ahead of them. Sky dug his fingertips into Titan's muscle. Titan slowed, and eventually ceased to move. Sky straightened, stretching aching back muscles as he stood; pretending not to be alerted. Shawnee was there in an instant, having been only a few steps behind.

"Machi (bad)?"

"I don't know," Sky whispered to her. "It was just movement, that's all, but I don't want to take a chance on anything."

"Stay here on the trail with Titan. I am going to make my way around through these tall reeds, and come up on the other side of the tree with the big knot on the trunk. I will check it out and call you from there if all is OK." Sky lay low to the ground, set a steel blade between his teeth, and belly crawled like a Gila monster into the reeds. In a moment, he had disappeared from sight. Titan made to follow him, but a word from Shawnee stayed him.

Chandler, Shawn, and Laura joined the two. Chandler's trained eye spied the nearly invisible entry point in the reeds. "Sky gone hunting?" he asked.

"Yes, he saw some movement." All eyes shifted forward.

A voice sounded from the other side of the knotted tree. "Andakwa (raven)!" Sky appeared on the trail, an adult Raven hanging by the feet from his left hand. Dangling the bird above his head, he joked, "Dinner anybody?"

Enamored, Shawn said, "How did he do that? I never heard a peep. You would think that bird would be screaming bloody murder."

"That's why he is considered the best scout my people ever produced," Shawnee answered. "Around our fires, they say you will never hear him coming, never know he is there, and not know he has killed you until after you are dead and asking the devil how you ended up in hell." Shawnee peered over her shoulder at the Irish detective. With bright eyes, she added, "He also has a way with birds." She grinned, then tapped Titan on the rump. He pounced, advancing with her at his heels.

"Creepy," Shawn said aloud.

Chandler slapped him on the back as he passed, causing the tall man to jump slightly sideways. "Don't worry, he will let the bird go unharmed, he's just fooling around, he has a way with birds."

"So I heard," Shawn retorted sarcastically.

"That's why he was named Sky," Chandler called from a few paces ahead.

"I guessed that much already," Shawn quipped in response. Chandler ensued down the trail, leaving the startled detective to ponder what he had gotten himself into with this strange bunch.

Laura, undeterred, caught up with Chandler a few paces ahead of the lagging Shawn. "What does that mean?" she asked.

"What?" He kept walking, but eyed her curiously.

"What he said, I heard Sky whisper it to Titan earlier."

"Nepoowe Wisi?"

"Yes, that," she confirmed.

"It means Death Dog. What the modern world may call Cadaver Dogs, the ancients of the Makujay called Death Dogs."

"How is that possible? Cadaver Dogs are a twentieth century homicide and disaster tool. They have only been in real use for the last 15 or 20 years."

"Have they now?" Chandler remarked sardonically. "Perhaps that's only as long as they have been in the public forum, but I assure you they have been around much, much, longer."

Sensing she would get no more information out of him, she drifted back, walking single file in silence, looking back every once in a while to make sure Shawn was keeping up.

Two hours had gone by before they stopped for a rest. Shawn

plopped to the ground on his butt, lying back flat on the ground, his arms stretched out above his head. "My feet are killing me," he complained.

Laura kicked his loafers with her hiking boot. "No wonder," she commented. "You are wearing street shoes."

"I know. I forgot my boots!"

"Live and learn," she retorted without sympathy.

"And to think," he grimaced, "I was always the one complaining about Lizzey's shoes."

"Ready everybody?" came the call from Sky.

"Ugh, not yet, we just stopped," Shawn spouted.

Laura kicked him again. "Come on wimp, you are making us white people look bad."

"Moving out," Chandler waved to them to hurry and keep up.

Shawn rose to his palms. Rolling over on a hip, he pushed up on sore feet. Hopping a few steps, and grumbling under his breath he turned up the trail to follow the others. The trail eventually opened wide enough again for two people to walk side by side. Sky moved up to Titan's left, no longer having to trail the dog with a hand on his rump. Sky knew they were heading in the right direction, he could see the telltale signs of tree limbs having been raked across the ground. Shawnee took up the rear position behind him. Chandler and Laura were close behind with Shawn bringing up the far end.

Sky's eyes were always moving, searching vertically and horizontally for any outward sign of danger. His instincts kept him alert, his training kept him alive. The six blades hanging from his belt were shaped and honed by the best craftsman among the Makujay. He could place one between a man's ribs and cut his throat with another before the unfortunate victim even felt the sting of the steel. Three were daggers made for throwing from a distance. Sky had been trained well with those also. He could extract a dagger from his belt and throw it into a man's heart from thirty feet away before the culprit could draw breath to run. Killing with the blades was only one skill he possessed. He was first and foremost a tracker. Sure, he knew all the animal signs, but his specialty was the tracks of man; the slight heel mark or canted toe. And like his entire tribe, he was an avid woodsman. He had been taught to survive in and on nature alone, to know the weather, the insects, the trees, the earth, and how all of them could kill you or help you survive.

As a part of his duties, he often worked closely with the Death Dogs, teaching them the Death Dance. He had a special fondness for the Death Dogs of the Makujay. They were the special of the special, so very few were born each year out of the litters of security dogs, and none of them would live up to the caliber of the one who paced beside him now. Titan was very young, yet he had surpassed all expectations, proving to be knowledgeable beyond his years and experience. Regardless of his tendency toward stubbornness, it was said among the elders that Titan had been touched by the Sacred Hand more than any Death Dog before him.

Titan had not yet smelled anything that would lead them to the missing dead. It was time to switch direction, but he saw no other viable heading, the shrubbery was only getting thicker. The plan to search in a crisscross pattern had been abandoned since the trees and foliage were too dense in most places. He whined in frustration. He could go on by himself without a problem, but the humans would not be able to follow, and only he could find a shortcut. Sky slid to a stop beside him. Leaning down, he whispered, "Calm your mind, young one, do not allow your circumstances to control you….control them."

Titan licked his teacher across the face, drew cool air into his lungs, and cleared his mind of anguish. A tingle went through his muscles filling his body with renewed vigor. He shuddered and shook himself all over. Sky and Shawnee waited. Titan scanned the rocky crags and the ditch-laden landscape. He peered between each individual tree and around every bush. Not finding what he didn't know to look for, he did it again. Something caught his eye as he skimmed over a wild persimmon bush nearly picked clean by migratory birds. Intensifying his focus, he noticed a wide deer and boar trail nearly hidden behind the bush. Stepping off the current course, he wound his way through the cactus and Black Jack Oaks, not finding places the humans could get through until he came upon the trail he had spotted. It jutted off at a parallel angle to the skinnier trail they had been using, which was perfect for allowing them to continue to cross over the property from one end to the other, providing it didn't take a drastic twist somewhere along the way.

Sky's instincts prickled, a trained eye caught the tops of the dry reeds and rushes edging the trail. The tops were bent forward, not in a way displaying that something weighed them down continually, but showing that something tall enough and heavy enough to disturb them had passed this way. Titan's nasal passages tickled. He sneezed, thinking the hackberry was getting the better of him again. No sooner had he cleared his thoughts of allergies before the tickle emerged again. Instead of ignoring it, he tested the irritant in the moist lining of his nose. *Dust, fungus, trace – very small trace of dried blood.* He bounded forward.

Sky, who had been examining suspicious tracks in the trail, was nearly knocked over by the dog. Titan stood on hind legs, and reached as high as he could to the tops of the tall spindly reeds. Shawnee joined him, letting him place his front paws on her shoulder, using her body to balance. He stretched his muzzle out over her shoulder, sniffing the reed tops on each side of the trail.

"I see it," Shawnee told him.

Titan turned his head back to see where her finger pointed. He jumped down, twisting himself around as easily as a ballerina to the other side of the trail, and stood once again on his hind legs, reaching up with his nose to smell the reed tops. He settled his nose on some pin-head sized dark stains on a section of reeds. Shawnee pulled the reeds down to permit him to stand on all four paws. He sniffed the stains, processing the odor. She examined the stains visually. Titan's brain admitted the presence of dried blood. He immediately dropped his belly to the ground, cocked his head, and stared at his mistress. She felt in the canvas bag tied to her hip, and pulled out his ball. In his frustration, he did not wait for her to throw it. Instead, he snatched it from her hand and took off up the trail.

"Titan, don't go far!" she yelled after him.

Sky and Shawnee squatted, examining the reeds they had pulled downward for a better look. Chandler, Laura, and Shawn arrived. They too bent down to see the evidence Titan had located. Chandler pulled a blood test kit out of his shoulder bag, broke a tube in half containing a

Q-Tip with a special chemical on it, and swabbed it on one of the small stains. The end of the Q-Tip turned pinkish. "It's human, alright," Chandler confirmed.

Sky, suddenly realizing Titan was nowhere to be seen, stood with a frenzy and exclaimed, "Geah Tula (mother earth), where is that dog!"

9

Trotting along the trail, Titan rolled the rubber ball around in his mouth, enjoying the results of his hard work. Lost in the revelry of the moment, he was scarcely paying attention to little else until the strong smell of animal death reached his nose. He maintained his stride up the trail as it veered just slightly off to the left. It was there beneath a tall, mostly leafless Red Oak that he found the dead beast he had smelled. A hog's head was wedged ruthlessly between two of the lower branches. He studied it. It reminded him of the deer head he had seen jammed on the top of the pole at the other place. The hog had not been dead for long; but like the deer, it harbored an eerie aura of intense fear that accompanied its demise.

A little Seraph made its appearance, flapping its tiny wings in fervor to get his attention. Titan made his typical facial expression when coming in contact with the pest, diverting his eyes as if something else of more importance required his attention. He spoke to the Seraph: *You are like an insect sometimes, a mosquito to be exact. I can see the hog head, its right in front of me. I know the evil one has been here, Seraph, but he is here no more.* He dropped the heavy ball to the ground, drew in a heady breath, expelling it in a forceful bark that sent the Seraph tumbling away. He grabbed the rubber ball as it bounced back up, then persisted down the trail.

Annoyed at the Seraph and distracted from rolling the ball around in his mouth, he did not sense the string, pulled taut across the trail and covered by a fine layer of dirt. His toenail slid across it, barely applying any measurable pressure, yet it was enough. The wired crate came crashing through the foliage where it had been hidden. Attached to a horizontal catapult, it swung sideways across the path, scooping Titan off his feet from the side. The weight of his body sprung a latch that slammed the side door closed, dropping a bar in a customized groove that secured it permanently shut. The force of the crate being swung across the trail on the catapult created a momentum that kept the dog and crate flying through the air as it was released from the arm of the wooden structure. The flying crate that jailed him went crashing through the shrubbery on the opposite side of the trail, never touching the ground until it unceremoniously dropped off an adjacent hill and into a small stagnant pond.

Sky had no time to check the trail for the tracks of men; he had to follow Titan. The dog was always unpredictable when he was let loose with his ball. He knew better than to wander off, but somehow he always managed to defy the rules. He was in danger, and it was Sky's responsibility to see to his safety. That is why the elders sent him here, and now he fumed at his incompetence. He jogged up the trail with Shawnee and Chandler close behind. Shawn and Laura were near as well with guns drawn, the blood evidence putting them on edge.

Sky lengthened his legs, feeling confident that Titan had stuck to the trail. He heard what sounded like elephants thrashing through the woods ahead of him, while beside him Shawnee dropped to her knees in pain, grasping her head with one hand and covering her mouth with the other. He retreated, grabbing her by the waist to hoist her up, when he heard the subsequent heart wrenching wail that coursed ice through his veins. Fear momentarily paralyzed his legs, causing him to drop down beside her.

"Go," she said through gritted teeth.

Regaining his composure, he leaped to his feet, shook off the fear that had gripped him so violently, and launched into a long endurance sprint. "Weshimaneto, hear me, give lightning to my feet," Sky puffed out the words. He ran with speed he should not have had and lungs that should have collapsed from such sudden and extreme exertion.

Shawnee gathered her feet beneath her as Chandler reached under her arms to lift her up. Shawn and Laura ran past, guns still drawn and at the ready. The position they took with guns held in both hands at head level did not lend itself to speed of the feet, but as the rear guard they had their purpose. The problem was that they were not at the rear anymore.

Chandler held a palm to Shawnee's brow. "Better?"

"Yes, but we have to get to him now! He is in real trouble," she gasped, then took off running with Chandler catching up fast.

They passed Shawn and Laura, shouting a verbal warning before they overtook them. Seeing they were being left seriously behind, the two holstered their nines and took off, intent on catching up to the fray.

Sky veered left on the trail, saw a bloodied hog head in a tree, and kept going. He fell to one palm, pushed off, and resumed the race. Before him, a large swath of destroyed vegetation came into view. He could see it cut horizontally across the deer trail. Before he even reached it, he had already analyzed the path and determined it was fresh. He jumped off the trail, running straight down the path of the ruined shrubs, screaming out a pack call at the top of his lungs in the hope that Titan could answer. He was rewarded by a faint gurgling howl just as he reached the top of a small hillock.

Shockingly, he saw Titan's muzzle barely protruding above water in what appeared to be some sort of cage with heavy wire. Still running, he bounded off the hill into the pond. Landing in the scummy water beside the cage, he began treading with his feet. Pressing arms against the sides of the cage under water, he pulled with all his might. But the dog weighed too much, and he couldn't lift him and the cage together. He tried to tug the cage toward shore, but it would not budge. He felt for a door, but could not find one. The top of the cage seemed to be reinforced with heavier wire than the sides. The cage shifted as he tried to manipulate it, and Titan sank further, leaving just his nostrils above the water's surface. Green bubbles of algae rose from his nearly submerged nose. He reached to his waist, ripping a special knife from his web belt.

Punching the short blade through the wire, hoping he would miss the dog, he then fastened the wire on a hook of the blade with a powerful pull, slitting the wire a good eight inches. Expending precious time he felt he did not have, he cut an additional six inches in a plus sign configuration. Reaching in with both arms up to his elbows, he felt for the dog, grasping him around the neck. Hoping Titan understood, he was about to jerk him all the way under in order to pull him through the hole, Sky tugged him once, hesitated, and then jerked him with all the strength he had, pulling his head and neck through the hole. The dog's shoulders jammed against the wall of wire. He struggled, pushing against the other side with his hind feet digging his front claws into the wire bottom with extreme panic. Sky continued to pull the dog, knowing Titan's head was now completely under water. Two large splashes occurred one after the other. Titan saw through the murky water that two more sets of shifting legs had joined Sky's. Appreciatively, he felt the crate being heaved up and tilted out of the water as Sky, Chandler, and his Mistress lifted him above the surface where he could breathe.

"Can you hold him?" Sky breathed, still clasping his dagger.

"Try it," Chandler blew.

Sky let go of the cage. Immediately the crate dropped, and he grabbed it again, his own head momentarily submerging beneath the water as he continued to paddle with his feet and lift the trap upward. Shawn jumped in beside them. Now with four of them treading water and hanging onto the crate, Sky tried again.

"Have you got him?" Sky struggled with the words.

"Do it," Shawnee grimaced, blowing water out of her mouth.

Sky reached the blade into the wire again, and cut it from another angle. He grabbed Titan by the skin around his neck, jerking him forcefully through the hole. With Titan free, they let go of the cage. It tilted over, sinking instantly.

Titan came to the surface, gagging and coughing water from his lungs. Sky and Shawnee hooked curled fingers into his loose skin, and propelled him toward dry land. Laura was poised at the top of the hill with her back to the pond, gun drawn, and eyes scanning the woods. Hearing paddling below her, she stole a quick glance. Seeing everyone was free and swimming to shore, she gusted out a stressful breath then turned her attention back to the woods.

Shawnee and Sky heaved Titan, wet and soggy, onto the edge of the embankment. "Come on you, wet bag of carpet!" Sky puffed encouragement with a bit of humor, but Titan was done in from the fight.

Out of breath, Chandler huffed, "Why was that thing so heavy?"

"Weighted." Sky blew water droplets through bluish lips. With a grunt, he hoisted Titan further onto the sloped embankment. If he slipped, they both would wind up back in the pond.

Titan dug back claws into the muddy soil, pushing the rest of the way up, flopping atop Shawnee, pinning her back to the ground. He pressed his muzzle into her neck, too tired to lick her face. Arms wrapped completely around the dog, she squeezed him tightly toward her, expelling water from his fur as if he were a wet sponge. "Nitehi (my heart)," she whispered in his ear. He stirred but did not move further.

Sky lay back, spent. After a few moments, he explained how he had found Titan in the cage with only his muzzle and nose sticking out of the water. "I don't know why he wasn't completely under; the cage was so heavy and with him in it, too…." Sky let out a whistle.

Shawn spoke up, not at all winded like the rest, having just joined the rescue. "The cage landed on a tree branch sticking up from the bottom, and got stuck on it. I kicked it while I was treading water. Otherwise, he probably would not be here with us right now. There is no way we would have been able to lift that cage from the bottom of the pond – or hold it up like we did, for that matter. That tree limb saved his life."

Chandler, Sky, and Shawnee exchanged knowing looks. "Howesimanito (good spirit)," Shawnee puffed under Titan's still weight.

"Uhdyenahuk (blessings)," Sky responded, propping up on one elbow.

Chandler, sitting up, pressed an open right palm to his heart and replied, "Niyaawe (thank you)."

Shawn watched as he ended the act by presenting his open palm at an angle to the sky above, fingers somewhat bent and slightly apart, with his index finger pointing straight up; as if the act were to make it certain who was being thanked.

Shawn, lying face up, bent his head back. Looking upside down at Laura above on the hill, he called, "Don't you feel like a total stranger sometimes?"

Laura peered down the sloped hillside. In an act of ignoring him completely, she resumed her vigil on the hill.

"Humph," he muttered. "No one wants to include me in a conversation, it seems."

Titan sprang up on wobbly legs, his body heat returning, which made steam rise from his back. He moved to climb up the hillside when Shawnee tackled him around the hind legs. Sky also grabbed for him, while Chandler cut off his exit with a dive in front of the dog.

Out of my way, brain picker! Titan growled. Chandler may not be able to read my thoughts, Titan seethed, but he certainly understands my snarl.

"No way you are about to take off, Wisi, you stay with us from now on," Sky demanded, curling thick fingers into the fur of Titan's haunches.

"Absolutely going to happen that way, Titan, don't even think about going off on your own," Shawnee instructed.

"In fact," Chandler added, prone on his front, "I think it's time we all backtrack to the RV and get some dry clothes on."

Titan growled again.

"Best advice I have had in days," Shawn included, getting to his feet to start the climb up the hill, water running off his pants legs and over his loafers.

Titan turned angered eyes to Shawnee. She met them, felt the cross birthmark on the back of her tongue begin to burn with intensity, and knew that Titan was opening the mind bond again. Twice in one day, she grumbled to herself while waiting for the tirade.

"I will finish this Mistress, and now."

"It will do you no good, my heart, you will not find this man here, only his victim. Would it not be better for us to get ourselves dry and pick up the trail after?"

"He has tried to kill me twice now, this time he almost succeeded.

What if it were you? Would you stop now that we are so close?"

She hesitated before answering. *"No, Death Dog, I would not. Let us find this missing dead; then let us go from here and plan what we do next, plan what we do to stop him. But we will stay together, are we agreed?"*

"Yes, we are agreed, Mistress."

Freeing themselves from the link, they momentarily bowed their heads, waiting for the intensity of the headache to pass; it always followed the release of a sudden or angered connection.

Shawn stood atop the hill with Laura, who still held vigil while he looked on in disbelief at the scene before him. "This bunch gets weirder all the time," he quietly muttered, shaking his head.

Her blonde hair drifted to one side as she shifted her body to look. "I don't know," she said. "I kind of like all this native hocus pocus." He threw her a despondent look. "Well I do," she shrugged.

Seeing that Shawnee and Titan were breaking the connection, Chandler and Sky each reached down a hand, placing a palm upon the forehead of the one before them. The step eased the pain of the break more quickly and left less of a lingering ache.

"There is a reason I rarely do that, that way," Shawnee complained, rubbing her forehead with the heel of her palm.

Titan whined, shaking his head back and forth.

The two men remained silent, waiting for the result of the private conversation to be revealed. It was Shawn's Irish impatience that interrupted the quiet, even though he did not know exactly what had just occurred. "Well?"

Shawnee looked up the hill at the thin, tall man in dripping wet clothes. "We go on," she said matter-of-factually. Gazing over at Titan, she incorporated, "We finish this, at least for today."

Climbing onto the trail once again, Shawnee grasped Titan around the cheeks, pulling his wet face to hers. "Stay with me, no wondering off."

Titan whined, and then licked her across the nose, as good as saying OK. He pointed front paws solidly in the direction he was headed, anger fueling his concentration. Drawing in cool air that tickled the membranes of his nose, he swirled the odors softly across nasal sensors, nearly stopping time in his nostrils. As the rafts eddied, he waited for his nose to provide the diagnosis before analyzing the data it produced. *Pond scum, water, wet humans, wild grapes, deer herd, birds, nothing, nothing here.*

Titan stepped out, knowing he would have to keep moving, keep testing, and wait for the unseen air to bring him the death scent. The terrain finally became flat, giving the five the ability to fan out, no longer forcing them into single file on the deer trail. Sky drew one of the long blades on his belt, and stayed to Titan's far left no more than five feet away. Shawnee stayed glued to Titan's right hip, refusing to distance herself from him at all. Chandler spread out to Shawnee's right, placing a gap of no more than ten feet between them. Shawn and Laura did the same to Sky's Left. The trees and shrubbery, though less dense, made it impossible to stay in a straight line; but with no more ditches, hills, and mounds to deal with, they could at least keep an eye on each other. Titan and Shawnee remained on the actual deer trail. Chandler had explained it was in their best interest to keep it in sight, since the killer would have had to use one of the many trails to carry the victim into the interior. Titan's nose would find them a shorter course, one more directly to the victim; it could make all the difference in whether the elements overcame them.

In the middle of the trail, Titan dodged a cactus the deer were in the habit of jumping over, his nose seizing upon the undeniable smell of blood accompanied by an infinitesimal amount of human cell decay. He pivoted left, sniffed, pivoted right, and sniffed again. *The death scent is to the right.* He veered off the deer trail around a short stubby Weesatch tree, trotted several feet, and tested the air again. *Stronger here, the victim is not far and barely out of stage-one of the freshly dead.*

Noticing his body language, Shawnee called to the rest, "He is onto something!" They clustered around the dog. He took off, but steadied his pace to permit the humans to remain with him.

Shawn was shivering despite the exertion of the search. His thin body held no stores of fat to keep him warm in such circumstances. Laura, dry, shed her winter coat, slinging it over his shoulders to warm him. He cast an appreciative glance her way, pulling the coat close around his neck. The others, he noticed, seemed indifferent to the elements despite them being just as wet as he was.

Titan swerved between trees he picked especially to allow the taller searchers behind him to follow, while still staying on a course with the death scent. He broke onto another deer trail, quickly assessing that the scent was at its strongest level of odor so far. Each of the others came onto the deer trail, once again taking up a single file position. He increased his speed, but did not out-distance himself from Shawnee or Sky. They were swift and could almost match his speed, of that he had no doubt. Sky, feeling the dog's excitement, kicked it up a notch and equaled the dog's gait, coming along his left side. Shawnee joined him on the opposite side. None of the three were breathing hard, enjoying the run and the feeling they were about to succeed at their mission. Titan's senses were pulsing; they were so saturated with odor. All three of them saw the girl at the same time, and struggled to stop themselves before running right smack into her; they were barely successful.

Her tattered body hung in the expected upside down configuration. Her naked remains may have been void of clothes but not color. Her black, purple, and blue skin removed all trace of race, as her swollen features hid any viable indications of what she had once looked like.

A small, elderly appearing buzzard was perched above her feet, which in turn were affixed with braided hay twine over a hook. The buzzard was working on her right big toe, reminding Shawn with disgust of an old man gumming a piece of overdone steak. The tree she was fastened to grew in the middle of the trail. A closer inspection revealed how the deer had cut swaths around it; one on each side of the ten inch diameter trunk.

"How does this sicko find these places?" Shawn remarked angrily.

"He does his homework," Chandler provided, "and probably enjoys doing it."

Laura slid a radio off her belt and switched the knob to a private channel. "Wade, come in."

"Wade, go," came a response.

"We need you at T&W (Trail & Water)."

"I am already here, figured you would be calling me soon enough. The bone-man is with me, no need to call him."

"I will go get them." Chandler moved off at a trot down the deer trail.

Laura hit the radio call button. "Chandler's on his way. Did you bring that chainsaw?"

"Yes ma'am," Wade confirmed.

Hitting the button again, "Give it to Chandler when he gets there, he will make you a shortcut."

"Copy, Wade out."

Titan ambled off with his ball. He did not go far, having gotten into too much trouble already for one day, even for him. Looking up through the bare canopy above him, he could see the day was wearing on. The winter months caused the sky to harbor a gray scheme, keeping the sun from finding the earth that was so hungry for it.

A slow moving glow glided its way around the tree where he lay rotating the blue rubber on his tongue. He smiled to himself, reaching out telepathically to touch the essence of the presence. *"You are still here?"* he asked soothingly.

The voice responded lazily like it was not used to speaking, *"I am not sure where I am to go."*

"Do not anguish, I can help you," he offered. The glow hesitated, not wanting to leave the warmth of Titan's calmness. Understanding her emotion, he offered, *"It is warm and peaceful there too, I promise, sweet spirit. You really should go now. Fear not the way, my mind will guide you."*

Concentrating, he willed the girl's light upward. The glow momentarily brightened, and then dissolved into thousands of brilliantly illuminated specks. Titan sensed the spirit leave, and subsequently felt her joy at finding her way. He always refrained from asking them about the circumstances of their demise, knowing how confused they could be in that state of transition. He was not at all sure they would even remember, and if they did, he felt it cruel to remind them of the tragedy they befell. *Better to let my father counsel her, and allow me and my people to accost this Death Dealer our own way.* The grind of metal teeth cutting into dry winter wood brought his mind back from the spirit realm. Chandler was making his way with the evidence team.

Steve shuffled up on thick legs, nearly out of breath from the haul through the woods. The overzealous accumulation of fat cells around his middle did not help either, thought Laura.

"So here we are yet again," he sighed, then reached pudgy hands down to hoist his pants back up around his hips.

Wade, staring up at the corpse, said, "I don't think I will ever get use to this."

"Get the camera going, Wade, so we can get her down from there." Shawn sneezed out the last word.

Two emergency rescue technicians – one pushing and the other pulling a wheeled gurney through the man-made path – broke onto the trail, and stopped cold at seeing the body dangling from a tree.

Wade, catching their distressed expression, tossed them a somber note of courage. "If she could live it, boys, we can endure this." They shot saddened eyes his way, nodded with puffed lips, and took up the gurney once again.

Wade, unrelenting, kept snapping pictures, taking measurements, and collecting any odd piece or particle that he even remotely thought could be evidence. Steve walked around and around the tree, looking the dead woman over from ruined toe to ruined scalp. Shawn sat huddled under Laura's coat, sneezing out a complaint now and again about the cold and how long everything was taking. Laura worked alongside Sky exploring unsuccessfully for any tracks they could make plaster molds out of. Chandler and Shawnee sat close by on a log, involved deeply in private conversation. Titan had stuck to his promise and was drowsing nearby, staying within sight of his Mistress. The two technicians stood nervously waiting for Wade to usher them into helping him disentangle the corpse from its hook in the tree. The younger man, a dark skinned Hispanic, reached every few minutes for the gold cross about his neck, bringing it to almost trembling lips and muttering an indistinguishable prayer before releasing it again. The day was getting colder.

"She's very, very badly beaten this one." Steve cocked an eye at Wade. Pointing to the woman's upper torso with a gloved hand, he added, "She's not all contorted like this from hanging here either, her bones are all busted up."

"Plus look at her scalp, Doc," Wade almost choked out. "The

gashes this time are so much deeper than the others were. I think she has suffered the most so far."

"He is getting bolder," Chandler supplied, walking up to view the body once more. Both Wade and Steve turned to the profiler, who continued, "He is getting angrier and less fulfilled with his past efforts. He needs more excitement, so he is getting more brutal. Unless something in his personal or professional life slows him down, his killings will become more frequent, or at least more vicious."

Chandler left the two men staring after him as he stepped out a few paces, reached down, and pulled Shawn up by a wrist, and ushered the man toward the chain-sawed pathway. "Let's go get you dry and warm, Irishman, you look paler than those two Evidence Technicians over there, and they at least have never seen this before."

Shawn ducked his head inside the coat and sneezed again. "You'll get no argument from me," he agreed miserably.

Wade snapped his last picture. "You done, Doc, can we get her down from there now?"

"Yes boy, let's get her back to the house where we can take a better look at her. I want to get her out of these woods before we lose the last of our light." Staring upward he added, "Looks to get dark early."

Wade tucked his camera in its case, and set it aside with his evidence kit. He whistled toward the fearful pair of young technicians. They did not jump to the call, but made each motion deliberately as if counting the steps off to the atrocity before them. "Remember what I said Jose, Jesse....she lived it.... gently as we can, OK?" Neither man spoke; rather they made the sign of the cross on their chest, finishing by kissing the gold emblem around their neck then pulling latex gloves onto their hands. Despite the cold weather, they were sweating.

Jose, being the taller of the two, climbed the ladder they had stowed on the gurney, and was able to reach the hook the woman was suspended from. While Wade and Jesse lifted her upward from the shoulders, Jose released the braided twine from the hook. Keeping her feet propped against the tree with Wade and Jesse still in position below her, Jose climbed down the ladder. Slowly, they slid her feet down the tree trunk until Jose could grab hold of them again. Together, they slid her into the plastic body bag on the gurney and zipped it closed. Jose used his sleeve to wipe the sweat from his forehead, jagged black strands of straight hair staying plastered to his face.

Grasping the rear handle of the gurney while Jesse did the same at the front, they quietly and somberly pushed and pulled the cart with the woman on it back up the man-made course that brought them there. With the weight of the dead body, the gurney did not bump and bounce as much, but neither was it as easy for the wheels to roll on the uneven surface. Finding it too difficult to continue, they folded the wheels up and carried the gurney with sheer will and pure manpower.

Stopping only occasionally for a few seconds of rest, they soon found themselves out on the roughly paved rural road. Releasing the wheels to the ground, they sighed with relief, muscles quivering from the strain.

Reaching the ambulance, they pushed the piece of equipment through the doors, the wheels folding automatically underneath the gurney as it slipped easily into place inside the van. They closed the doors with finality. Leaning their backs against the cold doors, they both stared dull-eyed at each other, breathing heavily.

Steve came around the corner of the van, puffing even harder. He poked a thumb toward the van and blustered, "Get her to the house, boys!" The two technicians scuttled toward the cab of the van, jumped in, and hastily drove the vehicle away.

Sky, Chandler, and Shawnee sat around the small table in the RV sipping hot tea with honey. Titan lay on the floor gnawing on a buffalo knuckle with thick warm strips of meat hanging loosely from it. Chandler had warmed it in the microwave, having saved it days ago for just such an occasion.

"Are we free to talk?" Shawnee asked.

Chandler tossed his loose hand toward the back room, where the door was firmly shut. "Shawn is fast asleep, and he won't wake up for hours. I gave him some of Grandmother Spirit's sleeping tea."

Sky grinned widely. "She gave that to me one summer moon when I fell from the swinging rope and broke my ankle. I didn't wake up for three days!"

"Exactly my point," Chandler smirked over the rim of his cup.

Shawnee spoke. "We will have to let my father know what has

happened. He is sure to be concerned. So concerned, I'm afraid that he will send the whole Spirit family, if not the whole Makujay sect down here to find this guy."

"May not be such a bad idea, considering the damage he is doing to the public at large and the damage he is trying to do to Titan." Chandler looked at the dog.

Titan ignored them; he had other concerns at the moment.

"We have to think about what we really need from my father, and tell him rather than letting him go off halfcocked."

"Your father never goes off half-cocked," Sky reproved. "Our family has not remained secret for this many centuries within the walls of the Maykujay people for little reason. He knows his duty to the clan and to Weshimaneto."

Shawnee accepted the rebuke; placing a hand on Sky's arm, she squeezed it lightly. Peering over at Chandler, she explained, "Forgive me, cousins, I lack faith sometimes, in all things. It is good to be reminded."

It was Chandler who spoke next. "So, what are we going to tell Bear-who-will-not-hibernate?" Mention of the name brought a trickle of anticipation down the spine.

Shawnee straightened and cleared her throat. "I say we decide what to tell him, and draw straws to see *who* will tell him."

"No," came the strong reply from Sky. "I must do this. The council sent me to act as Titan's shield. It is I who must convey that I failed."

"You did not fail, cousin," retorted Shawnee. "He is well and alive as you can plainly see." She cast eyes toward the slobber faced dog, which lay on his belly with one huge paw flayed across the top of the bone. He was clinching bits of flesh with his front teeth, tearing them off the bone and tossing them down heartily. Fully engrossed in his endowment, he cared not that his muzzle was covered completely in grease from eyes to chin whiskers. One look at the dog, and all three of them burst out in laughter.

Once again, Titan ignored them.

10

The next day, Steve went to work, performing an autopsy on the third victim. He slipped his arms through a gown, and fitted a mask over his face, looping the elastic straps behind his oversized head, and stuffing unruly and unkempt gray hair into a baggy cotton cap. Retrieving a thick pair of large gloves, he wiggled them over his hands. His assistant that morning was a round-eyed young man who was still in his internship at the morgue. Carlton tied the gown off behind the older man's back, having to pull it tight for the strands to reach.

"Thanks, Carlton."

"No problem, Doc." Carlton began to take swabs of the woman's mouth, fingernails, and genital areas.

"No mistakes on those labels, lad. Hear?"

"No way, Doc, no mistakes, I know we can't afford them."

"Good boy," Steve said approvingly.

The Medical Examiner stepped toward the table, placed knowing hands on the blue and black splotches on the body, and felt the bones beneath. He continued this way until he had made a basic assessment of the entire structure of the body, again noting the burn mark where a Taser had been used. Carlton leaned in to look at a section of black swollen arm, palpating it. Pressing fingertips into the bone, he grunted in unbelief.

"I know," Steve voiced, acknowledging the intern with upraised eyebrows. "Nearly every bone in her upper torso, including the arms, is broken in several places. Even in my vast years, I have never seen such viciousness."

Carlton was silent.

Steve pointed to the outline of the black and blue marks. "What do you make of the bruise pattern, young man?"

Carlton removed a magnifying glass from a metal tray. Pulling an overhead light closer, he bent over the ribcage and peered through the glass at one of the bruise patterns. "The weapon used was round. It is about six inches in diameter. Too large for a hammer head; but the fact that it can be applied with such force suggests it may be a tool of similar use."

Carlton pushed the overhead light away and stood erect. Steve stood opposite of the body eying the intern, his arms folded over his chest and resting on his belly. Carlton looked down at the floor, thinking hard about his next answer. "It could be….a wood or rubber mallet." He looked up quickly, meeting his mentor's stare.

A smile broke across Steve's roughly bearded face. "Yes. Well done. My guess would be a rubber mallet." He moved around the table to stand next to the intern. Tracing a gloved finger around the outline, he remarked, "I find the impression of the bruise to be deeper than I would expect from a wood mallet. So, my guess is a rubber mallet was used"

Carlton gave the older man a discerning look.

Steve turned to him. Noting his extreme concentration, he explained, "You see, a wood mallet is lighter and would require much more energy than one may want to expend to wield it for this kind of work. A rubber mallet, however, weighs more and can cause more damage with limited force, allowing for a longer period of use by the person wielding it."

Carlton absorbed the information eagerly, writing down every word the good doctor uttered.

"Turn off the lights."

The intern stuffed his notepad and pen in the pocket of his lab- coat. The room went dark as the young man tapped the wall switch downward.

Steve flicked on a black light, swinging it slowly over the young woman's chest and stomach. "Turn her over," he told the intern. Steve repeated the act on the dead woman's back. "Nothing," he commented. "No glow in the dark paint, no message. Take her prints, clip her nails, and then get her over to x-ray. We will start the organ work when you get done."

Shawn awoke in a strange bed. Despite not knowing where he was or what day it had become, he felt great. He stretched, found his trousers and shirt clean and neatly folded on a small chair by the bed, slipped them on, then found his shoes and did the same. Opening the door he found sunlight spilling through the window in the next room. Chandler sat sipping coffee and pouring over forensic faxes he had just received from Steve.

"Good afternoon, sunshine," Chandler said sarcastically. "How do you feel?"

"I feel great, actually," Shawn responded. "What did you give me?"

"Oh, that is an old family recipe. I would be in violation to reveal its properties, I am afraid. I see it did the trick, though."

"For sure," Shawn confirmed, stretching above his head with a groan.

Bending over to look out the window of the RV, he exclaimed, "I guess I better call in, it looks like I am late getting to work."

"You are about two days late, my friend. But it has been all taken care of. You are assigned to the FBI task force now for the Upside Down Killer. We have officially taken over the case."

Shawn feigned disappointment, and then asked, "Laura?"

"Yes," Chandler substantiated. "Laura, Steve, and Wade. Shawnee and Titan, of course, are always on call."

"Wait, did you say two days late?"

"Yes, well, you seem to be easily sedated."

He had intended to interrogate Chandler further but the paperwork the man was pouring over caught his eye. "What do you have there?" Shawn extended a long freckled finger toward the stack of papers.

"Steve's preliminary report on our last victim," Chandler responded.

Shawn sat down across from Chandler, folded his hands on the table, and asked, "Anything we can go on?"

"Not really. Same hay twine, dog stake, washing of the body, no seminal fluids, and no skin cells beneath the fingernails. Her head, you already know, was shaved....brutally. The blood samples on the reeds match our victim. She is in her early twenties – nothing unexpected there. We don't have the fingerprint analysis back yet, but I will get a call if there is a hit. The only new development is that this poor young lady had all her bones pulverized; except her legs, which were only broken in one place."

Shawn winced.

"Steve thinks our killer is using a rubber mallet as his weapon of choice, and still using a Taser to subdue them."

"What did the message say?" Shawn prompted.

"No message," Chandler shook his head in disappointment. Continuing, he added, "There was no message at the hog's head or painted on the body. It is very odd for a serial killer to change his mode of operation midstream like this."

"Are you sure we are dealing with one man?" Shawn asked.

"Yea, I am sure it is the same guy." Chandler swirled the liquid in his cup, then set it back down firmly, sloshing it over the rim. "He is just different, this guy, he defies all the traditional rules. It is as if he is changing his behavior purposefully to throw us off, to make it harder on us, but serial killers just don't behave this way."

Shawn reached across the table, slid Chandler's coffee cup over, and brought it to his lips. He sipped the hot liquid setting the cup back in front of his friend when he was done. "It is obvious, don't you think?"

"What is?" asked Chandler.

"Our killer is hot under the collar about your Death Dog."

In the ancient manner, Shawnee's father held a long descriptive name. It was a name given him at ten days of age, as was tradition; a name that described his ill-tempered refusal to miss any waking moment for the option to sleep. Later in life when so many young men were renamed to correlate with some life-changing event or act, his name – seeming still true to character – remained.

Bear-who-will-not-hibernate was a strong thick man of six foot. He was tireless, fearless, and known for his temper; even though all agreed it was usually only seen with reason. No one who knew him intentionally provoked it. His mental prowess, logical thought, and ability to plan war-like contingencies explained why the elders of the sacred Maykujay sect depended on him more than any who served before him. As head of the Spirit family, the most secret aspect of the Makujay clan, he was of course the sect Chief. Even the sovereign Chief of the Shawnee Nation did not govern here. It all added up to one thing: Bear-who-will-not-hibernate answered to the Great Mystery alone.

The Makujay council made decisions within the sect, such as selecting Sky to go to Texas to protect Titan, but it required his approval before any action could take place. Bear-who-will-not-hibernate paced the floor of his expansive two story log home in Moluntha Village. The stronghold, situated near the banks of the old Licking River in the secluded hills of Kentucky, held great significance to his people. The place, the site of an ancestral battle, was believed to hold boundless power and a spiritual connection to the Great Mystery.

The two advisers stood still, not wanting to interrupt their leader's thoughts or inflame his anger. His muscles constricted as he spun around. "Titan was unharmed, you say?"

"Scratches only, great Hokima (chief)," answered his second in command. "He was nearly drowned as I have told you, but the misdeed was not successful."

Bear-who-will-not-hibernate rushed forward, stopping directly in front of the man. "My daughter, was she harmed in any way?"

"Sky tells me no, Hokima. She was involved in the rescue, but all were OK."

"This killer," the Chief began, "is proving somewhat of a challenge Sikona (stone). Targeting a Death Dog is a death sentence; one we will carry out swiftly if we must."

"But, my Chief," spoke the wiry man beside Stone. "It is not the Makujay's purpose to remove the evil on our own? Our ancestral purpose is assistance not annihilation; unless a Makujay life is in direct danger."

Bear-who-will-not-hibernate turned swiftly on the smaller man. "I know full well what our purpose is, Hoqaskwa (opossum). Our integration into this wabi world (white) has always been for the sacred purpose. But I will tell you this: A man needs not hold a knife to my throat for me to know when my life is in danger. Just because this killer stands not before our Death Dog or my daughter, does not diminish the fact that he has indeed placed their lives in danger from afar." With an explosion of anger, the Chief butted the bridge of his nose against the man's brow. "Direct threat, you want me to wait for a direct threat!" The big Chief glared down at the skinny man with clenched fists.

"M'kwa (bear)," a soothing voice interrupted. At the mention of his abbreviated name, the Chief relaxed tense muscles. Uncurling his fists, he turned to kiss his wife on the cheek. Opossum inhaled a ragged breath while taking a voluntary step backward. Inserting a light hand into his, the Chief's wife intertwined their fingers. Turning to the two men, she voiced in a subdued tone, "Respected advisers, let us think on this no more for the moment. My husband needs time to think and quell his burning mind on the matter. Come to us in an hour or two, and let us speak of it then."

Reaching a right palm to their hearts and then to heaven, the two men smiled warmly, then departed.

"I can always count on you, wife, to know what is best."

"I know when my husband is about to remove the head from a man's body and kick his corpse," she smiled in humor. "Where our daughter is concerned, and a certain Death Dog to be sure, you are always a father first and a Chief second. You must learn to separate yourself from your emotion if you are to make the right decision."

"You are right of course, Bear-Star, as always."

Pulling him toward the kitchen, she said, "Come husband, let me make you fry bread and buffalo bacon, that will settle your mind and your stomach."

"Another excellent idea, wife!" He pulled her close, tucking her under his shoulder. Together, they strolled to the kitchen.

Bear stood on his second story porch overlooking parts of the 2,000 acre Maykujay countryside. It was a cold morning. Dark as it was, he could still tell that new snow had fallen overnight. He knew without seeing them that Makujay Horseman were patrolling the boundaries, carrying modern composite bows with metal-tipped arrows. Amongst them were the Makujay Guardians and Security Dogs; The Guardians being the ones who trained all the clan bred dogs – even, for the most part, the Death Dogs. Guardian dogs were born without the sacred mark and no special powers, but retained a close genetic bond with the Makujay and were trained to protect nonetheless. The specially trained Guardians carried sniper rifles, and were equipped with uniquely honed throwing knives; knives that were distinctively fashioned by a particular faction of women within the clan, and molded from special metals dug from the very ground of the compound. All in the Shawnee nation guarded the secrets of the Makujay jealously and with conviction.

Bear's eyes shifted to the peak of a mountain just becoming visible in the dawning light. Within the wooded hills beyond that peak were gem mines, rivaled only by those in North Carolina. The difference was the North Carolina mines were not owned by the Maykujay, and were well-known to the public. These were not known to the outside world and were all on Makujay land, their location undisclosed until Bear's great-great-great grandfather was told of them in a dream. Now as then, they served as the source of their seclusion, security, and to help attend to the purpose for which the clan had always been born. Within and around those mines, Bear acknowledged, there were many Dogs, Guardians, and Horsemen fiercely guarding that secret.

He drank his coffee and thought about what to do. Despite his wife's offer he had forbidden his advisers from returning to speak with him further the day before. He needed more time to prepare his thoughts. Perhaps, he surmised, he should go to Texas himself, but the council would be highly against it. He could send his best warriors trained in the arts of hunting and killing, but that too would be met with argument. He could decide the issue no matter the discontent, but a good leader tries to keep his people happy. He could order his daughter home, but that would be the father in him, and Bear-Star was right: He should not prejudice his decisions with his feelings.

Setting the now empty mug on the table beside him, he reached in a coat pocket and pulled out a cell phone. Pressing the speed dial number that brought up COFBI (Chief of FBI), he listened for the connection.

"Not that I don't like to hear from you, Chief Spirit, but it is never good news when you call," the voice on the other end greeted.

"Good morning to you too, Wendall," Bear responded. "I need to pull in another Maykujay field agent on these serial cases in Texas. This killer is targeting operatives, now."

"Will one be enough?"

"Yes, the one I have in mind will be."

"Send me a text with the agent's code, and I'll draft the order myself. Let me know if you need anything else?" The dial tone went dead.

Satisfied, Bear tucked hands in his coat pockets and finished watching the sun rise.

The next day, dual FBI Field Agent and covert CIA Operative Quinton Beaver arrived at Moluntha village. He was escorted right away to Chief Spirit's residence. It was the first time he had been inside the building. The elderly attendant left him waiting nervously in what appeared to be a room spaciously built for just such occasion. Quinton took account of the interior. The parapets had not been paneled or dry-walled, but left with natural wood logs exposed; even though they were hand sanded until they shone. There were none of the animal head trophies he had seen in the world outside that so many of their white brethren seemed to cherish. The Shawnee believed such displays to be disrespectful to their animal sisters and brothers. Instead, the walls were draped with beautiful hand-crafted rugs and paintings from village artists.

Quinton loved returning to the village. It was a completely self-contained city with crops, herds, mills, water, smoke houses, stores, schools; it was all here. Not until a Makujay was pressed into specialized service did they need to venture outside these protected ramparts. He mused how both he and his friend Chandler were born of Kishpoko mothers and Makujay fathers. Both had been selected at an early age to go into law enforcement, where they would support the Makujay operations from the outside. This continuum was an arrangement as old as good and evil, and was secured within the highest halls of the United States Government; the Makujay being as important to law enforcement as bullets were to a gun. Quinton dropped his rucksack on the floor.

"I understand we caught you on your way back to the Middle East." Bear strode into the room, his blue-black hair loose and swaying near the waist of his pants. His denim jeans fit securely to formed legs. Wearing no shirt, his muscled arms and chest made Quinton – although he himself was sizable – feel small. "Washicatwelo Nihokima (my chief). Yes, I was on my way back overseas when I was diverted. I am grateful; actually, I have missed being home. It has been too long."

Bear clapped Quinton on the back with gusto. Quinton winced from the sting. "Let us talk, you and I, then go visit your mother and father. They are eager to see how you look after so long. What has it been, three or four years?"

"Four, Hokima."

The two moved across the pine floor to another room with ample windows and a tall rock fireplace with a roaring fire in it. They both sat in plush oversized chairs.

"Have you completed all of your training with the FBI, then?"

"Yes, I have accomplished all my profile training and completed my firearm certifications."

"What about your CIA training?" Bear asked knowingly, dipping his head just slightly in question.

"I also graduated with honors in my killing class, great Chief – all manner of….weapons," Quinton stated humbly.

"Good," Bear exclaimed.

"Spend four days with your family, then I must ask you to leave them once again. I am sorry, but we have some significant issues in Texas that need to be dealt with. I will have Stone brief you and get you any equipment you ask for. It is good to see you, Quinton.

Chandler will be happy to see you as well."

Quinton smiled at the thought of rejoining his old friend.

"Tell your parents I said they need to visit. I have not seen them in many moons."

"I will, my Chief. Thank you."

Bear watched from a large window as the confident young man closed the front door and walked across the compound with eagerness. Eyes still focused on the scenery through the window, he smiled knowingly and remarked, "You can come out now, wife."

Bear-Star entered the big open room, pushing aside a large heavy rug that hung on the wall, hiding the opening of a secret stairwell. "Are you sure he is the best choice, husband? You know he has always been taken with Shawnee. He may get distracted."

Bear turned his attention to his wife's lovely olive skinned face. "That's exactly what I am counting on. So distracted, that he sticks to her like glue. However, I plan to have her sent away for a week or so. It will give Quinton a chance to get some recon done. Sky will do his best to take care of Titan when they get back, but I want Shawnee looked after until this madman is dead or behind bars. If Quinton has to make him dead, it matters not to me."

"Still being the doting father, I see. Better not let Shawnee guess what you are up to; she will be furious."

"Let her," he retorted. "It was either Quinton or me. Who do you think she would prefer?"

"I see." Bear-Star turned her back, and ambled toward the kitchen. She stopped, shifting her weight onto a petite hip, causing the fringe of her soft Doe skin dress to sway slightly. Gently, she craned an elegant neck over her left shoulder and smirked with deviousness, "Quinton, of course."

11

Shawnee stepped onto the small deck off the backside of the spacious second story room. The sun was not yet up, barely peeking over the twin humps of two towering mountains; casting a promise of another unseasonably warm day. The high temperature for the day was expected to reach over sixty degrees. She breathed in deeply, feeling the crisp morning air fill her lungs. Behind her in the room, Titan yawned but quickly went back to sleep.

She set copper hands on the frost covered wood railing, peering over it to the ground below. A lone raccoon made his way across the frosted grass, crunching it under soft padded feet. In the distance, a dog barked. No house could be seen, but Shawnee knew that little shacks and cabins must be tucked obscurely away in the mountain crevices. A thick fog descended, settled in the ravines; valleys then rose randomly through the tree tops, creating the affect that caused the mountains to be called the Smokies. Hugging her shoulders, she shivered. Turning, she went back inside the warm room, shutting the door tight to keep out the cold. Titan rolled on his back, stretched out his neck, and kicked all four legs up in the air. She watched him fall back into peaceful sleep, and wondered how he could possibly be comfortable like that. She took a shower and readied herself to go downstairs for breakfast. Titan showed no sign of waking anytime soon, so she left him to his dreams.

In his bliss, Titan found himself cruising along a meandering path filled with rabbits darting past at every turn. He gave chase long enough to satisfy his sense of superiority, then returned to the path to find his next target.

"I am glad you are enjoying yourself, young one," the voice intruded from all around him. Titan sat respectfully.

"Good morning, Father, what brings you to me this day?"

"I need to speak with you, my special one."

"Yes, Father, I know, I have been avoiding the Seraphs again, I am sorry.... Again."

"That is not my course of discussion this day, but you are indeed stubborn on that subject. It is your undoing, you know; your stubbornness."

"Yes, I am sorry. I cannot seem to help myself."

"It is your age, Titan. It is why I do not bestow all the gifts I intend for you. You must mature before I empower you further. Do you understand?"

"Yes great one, I do. I will try harder."

"Despite that you are here to relax, there is trouble brewing. Trust Shawnee. This wilderness will challenge you, take care to respect it. Your quarry will know the way of it better and could use that advantage against you. The Seraphs will not likely abide you; in this, you have worn out your welcome with them. I could command them, but as I do not force you, I will not force them. In their own time, they may aid you again."

"Yes, Father, I understand. Can I go back to chasing rabbits now?"

"Yes, young one, do as you wish, since you will undoubtedly do so anyway." The voice faded, and Titan was alone once again. He padded down the path, looking for his next rabbit.

The front porch of the Bed and Breakfast was a massive pine master piece; stained redwood dark. It was polished and sealed to illuminate with the sunbeams. Small puddles of water pooled here and there where the evening rain had fallen. Raccoon prints trailed from the puddles: Evidence that the ring-tailed little fella Shawnee had seen the previous morning was still about. She stood sipping weak coffee, watching the local birds flitter here and there. Titan sat mildly by her right leg, enjoying the cool air.

Even though it felt no colder than San Antonio, the air possessed a certain thin and brusque quality. The sun was in full spectrum, although pockets of the smoky fog were still issuing between the mountain peaks. The B&B sat atop an expansive piece of property high up on a hill overlooking many of the one hundred foot treetops.

"Looks to be a pretty day," Shawnee peered down at her partner. The big dog whined and leaned into her leg. Instinctively, she reached down and threaded fingertips behind his left ear.

"Want to go hiking, T? Check out some of this country?"

Titan lifted his haunches from the deck and barked in agreement. "Alright, let's get our survival gear and head out. I have to check in with our assigned contact point in Knoxville, though, and let him know where we are today." Climbing the pine stairs, Shawnee cautioned Titan not to dig his nails into the soft wood.

Grabbing her bright orange survival vest from the small closet, she checked the numerous gear pockets, making sure the necessities were there. She tied the small sleeping bag on the back of the vest, even though she had no intention of being out that long; her training engrained the need to be prepared in a new environment. She dialed the number for the FBI agent in Knoxville. The grainy voice of an older man answered, "Calvin Nightdance."

"Mr. Nightdance, this is Shawnee Spirit, Washicatwelo."

"Washicatwelo Shawnee, it is good to hear from you this day. Are you well, I pray?"

"I am. Titan and I are going to go exploring the countryside. I wanted to let you know."

"Where are you two going?"

"Just around the Berry Nut B&B, not too far off."

"OK, call me when you get back, I thank you for that."

"I will, niyaawe." Shawnee hung up the phone. "I am all set big guy, how about you?"

Titan leaped into the air, heading for the door.

When she and Titan returned that evening worn and dragging from pure delighted exhaustion, the sun was arching its way down in the west. Shadows protruded over the B&B property as the tall trees blocked the sun's attempts to radiate more light. Only the distant mountaintops reaching above the behemoth foliage could yet make contact with the sun's rays. That would soon cease as well. In the ravine below the lodge, Shawnee and Titan stopped to listen to a loud voice from above.

"I don't know where she is, Boss, I am here waiting for her now." Shawnee recognized the voice from her earlier phone conversation. It was her FBI contact Calvin Nightdance. She urged Titan up the ravine wall.

"There you are," Calvin exploded from the front porch in a panic.

"Washicatwelo. Calvin, I presume," Shawnee breathed out heavily from the climb. The man before her was not the much older man she had expected. In his early fifties at the most, his gravel-like voice did not match his features or physique. He bore a chiseled jaw line; a common Makujay genetic. The deep-set eyes, however, spoke of Kishpoko lineage. She was aware of the Makujay practice of placing those mixed with Makujay and the blood of another Shawnee sect into law enforcement.

Calvin wore a thin plaid shirt over wide shoulders, atop the shirt he donned a worn leather vest opened to the unusually warm day. He stammered out an apology. "Washicatwelo Shawnee, forgive my disrespect."

Titan slid more than moved his body between the two. He breathed in the man's essence. Calvin grounded his feet. Having been raised in Moluntha village in preparation for the profession chosen for him, he knew the drill with Death Dogs. He waited for Titan to make his assessment. Recognizing the familiar smell of the sacred people, Titan backed up a step to allow the man closer.

Calvin nodded. "Death Dog, I am honored to be allowed so close to you and your mistress."

Titan remained fixed, but Calvin knew the dog understood his words. Turning to Shawnee, he explained his unexpected visit. "My Boss has his white hair in a tizzy over a letter he just received."

Shawnee arched an eyebrow, she knew what was coming. "I have been ordered on vacation, Calvin, I am to lay low," she grumbled.

"I know," he said in exasperation, "but we don't have a Death Dog assigned to this area yet. There are some unreliable fly-by-night folks in the white world who claim to be experts in the field, but none that we have found to be reliable.

"You have to clear it with Chief Spirit. I can do nothing for you without his say-so. He would skin us both alive."

"I called first thing, I spoke with Stone," Calvin remarked, flashing a fax at Shawnee.

Shawnee snatched it from his hand, and read it: *Daughter go, Notha (father).* She inspected the edge of the paper, looking for the automated code that would validate the source. Finding it, she let out a whistle. "Titan, we are back in business!"

"You see the mountain peak," Calvin asked, pointing across the wide valley from the balcony off Shawnee's room. "That's where we will be headed. The mountain is near a small town called Chestnut Hill. The letter written in a woman's scribe said that thirty years ago, she lived on the mountain on that side, when her father brought a young girl home with him late one night. From what we can glean from the letter, this woman – who is remaining anonymous – was about eight years old at the time. The girl her father brought home was about six. He told his daughter that he adopted the little girl to be a playmate for her. There is no mother mentioned in the letter. Anyway, she says the father always had the little girl sleep with him, and she often heard her crying. About a month goes by; then one night, she hears him stirring. She peeks into the living room to see her father wrapping up the sleeping little girl in a blanket. He picks her up and takes her out the front door of the remotely located cabin. She rushed to the window, and by moonlight sees him toss the bundle over his shoulder and grab a shovel with his free hand. Off he went down the mountain on foot. She pulled on her boots and snuck out after him. Running from tree to tree, she crept quiet as a mouse until she finds him digging a hole under the only purple sage tree she has ever seen on the entire mountain. She claims to have been quite the young explorer, having hiked all over the mountain; on her own, no less, at eight years old.

The letter says she was taken away from her father shortly after that by the state, when a hunter found her alone on one of her explorations. She was dirty, underfed and unkempt; she never saw her father again."

"Sounds like we have a good clue to go on, only one Purple Sage tree on the mountain," Shawnee expressed.

"Trouble is, it has been thirty years, Shawnee; there is a vast Purple Sage population there now, albeit contained to the east side. The other problem is that side of the mountain is totally unpopulated, so there are no roads or homes, very little in the way of cleared away brush-line. There has been no one living on that side of the mountain for the last twenty years or so."

"Why?" she asked suspiciously.

"The locals say it is haunted."

Shawnee looked at Titan, who returned the stare. "We will be ready in the morning."

Calvin visibly relaxed, like a huge weight had been lifted from off his back. "I will pick you up at 07:30, will that be OK?"

"We will be waiting on the front porch."

The next morning, Shawnee dressed, packed, and was ready to go. She and Titan impatiently met Calvin at the bottom of the lodge drive as he made the turn onto the property. Calvin checked his watch as Shawnee jumped inside the Jeep, tossing her gear into the back. Titan hopped in and settled next to the gear.

"I am not late, am I?"

"Nope," Shawnee addressed him, "we were just bored."

Calvin pressed a worn hiking boot down on the accelerator. He was dressed in a dark green colored long sleeve canvas shirt and a pair of tan hiking pants, the kind with multiple pockets. Shawnee unknowingly had matched his dress, wearing the typical 5.11 tan work trousers and a camel colored long sleeve hiking shirt. Her boots were military issue camel suede, although a year of use had worn most of the suede away. Even though the day promised to be warm again, hiking in brush with short sleeves or shorts amounted to stupidity. Branches and vines could slice and bruise unprotected arms and legs.

"We will meet a helicopter at the base of the mountain," Calvin yelled over the wind whipping through the topless jeep. Shawnee's black hair flew straight as a board behind her. "It is easier to climb down than up, so the pilot is going to basket us down to the peak. We will work our way down the mountain from there. It will take us several days. I packed the provisions we will need."

Shawnee peered over her left shoulder. Titan was huddled down on the seat, bracing against the bumpy ride. She observed he would have a hard time catching what Calvin was saying for the wind tunnel the racing vehicle was creating. She considered how she was going to get him in a spinning basket tumbled by high elevation winds. He could be mulish when he wanted to be. No, she corrected, he was always mulish.

The tree-line flew by. Calvin, familiar with the skinny winding roads, slowed down for no man or creature in his rush to the mountain. Gripping the roll bar tightly, she asked, "Many wrecks?"

"Sorry," he laughed apologetically. "I forget how squeamish outsiders can get on these roads." Still, he did not slow the vehicle, continuing to traverse the course ahead of him. Before long, the mountain came into view. It was smaller than those around it, not near as stately. Yet it contained a strange and powerful aura. On one side, life was evident in roads, houses, horses, and livestock. On the other, it was obviously void of human intervention; as if a giant troll had drawn a line down the middle and declared one half his own.

Sliding slightly as he pressed the brakes, Calvin pushed the gear shift into park and announced, "We are here."

"Where is the copter?" she asked, looking around. Before he could respond, she heard the whirl of the four bladed utility vehicle.

Titan popped up from the seat behind her, took one look, and wagged his tail. Shawnee got out of the Jeep and walked around the other side, where Calvin stood watching the helicopter land. Titan jumped out the open jeep door, and trotted in front of the pair, tail still wagging.

"Looks like he likes to fly," Calvin grinned broadly. She met his eyes but did not smile.

"What?" he asked instantly, losing the Cheshire grin.

She leaned in. "He loves to fly, but I don't know how we are going to get him into a basket hanging precariously over a mountain."

"I see."

Calvin's cropped black hair stood up, imitating the trajectory of grass as the wind off the helicopter blades forced eddies of air past him with vitality. The right-seater in the UH-60 Black Hawk waved an OK to Calvin. The cargo door slid back on its track. The Crew Chief leaned one hand on the edge of the opened door, waving his free hand at the group to come aboard. Titan, waiting for no invitation, bounded at high speed for the open door of the helicopter. The kneeling Crew Chief saw the big dog too late to move out of the way, and was bulled over. The man's helmeted head hit the cargo floor with a loud thud. He lay helpless as Titan stood on his chest licking his eye shield, mouth microphone, and any aspect of the man's face he could reach. Realizing he was not in danger of being eaten, the man good-naturedly patted the dog on his sides. The pilot in the left front seat looked over his right shoulder to see a scene right out of the movie Kujo or Pet Cemetery. Still secured in his harness, he scrambled to extract his nine millimeter from his shoulder holster.

Unable to get to his weapon readily, he was relieved to hear the man announce with mirth, "I guess he is ready to go!" Crisis avoided, the nervous pilot propped his head against the headrest behind him and cursed under his breath; his heart beating rapidly.

Gear flying into the cargo hold saved the crewman from further indignity. Titan, hearing the bags being tossed, did a capriole over the man, taking up a seat where he could see out of the window. He glared at the metal basket secured by hooks on the wall. Briefly, he wondered what the unfamiliar contraption might be used for, but gave it no further notice. He was ecstatic when the blades whirled faster, lifting the entire aircraft from the ground. The thrill of transforming into a bird was matched only by the pure joyful sensation of actually flying through the air. He exalted in the experience. So high he was in spirit, he failed to reason the scene before him moments later. The Crew Chief, having slid the cargo door open in mid-air, was now lowering the metal basket outside; although it stayed tethered to the helicopter. The basket, full of all their gear, was quickly falling to the mountain peak below, extracting more and more of the metal cable wrapped around a pulley inside of the helicopter. Titan watched as the Crew

Chief reversed the cable's direction. The basket soon reappeared and was pulled inside… gear dumped and basket empty.

He was horrified when, next, Calvin seated himself inside the basket. Realizing the Crew Chief was about to drop Calvin out of the aircraft, Titan jumped from his seat, closing sharp teeth around the man's forearm. He did not bite through the skin, only held him, threatening. The crewman became riveted in place. He stared blankly ahead at nothing and nobody. Shawnee, sensing tension, tore her eyes from the ground below to witness the scene before her. She opened the bonded link between her and Titan. The cross birthmark on his tongue suddenly flared into hot embers. Titan shifted narrowed eyes from the man's face to Shawnee's eyes, never letting go of the man's arm.

"Why are you threatening this man?" Shawnee demanded.

"Can you not see?" Titan asked bewildered. *"He is about to toss a sacred soul to his death!"*

"No, Titan, he is not. This is how Calvin will reach the ground…. safely. It is how we must all reach the ground." She let the words hang there, watching his eyes to see if he comprehended what that meant. Titan's whiskered brows unfurled in horror; he released the man's arm, abruptly closing the link and backing up several steps. The crewman nearly collapsed with relief at being allowed to keep his treasured limb. The dog shook the pain from his head, took another step back, and felt his rump hit the bulkhead on the opposite side of the cargo bay. He stared at Shawnee in disbelief.

"Yes, Titan. It is how we must go," she voiced aloud over the roar of the blades.

He recalled then what the Great Mystery had told him in his dream: *Trust Shawnee.*

Titan watched helplessly. Calvin, showing no sign of fear, was lowered from the door of the helicopter inside the basket. The cable wound out much slower this time. It seemed like a long time before the cable reversed and the basket reappeared without Calvin inside. Titan looked over the edge of the helicopter floor to the ground below. Hovering above the hundred foot tall trees, the helicopter was high enough that Calvin seemed like a tiny doll of a man. But Calvin was waving up to them, alive and well. Titan retreated.

Shawnee accepted a wide roll of gauze from the Crewman. She leaned into Titan's cheek with her own, and implored, "Trust me, T."

He whined, licked her right cheek, and whined again. Slowly, she began to wrap the gauze around his eyes – looping the roll many times under his throat, over his eyes, and between his ears to secure it in place. She positioned herself inside the basket, never removing her left hand from his back. After getting settled, she called him to her, guiding him by using the pressure of her hand. He stepped into the basket, one careful paw at a time.

"Lay down," she yelled to him, over the whup-whup-whup of the blades. He complied, straddling her legs. She held the basket lanyard with one hand while keeping the other pressed firmly on his back.

"Ready?" yelled the Crew Chief.

Shawnee nodded once. The basket lifted off the floor, then swung out the door into the free air below the whirling blades. The crewman set the controls for the cable to slowly lower the basket, never removing his eyes from the girl and dog in case the situation turned sour. He sighed in relief when finally the basket reached Calvin's able hands and settled at the bottom. He pulled the basket up as fast as the generator would allow, motioning to the pilot when it was stowed on board. The helicopter climbed out and over the mountain.

Calvin took his time marking charts, reading his GPS, and checking his communications radio for the availability of frequencies. "Not getting through on the radio, but I did not expect too much in these trees."

Shawnee felt the comment was rhetorical, so she did not respond. Instead, she busied herself with removing the gauze from around Titan's eyes. He shook himself, expelling the sensation of fear he had acquired from the trip down. Free, he took off to explore.

"Stay close. I mean it!"

He barked in response as he stretched out in search of rabbits. Calvin scanned the peak, looking for the telltale tops of Purple Sage. The large bushy trees had small grayish green leaves, and sprouted hundreds of very small dark purple flowers. Clusters of such trees made them impossible to miss. The unseasonable weather in the region had the flowering trees producing strongly.

With the binoculars still pressed to his eyes, Calvin remarked, "Looks like if we make our way into the interior about two hundred and fifty feet along this western parameter, we will locate our first stand of sage."

Shawnee stretched her throat out, lifting her chin skyward, letting out a pack howl; one long throat harmony followed by three short yips. Titan crashed through the brush, tongue lolling sideways out of his mouth.

"The air is thin up here, Death Dog, you may want to keep that in mind," Calvin informed him.

Now you tell me, he thought. *I was wondering why I couldn't breathe.*

Shawnee heaved her pack over her shoulders. Calvin did the same. "Titan," Shawnee addressed him sternly. He was still panting. "Calvin will be leading us. We are looking for a certain tree that is a marker of sorts. When we find the trees that is when we need you to go to work. Save your strength until we reach them. We have a lot of work to do over the next few days."

Titan pulled his dangling tongue into his mouth.

Calvin worked his way through the trees, looking back now and again to make sure Shawnee and the dog were still following. He knew the risk he was taking with the pair. One was Chief Spirit's daughter. If that wasn't bad enough, the other was prophesied to be the future of the Death Dogs: One who would become so gifted that all who came before him would be considered babes in comparison. He hoped he had not bitten off more than he could chew. If harm befell either of them, he wanted to be far away in a third world country when Chief Spirit learned about it.

Calvin pulled up, checking his GPS for signs of life. Slipping it back in his vest pocket, he turned to Shawnee, who had come alongside.

"I can't get a good reading in this cover, not enough atmosphere getting through."

Shawnee stared upward. The trees had bud quite a few leaves; some branches were bare, but sparingly. If the normal seasonal cold weather ever got here, she thought, the leaves would probably all die instantly again from the shock of it. Gripping the mouthpiece on her camelback, she slipped the rubber fitting between her teeth, biting down she pulled cool water into her mouth. Calvin took notice and did the same. Titan trotted over to her, waiting. Pulling the tube from her mouth, she held the opening over his upraised muzzle and squeezed the end. Water ran in a trickle down to his mouth where he lapped at it.

Calvin squatted on his haunches and peered into the trees. "There we are," he pointed. "Purple Sage, right over there." Standing, he stepped off quickly, heading for the sage he had seen.

Securing the valve and tube, she took off after Calvin, with Titan trotting alongside. When they stopped a few minutes later, they were surrounded by beautiful tiny purple flowers. The sage leaves grew all the way down to the lower base of the tree. By all accounts, it was probably more of a bush as far as its classification, even though the Purple Sage grew to some fifty feet high. No fragrance accompanied the hundreds of flowers, but that did not detract from the exceptional beauty they created. Tearing herself away from the feeling of being wrapped in Easter paper, Shawnee told Calvin they needed to set boundaries for Titan to search. "We need to mark the beginning and end of the sage trees, since those are our markers. Otherwise, he will just keep searching. Telling him to distinguish one tree from another is like telling him to distinguish one rabbit from another; they are all just rabbits."

I think I can smell the difference between a Texas jackrabbit and a tiny cotton-tail, he fumed to himself momentarily. *But, she may have a point about the trees,* he conceded.

Calvin and Shawnee departed in opposite directions, each marking the end of the Purple Sage tree line with bright orange fluorescent vinyl tape. By looping long flowing strands around a branch at each corner, Titan would be able to clearly see the end of the search parameter. Each satisfied with the result; they met back up at the starting point.

"OK Titan, let's do this. Stay within the markers we posted for you. We don't want to wear ourselves out, we need to work with the clues we were given."

Titan huffed in exasperation.

"OK?" she said more than asked.

Titan wagged his tail, then barked.

"Mean it!" she demanded, arching a thick black eyebrow. He answered by barking with force.

"OK then, listen carefully. We are going to start at that corner," she pointed in the direction she meant. "Where Calvin placed his first marker. Pattern yourself to search the length of the parameter continuously in twenty foot intervals, until you have reached the opposite boundary where my markers are also posted at each end. Got it?"

Titan barked, hopping on his front legs with impatience.

"If the thin air gets to you, stop. We will rest, and then continue when you are ready."

He bounded off in the direction he had first seen Calvin take. Finding the first corner marker flowing softly on a cool loft, he stopped, and turned knowingly toward the trail Calvin had left as he had made his way to the next corner. Titan looked back. They were right behind him. He lifted his muzzle, pulling thin brisk air into moisture lined passages. The scents here were cleaner, crisper, and more finely assessed than what he was used to. His testing found nothing to be acknowledged in the way of human decomposition, so he gathered himself into a steady canter, staying to Calvin's original course. Not enough sunlight was ever able to find its way through the mostly opaque foliage to reach the soil below, so little in the way of ground cover could manifest itself. Titan threaded over fallen limbs and a scattering of misguided leaves, but other than that the way was clear. Mostly, all he had to do was make his way around each tree that presented itself as an obstacle, assuring that his companions could follow easily enough. Soon, he reached the farthest marker, indicating his need to turn right and pace out what the Guardians had taught him to be a twenty foot interval. He was glad he had paid attention during those lessons, or it would most certainly be evident today that he had not. Achieving the approximate span, he turned upward toward his original bearing; eventually, he would wind up back at the top, twenty feet from the uppermost west marker, where he would start back down again, adding another twenty feet to the breadth of his pattern.

They continued this way for an hour. Seeing Titan slow and his sides heaving for air, Shawnee called a halt to the continuance and sat down for a short break.

"The temperature has dropped," Calvin pronounced.

"You think so? I had not noticed."

"That's because you are not from here. You think you are warm from these uncharacteristic temperatures. This country has lulled many-a-visitor into thinking they need to shed a few layers when that's the worst thing they could do."

"Is this drop something we need to worry about?"

Calvin rested with his back against a large Maple tree, one knee pulled up with a hand propped atop it. His fingers flicked up and down almost involuntarily, as if an insect were pestering him. Finally responding, he announced, "No, but we need to remain aware, make sure we don't get too comfortable out here and miss a sign of the weather changing for the worse."

"I'll leave that to you, lawman. As you say, I am not from these parts."

Calvin acknowledged the statement with a grunt.

Titan led the way, again picking his way through the trees and sage, maintaining the interval as best he could. As the second hour closed, he emerged past the upper eastern marker; he had finished searching the entire boundary without finding the missing dead. In fact, he admitted that since entering the dominion of the Purple Sage, he had not even smelled a scrawny rabbit – or a bird, for that matter. He scanned the tree branches above with far-seeing eyes, rotating his ears to catch the sounds of the mountain. He saw no life but the trees and heard no noise but the wind. Shutting out the light, the wind, and the place where they were, he turned his mind over to the bond that was he and Shawnee. He reached out lightly, avoiding the intense burn that came with a hurried connection. The cross mark on his tongue tingled with warmth, and she opened the link on her end almost immediately.

"Yes, my heart?" responding to his summons.

"Mistress, there is no life here."

"I thought you found nothing?" she remarked with surprise.

"No, I mean no living thing, no creatures, neither those who soar above nor those who occupy the Earth. It is as if they will not dwell

here."

Startled, Shawnee severed the link. Her eyes flew open; instantly, she twisted, scanning the forest about them.

"I thought I told you," Calvin interrupted somberly, realizing she now understood.

Shawnee turned on him. "Told me what Calvin Nightdance? That no person would live here, that it was thought to be haunted? You seem to have left something out, don't you think? Was there ever even a letter?" the accusation was shot out hotly.

Titan was confused by the affray. The two sacred souls were chafed with each other. His mistress was angry; a bitterness floating about her words that he did not understand. Titan tossed neural sensors toward Calvin; deception flowed back to him, no ill will but certainly the guilt of untruth. Finding no threat, he allowed the confrontation to take its course: If his Mistress came to need him, he was close.

"Please appreciate, Shawnee, I meant no harm, I...."

"Harm may be exactly what you have done, Calvin," she spat. "He is not ready for this," she hissed, lowering her voice. "What were you thinking?"

"I know what they say he is capable of. I thought he could.... end this." He swung his arms to the side, splaying his fingers.

"He is not yet aware of the many things for which he is capable," she gritted through clenched teeth. "He is only two years old. Baptism by fire is not the way the Makujay present such knowledge to them. It is not done this way. You know this!"

Shawnee flipped eyes to her feet. Titan sat serenely at her side, intently amused to discover the quarrel was about him. "How long have you been sitting there?" she expelled.

Titan twitched his ears. Facing Calvin once again, she slapped strained hands onto rigid hips, seemingly making an effort to hold herself still. "This is your fault, Nightdance, now I have to explain it to him."

Calvin bowed his head, no longer able to meet her glare. Pressing hands out in front of her, she drew in a rough breath and indicated for both of them to give her a minute or two. Stomping off in no specific direction, she ranted in a slang that Titan was sure he had never heard before. He stared after her, then to Calvin. *Not sure what you did, but I would not want to be you right now.* Calvin, sensing another set of glaring eyes, shifted his feet and found an indiscernible spot on the ground to focus upon.

Returning, Shawnee pointed to Titan. "You stay there, and it is not a request."

Titan plopped to his belly with a huff, regarding her coolly.

Wagging an index finger at Calvin to follow her, she cut him a look of umbrage to ensure he understood that it wasn't a request, either. Leaning against a Eucalyptus tree, she folded her arms across her chest. "How long have you known?"

"Only a couple of weeks, I swear!"

"How did you discover this?"

Calvin's shoulders slumped. "A woman I see on occasion over in Charlotte, well, we have become really good friends. She used to live in the area here. She had a little girl that went missing several years ago; it still terrorizes her dreams, and every day is a challenge for her to get through. I started doing some research and discovered that in the last thirty years, thirty young girls have gone missing; one for every year."

Calvin pulled a folded map from inside his leather vest. Unfolding it, he tapped the paper. "I marked every address where the girls went missing from, look...." He shoved the map toward Shawnee. She took it. Examining the little red dots marked on the map, she noted that they were concentrated in a huge circle, except for a tiny "x" in the very middle of all the dots.

"What is this?" She pointed to the "x."

Calvin leaned in to look. "That's us, this mountain rather. All the addresses of the missing girls sweep in an expansive circle around this mountain." He traced it with a fingertip. "He was careful, though... our murderer, he made sure he abducted them from numerous different counties and only one per year, as best as I can tell. The combination of those two factors made it pretty sure that the different agencies would never put it together."

"So you came up here to look around, and discovered all the wildlife gone?"

"Yes. I realized then that the rumors of this place being haunted weren't rumors at all. I was preparing to send a report to Moluntha Village, but then you showed up here with Titan. I started thinking about how much easier it would be for a Death Dog like him to find them all that much quicker, and I could help my friend heal so much faster. Then the letter came – yes, there really is a letter! It confirmed what I thought… I am sorry, Shawnee, I know that what I've done is wrong and I will face punishment."

"Your heart was in the right place, Nightdance, I will give you that."

Calvin lifted his eyes to meet hers, there were tears there. He rubbed a sleeve across his face to dry them.

"We have no choice, do we?" she asked.

"No, I am afraid there is no way to call anyone," he sniffed lightly. "The radio doesn't work this high up."

She sighed. "His first encounter should be done in ceremony, with elders sitting around a night fire chanting the old songs, imploring the ancestors to intervene for support." She lifted her arms in vexation, and then dropped them. "Numerous trapped souls at once can drive an immature Death Dog mad without aid," she finished.

"But….what about the tribal prophecy?" Calvin beseeched.

She lifted her face to the patch of tinted sunlight transposing its way through the leafy tops. "It is said… that he will be great. That, his abilities, his powers, will be like none before him. The Great Mystery will grace him with abilities that are beyond any a Death Dog has ever possessed. He will produce a new race of sacred instruments." Shawnee returned her stare once again. "But I do not decide the time nor the place of his learning that is not in our hands." She pushed her back away from the tree trunk with a foot. "But it seems I am forced into doing just that." She took several steps, stopped, then looked back at Calvin. Addressing him sternly again, she said, "Take care of him. See that he is fed and kept warm for the night. I will enter into solemnity and seek permission and guidance. I will build my own fire Nightdance, do not disturb me." Setting firm steps before her, she entered a coppice, disappearing from sight.

By the time Calvin made his way back to where they had left their gear and Titan, Shawnee had already opened the link, telling Titan no more than to stay and obey Calvin. Titan was of course perturbed about the lack of forthcoming information, but heard the tone in her voice and knew there was no negotiating. With respect to obeying Calvin, that was a farce as far as he was concerned. But he would stay put.

12

Shawnee gathered dead wood, piling it high for an enduring fire. She stacked smaller pieces nearby within reach for ease of feeding the anticipated flames. Rolling up dry moss in a ball, she placed it beneath the dead wood. Pulling a chain from around her neck, she gathered the Flintstone and striker from the clasp, then leaning over – struck the striker against the stone several times until it sparked. The small flame sped through the moss and bit into the edge of the dry twigs atop it. Quickly, the fire advanced onto the thicker pieces of wood, until the fire was in full bloom and spreading its warmth around her.

She stood, then made her way to the nearby creek, where she used a bark trencher, scooping up water to wash her hands and face. Returning to the fire, she extracted a small sage bundle from the deer hide pouch on her belt. She held it to the fire waiting for the ends to turn red. Pulling it free the embers quickly dissolved, causing the sage to issue smoke from the ends. She bathed her face in the smoke, using one hand to wave the cleansing mist onto her body while chanting ancient songs taught since childhood. The songs she sang sought to gain permission to enter into intercession with the sacred realm on behalf of another. She placed herself beside the fire, holding her arms and palms skyward while reciting invocations, preparing to enter into a deep trance of entreaty. She would spend the night this way, absently feeding the fire and praying for aid.

With the coming light, Shawnee gathered herself, kicked dirt on the remaining embers, and headed for the camp. Calvin was waiting with a cooked breakfast of powdered eggs, jerky, and hot coffee. Titan sat impatiently shifting his weight from one paw to the other. She ate without speaking to either of them. Calvin knew not to ask what had not yet been volunteered. Titan, however, was beyond containment. He barked several times in succession, voicing his full annoyance.

"Not yet," she said to him.

He snorted in objection.

She ignored his behavior, sitting back on her haunches, continuing to sip her coffee. At last, she set her tin cup down on the ground. "I don't want more of a headache than I have already, so do not open the connection with all the vastness of your impatience. OK?"

Titan barked loudly. Catching himself, he calmed his exuberance then barked again more softly. She arranged herself sitting on the ground, back leaning into a large chunk of oak tree that Calvin had rolled up next to the fire the night before. Calvin draped a fleece blanket over her shoulders. She wrapped her fingers in it, pulling it tightly around her. With arms folded across pulled-up knees, she rested her head on her forearms. With care, she drew her attention to the point of convergence; the birthmark at the back of her tongue tingled and warmed. Soon, she felt the electrical pulse of Titan opening the connection, too.

"Mistress, I have been worried about you."

"And I you, my heart."

"Why?" he asked without preamble.

"It is complicated, but I will try to explain."

"I am all ears." Titan chortled at the humor in his words.

"It is this... You are very special, I am sure the Great Mystery has told you this by now. There are things that you are yet to learn, things you may not be prepared to deal with, things that usually require pomp and ceremony to bestow. Yet you will be thrust into a situation here that has brought lesser Death Dogs to heel. I have spent the night in prayer seeking aid on your behalf. I trust the Great Mystery to provide

it. All I can do now is tell you what I know." She paused. Titan remained quiet, intent on hearing all she had to say. *"I know you have the ability to see and converse with spirits, all Death Dogs do,"* she continued. *"I am also sure you know that when a human is killed violently, the trauma often carries over into death, causing the spirit to lose its way; never walking the wind to the plains of the sky; forever taking refuge where last their body was. You Death Dogs possess the skill to help them find their way across the divide. You are a conduit for them. So far, it has been an easy task for you, only dealing with one spirit at a time, a walk in the woods. But when no conduit is available, and one of these confused lost becomes many, they cling to each other in the place of their demise, causing all living creatures to abandon home and sustenance. The senses of the living cannot abide the dismal suffocation of being so near so many of the bemused and lost. Creatures feel and know them for what they are. Most humans only feel the sense of oppression and unconsciously distance themselves from it."*

He continued to listen.

"Now hear me, special one. When so many in one place feel your presence, feel the conduit that you are, they will clamor for your attention all at once. The chaos in your mind could be shear pandemonium. It is an event that has driven some Death Dogs mad, beyond the realm of recovery, even with the aid of the elders' prayers."

Titan's mouth was dry. *"What must I do to avoid this?"* he asked.

"You cannot, you can only contain it. You must compartmentalize each deafening voice, so that each becomes an individual. You must overcome the desire to shut your cognizance off from them, for they will not allow your mind to depart once they have made contact. Suppressing the cries of the many in order to control a conversation with one is the only way you will be able to help them, and save yourself."

"Can I do this thing?" he panicked.

"There are an elite group of Death Dogs who can, who have passed such arranged trials; but it has taken most several years to perfect the talent. They are limited in what they can endure, and even then they are never knowingly sent into such a place without the

supplication of tribal rituals and being accompanied by a host of spiritual leaders. You are said to possess abilities that none of us can fathom, Titan. But, it has been our Chief's ruling that despite the prophecy of our people, you are not to be pushed or rushed into something you may yet not be able to handle. It is his fear that because of the prophecy, others will unknowingly harm your young mind."

Titan was quiet for a moment, pondering how hard this thing before him might be. She waited. Finally breaking the silence, he reached out to her again. *"This is why you are coarse with Calvin?"*

"Yes, he has put you in this position. It has indeed angered me. But know that he meant you no harm."

"You will be with me?"

"Of course I will, I will not leave you."

"Then I do not fear it," he said with renewed confidence.

The day turned out to be hazy with a damp mist clinging low among the tree trunks. More than once, Calvin, scouting in the lead, tripped over some unseen obstacle, nearly tumbling off a cliff edge. After only half a day, Shawnee called a halt to the search and ordered the camp drawn up for the night. Calvin set about gathering wood; once a deep pile had been accumulated, he built a large fire. Not wanting to spend the night in the damp air, Shawnee pulled the tent from her backpack and began unfolding the canvas cover. She used several spruce branches to sweep an area free of pebbles and extraneous natural debris. Finding the quarter inch diameter foot-long metal rods, she threaded the male connections into the female ends, and inserted the rods into the cover. Hoisting it upright, she shook out the front flaps. Satisfied, she pulled the rolled up fleece blankets off the packs and tossed them inside.

Within his bag Calvin retrieved salt packed steaks, dehydrated peas, potatoes, peppers, and flour for biscuits, along with butter and blueberry preserves. Shawnee and Titan found their way to a solid rock face sprouting a natural faucet of dribbling water. The massive stone was split across the top; a four-inch diameter tree branch stuck out from the crevice, allowing water to run down the limb and drip cleanly off the end in a steady trickle. The near silence of the woods from the lack of wildlife activity allowed the trickle to be easily heard from far away. Titan lapped at the dribble eagerly. When he was finished, she placed the small metal pale underneath the stream. When it was filled to the brim, both slowly stepped off back towards the camp.

The haze was getting thicker. She could barely see Titan beside her, but Calvin's fire was a beacon lading them to the camp ahead.

Taking the water pale from her, Calvin set it beside the fire while unfolding the collapsible metal bowls he used to combine his biscuit mixture and cook his dehydrated vegetables. He placed freeze dried steaks on a spit over the fire, high enough to keep them from burning. Calvin watched as Shawnee withdrew a six-inch long, two-inch diameter compacted log from her pack and tossed it to Titan.

"What's that?" Calvin pointed at the log with a flick of a fork.

"It's a specially made protein bar of sorts for working dogs. The cooks at the village created them." She laughed for the first time since she and he had argued. "You should have seen the Death Dogs volunteering as testers!"

Calvin smiled, watching as Titan held the tasty meal between front paws, fervently licking at the meaty center. The ice seemed to break between the pair, the tension built up over Shawnee's mistrust of him eased away.

Finishing dinner, Shawnee set her bowl beside her on the ground. "That was good, Calvin, thank you."

"I like to cook," he said. "I find it relaxing."

"I'll start washing up the hardware and pans," she offered. "If you are happy with cooking, I will gladly do the washing." She gathered up the dirty dishes along with the utensils, and headed back to the rock face. She stole a peek back at Titan, who was asleep on the other side of the fire, and decided to let him stay that way. "Keep that fire banked so I can find my way back."

"He won't be happy if he wakes up and finds you've left without him."

"Then don't do anything to wake him up."

Calvin looked at the sleeping giant, and shook his head, wondering how the dog could possibly be comfortable sleeping with his feet in the air and his head flopped to one side.

She walked softly out of camp, trying not to make too much noise with the metal dishes she was carrying. She stopped, craning an ear to make sure she was headed in the right direction. Hearing the steady patter of water, she shifted her course to the left, finding the little water source a few minutes later. She scooped dirt into the pans, scrubbing out the insides, and washing them out underneath the dripping water. She shivered, her hands were getting colder. Must be the water, she thought. Done, she gathered up the pans and headed back. The fire was much harder to see than during her last trip, even though the dark of the night should have made it easier. Eventually finding her way back, she sat the dishes near the fire so they could dry.

Calvin stood over Titan with hands perched on broad hips.

"What's the matter?" she asked, concerned.

"Don't know. He is jerking his feet and moaning. Might he be ill?"

She stood next to the man inspecting the dog. Titan kicked his legs out vigorously. "He is conversing with the Great Mystery," she said softly.

"You know this?" Calvin turned expressive eyes to her.

"Yes." She said no more. Turning to the pile of wood, she placed several more logs on the fire, building it up so they would be warm for the night.

He waded through the cold water, splashing along without much care, his big paws flew along aimlessly; Titan was enjoying the isolation of the woods and all the sounds that nature produced. A Red-Tailed Hawk screeched above him; Titan looked up, witnessing the pale underbelly of the large bird. The hawk followed overhead, watching the big dog as if it had never seen such a creature before.

"He is beautiful, is he not, young one?"

Titan stopped his advancement, standing still in the stream, the displaced water dripping from the long hairs of his belly. *"Greetings father, I was expecting you."*

"But hoping I would not show up too soon."

Titan bowed his head. *"It is true, Great One. I was hoping to have a long trot in the stream."*

"You may still yet, but hear me now."

Titan splashed out of the stream onto land, settling down on his stomach to listen to what he hoped would not be a long oration.

"You have but this night before you will encounter the spirits of those lost. Do not panic, young one, for it is due time I bestow upon you one of the many gifts I have yet withheld. It was my intention to wait, but circumstances in your world don't always go even my way. With this mental prowess, you will be able to communicate effectively with the many of the lost – just as you have spoken with the one, in the past."

"How will I receive this special ability?" Titan interrupted, licking his jowls at the prospect of hurrying along the conversation.

"Your impatience can be exasperating, Death Dog." The voice paused. Titan whined. Without malice, the voice began again. *"When you wake you will feel no different; but as each spirit rushes to communicate with you, their messages will enter a place in the heart of your mind, and you will automatically partition them off from one another. No other Death Dog has this ability, Titan. Each before you has had to force the essence of each spirit back, then mentally cubicle each message, closing it off to thought until such time as they could deal with it individually; it is an exhausting process. You will suffer no such vexation. I have evolved your mind with such fidelity as to process all of them nearly at once, reflecting back to each spirit and giving them instructions on how to depart this dark bedlam for the light of true life. Forget not what I tell you now – just like when you impatiently bombard the connection between you and your mistress; if you insist on closing down the link with the spirits too quickly, you will partake in agony. Heed not, and you will wish you were not the Death Dog of prophesy. I leave you now to dreams of cotton-tails and the uninhibited arrogance of your youth."*

Titan sensed the sudden absence. As much as he felt dismayed at the conversations, the parting created a deep void at times. Respectfully, he did not jump back into the stream right away but waited for at least a full minute. Feeling he had shown he was capable of extreme patience, he hurled himself off the shore back into the clear shallow tributary. Bounding happily downstream, several fish leapt into the air to get out of his path; he left a wake of scattered spray kicking up behind him.

Morning brought the promise of a clearer day. Titan flipped off his back, stood to yawn, then with rump in the air and front paws bowed he stretched. Shawnee sat by the embers of the fire, drinking coffee. She eyed him. "Have a good night?"

Titan yawned again.

She peered at Calvin packing the last of the gear. "Well, now that his highness is awake, we can get going." She tossed the last of her coffee from the cup, giving Titan a convivial smile.

Titan took the lead, somehow he knew his way without knowing it. He scooted under fallen trees, crawled along ledges, and stood atop a rumbling waterfall overlooking a vast barrage of Purple Sage. It was there he would begin his exigency. The day was only half gone when they reached the boscage. The copse was saturated with color so thick the sky itself appeared purple. The beauty transcended the eerie silence; even the sparse but dead foliage beneath their feet seemed to make no sound as they tramped across it. Titan's nose twitched. He thanked the Great Mystery for granting the sage flowers no sweet odor. The power of such an army of blossoms may have overtaken his sense of smell.

He breathed in the musk, searching for the smell of death. He advanced through the sage, winding his way around each massive bush, continuing to inhale the aroma of the place. A molecule of recognition entered his mind; he tested it in his nose, searching out its identity. He distinguished the death scent – *old, trace, and close by*. He slunk under a huge oak whose trunk was untouched by insects. Even they had abandoned the place; it had fallen decades ago, yet it was still intact. Looking back, he saw Shawnee and Calvin climb over the timber, and then he whined. Shawnee understood the message.

"He has found the odor," she voiced to Calvin. Calvin hesitated in his step, knowing what could be before them.

Titan tread deliberately, ever checking the air for clues. He caught it again, that knowing smell of the dead. Veering left he moved gracefully around one of the tall bushy sage trees… *the smell is old, very old, very faint*. He reduced his nose to the base of a colossal sage, then sat knowingly and waited for Shawnee. She made the turn, pushing aside flowered limbs, and located him sitting there waiting for her to find him. She asked him to show her where it was; he leaned down with his nose and tapped the earth in front of him. She reached in the canvas sack on her hip for his reward. Instead of a show of glee, he stood and barked with anxiety. Turning away, he padded off a distance of fifteen feet, dropped his nose beneath the base of another immense Purple Sage, and sat. He looked her straight in the eyes, barked, stood and trotted off, again dropped his nose, sat, eyed her, and moved off again. She followed, dismayed. She was not shielded by the fact that it was expected. She was in the midst of it now, and it burned in her heart to realize these were likely the remnants of children he was finding. This went on for an hour. Calvin, following behind, marked all the spots Titan alerted on using a short stream of orange ribbon he attached to a branch. When Titan finally lay down, weary from the effort, Calvin had counted thirty-five markers. Shawnee approached the dog to offer him his ball. He solemnly turned his head away, placing his chin on his paws. He slept.

"What now?" Calvin asked.

The mild warmth of the day had been lost as soon as the trio entered the expanse of the hidden graveyard.

"We build a fire." Shawnee inclined her head toward the sleeping Death Dog. "When he wakes, the real work will begin." They worked tirelessly, pitching the tent, gathering wood, filling the water pale.

With the fire raging, flames licked at the limbs eagerly, cracking the shell of the hard wood within it. Titan woke, found the bowl of water beside him, and lapped at it vigorously. Shawnee tossed him a protein bone, which he snatched from the air, and fixed fast between his front paws. Working on the bone with perfect fangs, he did not cease his pace when Shawnee spoke.

"It looks like this coming night, father winter will finally break the back of this unseasonable hold. It will begin to snow soon. Do you wish for us to wait till dawn to begin this folly, or do you wish us to get it over with?"

Titan gnawed the bone contentedly. Shawnee waited. He lifted his head, chewing a piece of buffalo meat he had dug out from the middle.

He opened the link slowly. The backs of their tongues warmed.

"I know they linger. I feel them, but they do not yet know that I can help them. I have closed off my mind, so they do not attempt to reach me," Titan concluded.

"As soon as we break open the first grave... its spirit will appear." Shawnee waited to see if he comprehended.

"I know," he answered back.

"Will you reach out to it, then?" she asked him.

"Yes, then the others will show themselves to me, and I will begin to send them home."

"Are you afraid?"

"No. I am eager to do my duty. This is what I was born for. I alone have this charge; you cannot help me in this, so do not try, Mistress." He gingerly broke the link, leaving Shawnee with a vestige of his adoration for her. She beamed at knowing this was a new ability - this feeling he had left her with. Placing a spread palm over her heart, she said, "I love you too."

Calvin unfolded the camping shovel to full length, twisting the threaded clamshell in the center tight to prevent it from collapsing. "You sure about this?" He directed the question to Shawnee, but knew Titan would understand him.

Shawnee looked from Calvin to Titan, then back to Calvin. "He is sure, that is enough for me." Night was falling; it was cold, and it had begun to snow hard with large fluffy flakes that obscured visibility. Shawnee pulled on the fur of the parka she had thought to pack at the last minute, bringing it to sit tighter around her throat. She shivered, despite the coat. The fire was bright, but it was too far away to warm them.

Calvin bit the edge of the shovel into the ground beneath the first sage that he had marked; the first that Titan had alerted on. The sharp edge of the shovel bit easily into the hard ground, and he flipped the dirt over his shoulder. He bent to the task again and again, repeating the effort for what seemed an eternity, until the tip of his shovel clanked off something hard. Pausing, he hunched over relaxing the shovel against his shins. Reaching for a flashlight, he pointed it into the hole, and let out a gasp. Two hollow eyes stared ominously back at him. He stood rigid, donning a blank gaze. Shawnee pulled the flashlight from his hand. Leaning over, she directed the light downward. The beam illuminated a tiny white skull. Titan walked over to the little grave. He smelled the decay of stage-four decomposition (bones only), from twenty-or-so years past. He whined, then pulled his head up toward the heavens and loosed a solemn howl.

He stood alone at the grave as was his desire; Shawnee and Calvin were expelled to the fire. Feeling a pulse of the spirit enter his mind, he opened his eyes and saw the faint illumination of the child's presence. She had been interned here a long time.

"Whhaat rrrr uuu?" she expressed in rubbery words. It was hard for her to communicate; she had not done so since her demise.

"I am a presence, much like you," transporting his thoughts through a void in time. *"But I am also a path, a steward."*

Her essence drifted, faltering in its soft glow, *"I duuu naaat knowww whhherrre iiii ammmm."*

Titan opened the communication wider, sending her a channel for speech. He knew not how he was able to do it, but that mattered little. *"I know,"* he projected. *"I am here to help you."*

"Will you help me to leave this gloomy place?" she asked fluently, her essence brightening.

Titan was overjoyed. *"Yes, little one. With my help, you will go where you will be safe and warm."*

"How?" she asked, with ease. *"I have been trapped here... a very long time. There are many others here, too."*

He concentrated, willing his mind to branch past this interlude to the beyond. Feeling the Great Mystery reach out to him, he was reassured he had done this thing rightly. He cast the wonder of the place through the portal of communication between them. The essence shuttered, not from fright, but elation. *"Follow the caress, little one,"* Titan conveyed. *"I will be with you as you walk the wind. You will not lose your way."*

The spirit ignited into pure light, softened, then dissolved brilliantly, scattering into a host of fire-fly-like fragments. Titan felt her escape the bondage of confusion, but then he was suddenly on fire, burning in the bombardment of the life force of the dead... so many dead.

Shawnee jumped from where she sat with Calvin near the fire, watching Titan in his otherworldly trance. He was swiftly and abruptly consumed with white hot phosphorescence. She saw him cringe with the heat of it, gasp, and then fall. Calvin grabbed her arm as she ran to his aid, but she fought him harshly. He wrapped brute arms around her waist, pinning her limbs and lifting her feet from the now snow covered ground. He screamed her name. "Shawnee! Calm yourself, you cannot help him."

"Nightdance, release me; he will not endure this, he is not ready!" She struggled to get free of his grip, but he was too strong.

"Shawnee, please," he begged. Breathing in her ear, he uttered quietly, "He is the hope of these children. He is the Death Dog of prophesy. You must begin to accept this."

She relaxed. He slid them both to the ground, still holding her tightly in front of him. As the snow gave way beneath their weight, the moisture penetrated the pants they wore, unsuited for this weather. Her tension ebbed away. "You can let me go now," she said with a tearful sniff that she tried to mask.

He loosened his grip. Lifting herself upright, she dusted off her canvas trousers, thankful she at least had on a warm coat. Reaching up, she rubbed wet eyes with the heel of her hands. Stealing a look toward Titan she noted he was again standing, but on shaking legs, the aura about him remaining aglow.

"I don't like it, Calvin, but... I know, you speak truth."

He was still sitting atop the small snow bank, legs stretched out before him, hands pressed palm-ward in the snow. He gave her a knowing nod. "At least you are calling me by my first name again," he said with a grin. They both chuckled with obvious tension. But the newfound acceptance was quickly vanquished in the midst of a precipitous lightning storm.

The irradiate whirlwind of the storm burst several trunks of trees into splinters, felling them all around the camp. Instinctively, they threw their arms over their heads. Lightning struck the snow in front of them in rapid succession, turning it orange and blue where it collided. The percussion was deafening. Once again, Shawnee made to run for

Titan. Calvin snatched her up around the waist. Flipping her over his shoulder, he turned his back on the dog and ran heavily away, carrying his burden. She screamed at him to let her go; but even had he heard her, he would not have done so. In the brilliance of the storm, Calvin could see a rock face jutting out. He willed strength into his burning legs, pushing hard through the growing and heady snow, still holding tight to a squirming Shawnee. He tossed her as comfortably as he could toward the base of the overhang, and slid in behind her. A big maple tree crashed down in front of the opening seconds after their abdication. She was pounding her fists into his back and screaming at him for leaving Titan. He took the beating, knowing there was no way for her to escape; she was trapped against the stone wall with him blocking the entrance, and now he was blocked by a tree.

Morning found them still imprisoned behind the splintered tree. Calvin could see light peeking through the branches. He reached out and took hold of two branches protruding off the trunk, breaking them off near the tree. The trunk was as big around as a good sized man. Fixing the soles of his boots against the trunk, he pushed mightily, but the tree did not budge. He swore.

"Get me out of here, Nightdance!"

He noted she was back to using his last name. "I am trying, give me a moment," he implored. He could see a mist had settled in, but the snow had stopped. Reaching beneath the trunk, he scraped away at the accumulated snow. A foot or so down, he hit hard ground. He swore again. He thought Shawnee could probably make her way under the tree, but there was not enough room for her to climb over him, with barely enough room for him to lie on his side. Using the light of the morning, he examined the rock shelter. Looking toward his feet, he could see there was space to move down and against the rock wall opening; there was a small gap between that and the tree trunk. "Shawnee, can you inch your way down?"

"Maybe, why?" she asked annoyed.

"You might be able to wiggle out down there."

"Say no more." She wiggled her hips, pulled with her heels, and pushed with her fingers pressed against the rock above her. The coat made it difficult, but after a painstaking ten minutes her feet touched the wall.

"Can you pull your legs up any, Calvin?" She was back to using his first name again.

Lying on his back, Calvin twisted over on his side as best he could. Reminiscent of some yoga maneuver he thought he might have seen somewhere, he pulled his knees up toward his chest with his hips at a half angle. It was just enough room. Shawnee continued the push-pull approach, shifting and scooting her way out between the tree and the rock wall, feet first. The sight before her took her breath away. For as far as she could see through the mist, there was not a tree standing. The splintered and exploded wood was strewn and piled like a deforestation had taken place, or an entire minefield had abruptly been triggered and simultaneously discharged.

"Shawnee, can you get me out of here?"

Eyes still frozen on the melee around her, she whispered, "No."

She took a step, hesitated when he called her name again, and then took the motion up again with vigor. She grabbed onto limbs to pull herself up and over the piles of forest debris. In several places, she had to crawl through the gaps in the fallen tree trunks only to find herself climbing over the next pile so tightly packed she could not get through it. Her attempts to connect with Titan through the mind link had so far failed. She could hear Calvin calling, but she pressed on. Standing atop a broken maple, washing the landscape with her eyes, she tried to get her bearings. What she recognized of the place was gone, it was totally expunged. Not one tree was left upright that she could yet see. But the mist had begun to burn off as the sun broke through, a sun she had not seen for days. She focused, trying to open the bond with Titan, but no response came to her plea.

Ahead, she was surprised to make out a single Purple Sage tree reaching for the sky. A Red-Tailed Hawk lighted on the uppermost branch, turned its majestic head toward her, and screeched. She tramped toward it, the hawk bent downward and screeched again. Stumbling forward, she fell against the upright sage. The bird fluttered and took flight. She stood inspecting the ground near the tree base. Oddly, ten or more pine-sized trees lay side by side, perfectly touching length-wise with a fine dusting of snow layered across the top. She began rolling the trees apart. As each log was pushed away, pale light spiked the blackness, highlighting the hole beneath. Finally, she could see Titan on his back with his paws in the air. Instantly, she knew he was alright.

"Titan," she called. The dog smacked his lips together – a very human gesture, she mused with relief. "Have a good night?" she asked sardonically. He barked, quickly regretting it, his head hurt. "To think I was actually worried about you. Let's get you out of there," she said, pulling at the logs to open a large enough gap for him to jump up through.

13

After helping Calvin drag himself out of the crevice he was trapped in, they scrounged through the battle zone to recover any supplies they could find. Locating her pack, Shawnee let out a yip of delight. Calvin grumbled, having not located anything of his at all. Shawnee pulled her radio out of her bag and tossed it to Calvin. In spite of reaching high, and balancing on one set of toes to catch it, Calvin came away with no radio, three less fingers and half a palm.

The shot had rang out at the same instant he reached to wrap his left index finger about the radio. Blood splattered and sprayed from the destroyed hand. Shawnee had looked away; secure she had thrown it within his reach. At the echo of the rifle shot, she turned in a defensive profile, instinct taking over. Before she could dive for cover behind a pile of broken trees, another bullet bit into a tree trunk directly in front of her.

"Another step and the next one goes in your head." The voice had a grate to it like sand being pulverized between raking granite slabs. It was aged, rough, bitten with years of hard living. She halted. Her eyes roamed left then right, she did not see Titan; she opened the link.

He heard the echo of the shot through the newly made openings in the forest, it reverberated past his ears with force. Just as suddenly, the birthmark lit up at the back of his tongue; it was so hot it stole his breath, causing him to gasp for air. His head pounded from the quick connection and the exertion of the night before.

"Do not come running in here, Titan!"

"Could you have come to me a bit easier?" he fumed.

Foregoing the opportunity to ask him how it felt for a change, she instead spouted, *"Calvin has been shot! He looks bad, losing a lot of blood."* He could tell she was fighting panic. *"I cannot see the attacker; I only heard his voice, no idea who it could be. Be careful!"* She closed the connection.

Titan took a deep breath to clear his head, but the pain did not subside.

Feeling the breeze on his damp nose, he calculated whence it blew. He wanted whoever had fired that shot to be upwind of him so he could catch their smell. As he moved, he stayed within the scarce tree-line of the parameter around the fallen and shattered piles of destroyed wood. The result of so many seeking his aid the night before had produced an electrical storm of catastrophic proportion. Only sheer luck must have prevented an all-out fire from flourishing. As the last child's spirit had risen skyward, a hawk screeched overhead followed by a forceful gust of wind. The squall pushed Titan into the grave Calvin had dug the night before, now deeper and wider from the torrent winds. Logs fell gently astride the opening until every sight and sound was sealed from his sensitive ears and eyes. He fell asleep from exhaustion, at peace with all he had done, until Shawnee extricated him that very morning.

Carefully, he pressed his weight into the fleshy loam. Treading heavy paws, he crawled and climbed well into the debris field, sniffing quick bursts of fresh air, testing it for live human odor. It was a different task than he usually undertook: By all reason, he should be ignoring the cell structures of the living and seeking those lost. But now he must reverse his role and ignore the smell of the long interned dead whose bones still lie beneath the cold earth, and seek out those who still breathed. A flake of odor crossed his nose, he caught it, examined it, found it foreign; *man, filthy, old, not many years to live, angry, evil... so very evil.* His muscles constricted. The man among them was the very murderous beast who had been killing these innocent children since so very long ago. Titan's lips peeled back from his teeth threateningly. He growled deeply in his wide chest, blowing out hot breath. Curling claws into the brush beneath his paws, he opened tightly pressed eyes. Anger like he had never felt before flared within him.

Without knowing exactly how, his eyes shifted focus, eliminating the hues and contrasts of normal color, converging on any heat source produced within sight. He rounded a hill, climbed to its height, then smelled the filth of the man unwashed for many months, but did not see him. In the distance, he could see the shape of Shawnee's heat signature standing erect and unmoving. Titan looked over the top not bothering to lay low on his belly. He was at that moment a savage centaur bent on the destruction – nay, the elimination of an abomination – and he stood prepared to discard the monstrosity. He saw the heat of the gun barrel protrude from the cliff base followed by an arm, leg, and then the retched man himself. Titan blinked heavily, clearing his vision, reinvesting in the colors of the natural terrain.

The man was ruddy looking, his hair long, tangled and gray. He wore rags mostly, layer upon layer of torn and filthy material sewn crudely together. After a moment, Titan realized the man's clothes were a patchwork of the clothing his young victims had worn at their death. It sent a chill across his spine, and hot blood rose through his already embroiled veins. The rifle was pointed toward Shawnee, who stood immobile, never betraying Titan's position with her eyes – for she had seen him there, prepared to take the killer down.

Calvin was pitched in the throes of his injury, grasping red spurting fingers in his good hand, writhing on the ground in pain. The man walked up to him, rocking back and forth on his side. The rifle barrel dropped casually, and the man shot him point blank in the head. Titan, abandoning all reason, pressed trained leg muscles downward to jump, but was held fast in his fury. Above him the hawk screeched. Titan fought a battle of grief and anger as the force that held him bid him to stay. The wall of Seraphs was so thick, so strong, that he was unable to move it even in his state of physically powerful rage. *Let me go!* He screamed at them. *He must be made to pay!* The screech of the hawk sounded again and in that instant he was released. The force of his forward struggle propelled him off the hill over Calvin's body, and exposed him only paces behind the madman. The man strode harshly toward Shawnee, stepping hazily but with purpose over fallen trees as if they were but a step on a staircase, the rifle barrel swinging up and down as he went. In three bounds, Titan was in the air, claws fixed fast into the man's shoulders and lower back, teeth clenched tightly into his neck. The man screamed in agony, tossing his arms wildly about, losing the rifle amongst the carnage. He fell hard from the weight of the dog, breaking several teeth as he hit, the air in his lungs expelling from the thrust of the impact. Titan wasted no time and had no mercy. If the Great Mystery himself had chosen to intervene, it would be doubtful if he could have been contained. Titan was... possessed. He came to himself with blood oozing between his teeth, human flesh squeezed between fangs. No life stirred in the form he held, the man had expired.

Shawnee tugged at him firmly. She stroked his head and spoke to him softly in the language of the Makujay, asking him to let the man go. Her words coursed through his mind, finding a cell still attached to reality and stirring his consciousness. He let go. He could still taste the vileness of the man's existence in the blood that fluxed on his tongue and down his throat. He looked at the ruined form that lay beneath him, eyes glassed over, throat destroyed, blood dispersed. Shawnee pulled his head around, gripping it, solidly pulling his forehead into her cheek.

"You did what you must, thank you for not dying in the doing of it!" She kissed his head, pulling him closer and wrapping her arms around the barrel of his body.

The downward gust announced the arrival of the helicopter that woke him. There was no vertical timber to foul it, so the pilot was able to descend closer to the pick-up point. The blades whipped fragments of wood into a whirlwind of tiny rubble. Shawnee and Titan rose and stepped back, squinting their eyes against the trash in the air. The basket came down slowly but landed with a loud thud. Titan jumped back with a growl. Despite his abhorrence of the chosen conveyance, he accepted the subsequent nudge from Shawnee stepping into the metal crate. With ears pinned against his head in annoyance, he lay length-wise on her legs with his blood streaked face pressed to her lap. She rubbed the groove behind his ears, which calmed him.

Calvin's body had already been delivered to the morgue where it would be held for the Makujay to retrieve. Though Titan and Shawnee had not known him long, pack was pack and they felt the loss. As the basket lifted, Shawnee could see the still bloody form of the man Titan had killed. She would tell her father all that happened. But she also knew that despite Calvin's misleading him and endangering her and Titan, her father would not allow that to take away from the tribal ceremony that would send his spirit home with dignity. Had Calvin lived, however, she could not say what her father would have done. The remains of the children would be seen to. Her father would make sure the proper expertise was made available to correctly excavate and recover each tiny skeleton. First, though, the mountain would have to be cleared of all the fallen trees; plenty of firewood for the poor, she surmised, and a clean start for the mountain.

Titan lay down on the floor of the helicopter and fell trance like into a very brief conversation with the Great Mystery, before falling deeply asleep.

"I don't understand why the Seraphs impeded my way once again," Titan bellowed in his dream, still angry.

"I could not abide your death, young one, the time was much too soon. Sometimes, a sacrifice must be made for the good of all, and you avenged Calvin. But if you had engaged the demon when you had first tried, Calvin would still be gone and you... you would not have lived long enough to save Shawnee..."

The following day she watched from the window as the pilot set the fixed wing airplane down on a secluded dirt runway in the middle of nowhere. The light was fading, but she could see a few vehicles parked nearby in a partially winter-dead field. As she descended the short set of steps, she was greeted by Sky and Chandler.

"It's good to see you both." She reached for the men, wrapping an arm around each of their necks. They hugged her, and watched as Titan emerged from the stairway, seemingly bigger in brawn than when he had left. He too descended the stairs; but instead of the immature bounce he would normally display, he stepped lighter and stouter than ever before. He brushed up against Sky, then Chandler, before striding off on his own.

"He is different," Chandler analyzed.

"I sense it too," Sky agreed.

"Yes, he is different. He is becoming the Death Dog he was born to be," Shawnee confirmed.

"We read the report. Sounds like you two don't know how to take a vacation," Sky laughed.

Shawnee forced a small smile.

"What is it?" Chandler placed a hand on her arm, conveying concern.

"Oh, nothing really, I just… I just didn't want him to embark upon this path so soon. He will be forever burdened from that day in Tennessee, to the end of his time. I feel like… I will lose that sweetest part of him."

Chandler patted her hand several times. "He gets to you, that one does," Chandler admitted, eyes diverted toward Titan exploring the grounds.

Ever the consummate reminder of duty, Sky remarked, "We are born to a service. All of us, our lives are burdened in one way or the other. Yet, we still cling to the simpler parts of ourselves, the fondness of friends, the love of family, and the pleasures of life." Sky too looked Titan's way, "So will he, you will see."

14

Corin's eyes twitched. He was sleeping restlessly, dreams filled with real memories of deeds past. He was five years old, living in Abilene Texas with his mother and father. His father had come home from working their two hundred acre ranch and was tossing Corin in the air, then wrapping him in a bear hug. His father adored him. His mother, ever berating them both, was on one of her usual two day drunks. Jealous of the attention his father paid him, she smacked him across the back of the head and ordered Corin to his room; he stood fixed to his father's leg. His father protested the abuse; his mother responded by jerking the boy away by the arm and beating him bodily with a kitchen spatula. His father flew into a rare and uncharacteristic rage, planting a well-aimed fist on her right cheekbone. She picked herself up off the floor, calmly walked to the pantry, extracted a loaded .38 revolver, and – aiming it with precision – pulled the trigger. His father's head jerked back cruelly. Corin saw him fall dead to the floor. The police came, saw the bruises on the boy and the bruise on his mother's cheek, and called it self-defense. Corin was too much in shock to tell them any different.

He found it difficult to function socially after his father died. He did not shirk his studies at school, but he was always getting into fights. Each time a teacher called to complain, he suffered another beating from his mother; not that she needed a reason to beat him. He was not a large boy, not yet. But as time passed and he grew as much in muscle as in his hate for her, he began to give more than he got from boys at school. He had never retaliated against his mother; instead, he made dolls out of straw and hung them with hay twine from the trees around the old dilapidated barn, where only he ever went.

When Corin turned fifteen, his mother came home in a usual drunken stupor, packed her bags, and wrote a detailed letter about how she was taking off for Las Vegas and leaving the boy here to be a ward of the state. Corin saw his golden opportunity; a moment he had fantasized about since the day his father was murdered. As she tossed her bags into the bed of her beat-up truck, he carefully placed the dual prongs of his hog hot-shot against the back of her skull and pushed the button with delight. She dropped like a fifty pound sack of barley seed. He held it there against her neck for what seemed an eternity while she flopped on the ground, electrocuting her as much as he could with the device. He bound her wrists and ankles with hay twine, and dragged her by the hair with one hand into the thick woods near the house; in the other, he carried a carefully measured length of braided twine, something he always carried in his pocket like a good luck charm. She moaned from the pain in her head and the roughness of the ground against her back and buttocks; her skimpy shorts offered little protection. Rocks, sticks, and stickers scraped at her legs and feet. Reaching his destination, he dropped her heavily. Coming to her senses, she screamed at him.

"Go ahead and scream, Mother, no one will hear you at this time of evening, they have all left for the day. It's just you and I now."

He kicked her hard in the side. She groaned, bending sideways to clutch her ribs with bound hands. "That is for my father, you murdering bitch." He kicked her again, she wheezed. "That is for me."

He flipped his hand out that held the twine, clasping one end with his thumb and index finger. Bending down on a knee, he tied a loop of it around her neck. She spat at him, spreading spittle across the left side of his face. He hit her hard against the temple, she blacked out. He backed away quickly, shaking his hand, screaming at her that he had probably cracked his knuckles. After a few minutes, the pain subsided, and he resumed his work with his mother still unconscious.

He picked her head up by the hair. "This loop counts as one," he said out loud, wrapping the twine around her neck nine more times. "That makes ten," he counted when done.

"Ten for the ten years it took me to get to this." Continuing, he tightly wrapped ten more loops around her throat. "Another ten, for the ten more years I would have waited, but I vowed you bitch that I would wait no longer than that. On my twenty fifth birthday, you would have died. As it is now, I am truly gratified to not have a need to wait that long. I sincerely thank you for the early birthday present, that letter you wrote is pure gold." He smiled, broadly pulling the twine tighter.

She woke again, gasping for air, scraping at her throat with near numb fingertips, looking for a perch to release the tension. She wheezed one ragged breath after another. He stood over her smiling, truly content for the first time in many years. Taking a measuring tape from his belt and a knife from his pocket, he swelled with excitement as her eyes grew wide at seeing them in his hand.

"Oh, don't worry about this, Mother," he waved the knife at her. "I don't intend to use this on you. That would be too merciful, I think."

She wheezed heavily, still clutching at the tightly tied twine around her constricted throat. He hooked the metal tab at the end of the measuring tape behind a strand of the tight twine at her neck, and then extended the tape outward along with the rest of the twine until he had reached twenty feet. He pressed his thumb to the twine over the knife blade pulling it upward to cut it.

"Twenty wraps around your throat, Mother, and twenty feet to help you die. I have practiced this hundreds of times," he said. "I started with dolls, then deer, then hogs… well, you get the picture. Over the years, I would say I have developed a perfect picture in my mind of how I want you to die." She rolled to and fro on the ground, trying to escape her internment.

"Tonight, you gave me the perfect alibi to get rid of you. See, I had not quite figured that part out yet, the part where I explain what happened to you." He jerked the length of twine in his hands, snapping her head sideways. "Twine is an amazing thing," he said. "It is so small in diameter; yet it is astonishingly strong, and here on the ranch there is an overabundance of it."

Knotting another length of twine into the bonds around her ankles, he tied a small rock to the loose end, and tossed it over a thick tree limb. It swung over easily; he caught the rock and removed it quickly. He heaved with his weight, watching his mother's body as it dragged closer and then lifted upward. His muscles bulged; he was afraid he might tear a tendon, but did not stop – he was committed now. He pulled until he had to sit on the ground and wrap the twine about his elbow and forearm to hold her.

"You are far heavier then these skinny hill deer and scrawny rock hogs, Mother. You challenge me," he puffed from the exertion. "Now what?" he considered. Hanging upside down from the tree limb, she was scratching at the ground, trying to push herself up by her fingertips. "Hmmm," he thought aloud. He let go, letting her drop face first to the ground.

"Well, that did not work as I planned. I should not have tried to drag you and hoist you up all at once. At least, I have you over here now," he remarked happily.

Scooping up the same small rock, he re-tied it to the end of the twine, tossing it around the limb three more times. "Now that should create enough tension to hold you while I tie this off."

He pulled back forcefully on the twine again. It coiled around the limb as his mother's feet closed the gap between her shoeless feet and the tree limb. Her toes touched bark. He wrapped the twine around his elbow and forearm to shorten the length so as to tie off the braid at the tree limb. Making a loosely bound knot and pulling on it hard, the knot climbed the distance to the limb, tightening as it traveled. When he let go, his mother dropped only a couple of inches. He smiled, pleased with his ingenuity. Feeling for the knife in his pocket, he used it to cut away the extra coil. He returned the knife to his pocket, and dropped the extra twine to the ground. Snatching up a wood stake as big around as his wrist, he paced off twenty feet. Reaching, he extracted the hammer residing in the loop at the seam of his trousers; ranch life made easy access to tools a necessity. He pounded the stake into the ground until it felt secure. Walking back to where his mother hung upside down, he seized the twenty foot strand hanging loose from her throat.

He held on to the end, wrapping it around his palm several times as he closed the distance with the stake. He felt her weight grow heavy as she was being pulled toward him by the throat at an odd angle to the ground. He held on. Bending into it, he struggled to pull her full weight until he could turn, sit, and plant his feet against the stake while facing her. "I must face her," he grumbled.

Leaning forward allowing her some involuntary slack, he wrapped the twine about the stake, then pulled it tight again and tied it off. Finally, placing palms flat against the ground behind him he blew out a deep breath. "Whew, that was hard work!" He swiped the back of one hand across his forehead, making a show of it.

"Your eyes are bulging, Mother." She twisted, fingers clawing furiously at her throat. She writhed in agony only a few moments longer. Eventually, her arms sagged downward past her head as she ceased to struggle. He stood suddenly upon her death, reached upward toward sky and howled his joy. He felt empowered beyond measure, relieved beyond endurance… vastly alive!

He slept well that night knowing he would not wake to her endless taunts and frenzied harrowing. He ate breakfast, took a shower, and watched a few Saturday morning cartoons. "Well," he said aloud to no one but himself, "I guess I better get myself to work." He snagged the handle of a shovel as he made his way out the front screen door, letting it slam closed behind him. He whistled all the way to the woods where he had strung her up.

Cutting the twine, he grinned as she plopped unceremoniously to the dirt. Her face he noted, was bloated and dark in color from hanging upside down. The sight pleased him. He dug a deep grave right where she lay. The ground was hard on the surface but got softer as he went. Satisfied, he dumped her into the hole and shoveled dirt on top of her. He jumped up and down on top of the grave, packing the soil tightly, refilling it as necessary and packing it again. He drove her truck into a large pit on the property where they burned all their trash and building materials, then he set it on fire. After it burned down and cooled several days later, he used their front end loader to cover it up, then dug another burn pit for the work crews to use; they would assume this one had gotten too full.

Several days later, he picked up the phone and called the police. When they arrived, he handed them her letter and told them how she had taken off only the previous night. He was subsequently sent to his grandparents' ranch in Bexar County near San Antonio, Texas. It was there that he bided his time till the day his grandparents eventually expired of geriatric causes. They were good to him, so he allowed them to live out their natural lives. He inherited their 100 acres. A legal adult at their death, he decided to keep the Bexar County property and sold the Abilene ranch, which had been held in trust by his grandfather, for over three hundred thousand dollars; land, house, equipment, livestock and all.

Corin woke in his apartment bedroom with a start. Instead of being drenched in sweat and trembling from a nightmare, he bent his head back breathing in deeply, enjoying the sensation of reliving the glorious details of his mother's demise and his very good fortune.

Tiredly, Shawnee unlocked the door to her house; it was well past dark, but Titan bounded inside full of enthusiasm, checking each room, making sure all was well and secure. Satisfied, he bounced back into the living room, wagging his tail excitedly.

"Yes I know it's good to be home. I am glad to see you are back to yourself, after all."

Turning abruptly for the kitchen, he stopped, revolved his head back towards her, and barked. "And yes, I know you are hungry. Remind me why I need the sacred link to communicate… I already know what you are thinking when you think it." She laughed a little. Exhausted, she pulled his bowl from the counter, removed the threaded lid from the 40 gallon canister on the floor, and scooped out two cups full of specially formulated dry dog food. He barked in complaint.

"Okay, okay." She reached in the canister again, pouring another cupful into his bowl. Sliding it across the floor with her foot, she announced "pig."

He ignored the comment, inhaling his food instead.

"I am going to take a shower," she informed him. Making her way down the dark hallway, she entered the bedroom, pulling off her long sleeved shirt as she passed the doorframe. She didn't bother to turn on the bedroom light, opting instead to flick on the bathroom light and turn the hot water up high in the shower. She removed her shoes, socks and trousers, tossing them egregiously into the corner. Stepping into the shower, she exhaled pent-up tension, letting the hot steamy water dissolve the ache in her muscles and her mind. She needed a rest.

The man sitting in the chair in the dark of her bedroom had been greeted warmly by Titan. He whispered to the big dog that it was a surprise for his mistress, and so her personal protector left him to himself. He stood now, slowly making his way to the bathroom where he knew he would find her in the shower. Turning the knob, he pushed the door slightly open, steam hitting him in the face, washing the smell of oatmeal soap across his senses. After washing her hair, she shut off the water and felt for a towel outside the shower door. Unexpectedly, a masculine hand held it out to her. She inhaled a shocked breath, unable to see who it was in the steam. Where is Titan? Her mind wondered, and why isn't he eating this guy?

Quinton voiced a small laugh. "I am sorry, Nitehi, I did not mean to scare you so."

"Quinton, of all the foolish things!"

"Again, I am sorry, here take your towel, I will wait for you in the kitchen."

She pulled on a pair of jeans, surprised that she had a clean pair, and then donned the only clean T-shirt she had in the house. She padded down the hallway in bare feet, still drying her hair with a towel. Stopping in the entrance to the kitchen, she witnessed Titan sitting by Quinton's side on the floor, getting his back scratched.

"Traitor," she accused.

Titan shifted on the floor.

"He knows I am harmless, otherwise I wouldn't have survived his search of the bedroom."

"Yea, well you could have given me a heart attack just the same," she complained.

Quinton stood, he towered over her. As he was powerfully built, she could see the pectoral muscles in his chest press the soft fabric of his tight shirt. He reached over her head and opened the cabinet door.

"I made coffee, thought you could use some." Handing her a cup, he wasn't surprised to see it had an infused picture of Titan on it. After pouring coffee and making sandwiches, they sat idly at the kitchen table.

"I suppose my father sent you."

"He did, but I am not upset that he did, are you?"

She looked at him, her green eyes taking in his beauty. Short but thick blue-black hair stood on end, while prominent olive cheekbones highlighted the strong structure of his jaw line.

"Do you miss your hair?"

Quinton inclined his head almost sadly. "Yes. It is a sacrifice, but I do it for my people and am proud to do so." He met her eyes again. "You evaded my question."

She sipped the hot liquid, never leaving his gaze. Setting the cup down, she said, "I know. No, I am not upset. You know I have always cared for you, Quinton; it's just that this life I lead and the one you lead, the one we all lead in fact, are not compatible."

"I will not always be away, Shawnee. In two years, I can ask for another assignment. Perhaps if your father knew we intend to marry, he will grant me a transfer where you and I can be closer."

"Do you love what you do?"

He did not have to think about his answer. "Yes, I serve my people and my country, I love that, but I can do that in other ways."

"And throw away years of training?" Before he could respond, she added, "Quinton, I do not know that you and I are meant for each other. I care for you, yes, but my life is complicated. I am committed to a Death Dog, and that brings with it a bond that I cannot share with you. I cannot give all of me to you; do you understand what that means?"

"I know that the Guardians as well as Sky and his kind train the Death Dogs in special skills, and they understand them like those of my craft never will. I know that all of you who handle and speak with the Death Dogs have a link with them that even Sky or the Guardians cannot grasp." Quinton turned his solid frame toward Titan, who was relaxing on the cool tile of the kitchen floor. He smiled broadly at the big dog. "But I won't be jealous if you won't, Titan."

Titan lifted his big head from the floor, lolling his tongue out of his mouth.

Shawnee rolled her eyes. "It's a conspiracy, I can see that now."

With the night growing late, she showed Quinton where he could sleep. "The spare bedroom is to the right. Everything should be made up; but if you need something, the linen closet is across the hall from the room."

Quinton reached a strong hand out, lightly folding it around hers.

"I have missed you," he said softly. He pulled her into his arms and kissed her on the forehead. Releasing her, he whispered, "Good night."

The next morning when Shawnee woke, Quinton was gone. Prodding groggily into the kitchen, she found a note that read: Have to meet with my contacts, see you tonight.

"Well, I guess we are on our own today, T. What do you say we be absolute vegetables and ignore the world?"

Titan rolled over on his side and yawned.

"I will take that as a yes."

Abruptly, the phone rang. Picking it up, she heard Chandler's voice. "OK Chandler, give me a couple of hours to pull myself together and get there." Hanging up the phone, she let out a sigh. "That takes care of our lazy day. We have to go meet Chandler in San Antonio."

Shawnee and Titan waited for Chandler in his office. He strode in solemnly. "Sorry to put you back to work so soon," he apologized.

"It's no problem. I probably would have just gotten bored anyway. So what do we have?"

Chandler paused momentarily in thought. Handing her a folded piece of paper, he waited anxiously for her to open it. As she read the photocopied letter, he stood rigid, hands clasped in front. He watched her face. Her jaw clenched more than once; eyebrows met in an aggressive clash against the canvas of her delicate face.

"He threatens him so openly now?" she voiced with venom.

"He does," Chandler admitted. "But he does more, saying that you will become a target too if Titan is not pulled off the case."

"To hell with him, and the sooner the better," Shawnee spat. Titan, listening to her words and sensing trouble, moved to her side. Instinctively, she reached a hand down and began scratching behind his ear, soothing his unease.

"Exactly what I told Quinton on the phone," Chandler grimaced.

"Damn right," she expelled, grinding her teeth.

He eyed her carefully, retrieving the letter from between her pressed fingertips. Reviewing the contents for the third time that day, he mused aloud. "He will provide no more notes with clues, no more markers like the animal heads." Chandler dropped the letter to his side, turned to her, and inclined his head. "I freely admit I am glad of that part, at least."

Shawnee nodded her assent. A quiet fell over them. She broke the lingering silence. "What will we do now?"

"We will hunt," an answer came from the open door.

Shawnee, seated, rotated toward the voice. Chandler pivoted softly on his heels, caught sight of the face that matched the throaty words, and stepped the three paces needed to grip Quinton by the shoulders. "Washicatwelo!"

Quinton returned the greeting, both men genuinely happy to see each other for the first time since Quinton's arrival.

As Chandler stepped aside to allow Quinton through the door, Shawnee stood to embrace him. Quinton softly pressed lips to her left cheekbone and whispered, "I will let no one harm you or Titan." Realizing she held his hand, she gave it a squeeze, and released it. Titan waited patiently for the two to finish speaking before planting huge front paws on Quinton's chest, washing his face with a wet tongue.

"He never greets me that way," Chandler appraised. As he walked back to his desk and observed the slobber swiped expression on Quinton's face – added, "Thank goodness."

Titan lifted an eye to Chandler and saw, for the second time since these events began; the slightest thread of aura shimmer about his torso, then vanish. He sniffed the air, but caught nothing out of the ordinary.

Settling into an office chair, Quinton addressed them. "His territory is too vast. We cannot hope to get ahead of him, having to wait for another dead girl to turn up, or asking Titan to search for one with no idea where to start until the perp tells us. We have to begin hunting this predator like we would a rabid animal; one that kills by no law under nature."

"There is no paper trail on this guy. I have run all the pertinent databases on this type of serial crime; conspectus of the victims, methods of possible transportation, types of dump sites, etc... I got zero," Chandler complained.

Quinton leaned forward, placing one palm flat on top of Chandler's desk. "Forget our internal databases, Mr. Profiler, go to the heart of the real network. Ask the village for a mass distribution." Shawnee shook her head.

"Only my father can authorize that, only he knows the secret codes to do such a thing."

"And," Chandler inserted, "it is only done under the most extreme of circumstances."

Quinton turned his attention from Shawnee back to Chandler. "Like his only daughter and the future of the Death Dogs both being on a hit list?" Both men stared at each other for a moment, breaking out in simultaneous grins.

Coming out of her chair, Shawnee exclaimed, "Now wait a minute!"

"Woe girl." Quinton pressed her back down into the chair with a firm grip. "I know you don't like it; but like they say in the world of the white: If you got it, use it."

"I don't think *this* is exactly how that phrase is meant to be applied," she griped. "Using the secret codes is not a common practice because even though a secure system is used, if they were to be intercepted it could relay the location of every Maykujay in law enforcement in the world." She stared at the pair with a lack of patience, like she was scolding two school children who should know better. They returned only blank expressions.

Chandler piped up impatiently, "Well?"

"I expect this from Quinton and Sky, but not you Chandler!" Realizing she wasn't going to get anywhere with the duo, she drew in an exasperated breath expelling it hotly. Looking from one man to the other, she grudgingly nodded in acquiesce. Pointing her finger vigorously at the both of them, she voiced loudly, "For the record, I don't like it."

Standing suddenly, Chandler smacked the top of his desk, "Duly noted!"

Quinton bent over and kissed her on top of the head. "You know we wouldn't if it wasn't necessary, Nitehi."

She looked up at him, voicing bitterly, "It still doesn't mean I have to like it."

Chandler closed and locked his office door. Shawnee and Quinton had said their goodbyes and left him to his duty. Slipping the odd looking little key into the slot on the secure phone, he turned it to the left. The phone clicked audibly three times, a small blue light lit up in the bottom right corner. He hovered a nervous index finger above the button marked *tribe*, pushing it until it settled in the detent, he listened as it automatically dialed the classified number. It seemed painfully slow.

The voice on the other end asked, "Greeting?"

Chandler answered, "Washicatwelo."

"Agency?" the voice prompted.

"FBI," Chandler responded.

"Badge?"

"3786," he supplied.

"Name?"

"Chandler Fox," he responded.

"All matches with the phone code you are using. Contact?" the voice returned.

Chandler supplied, "Sikona." Sweat started spreading between the plastic edge of the phone speaker and the rim of Chandler's ear. His nerves were stretched thin. This was a risky move. Just asking for such a thing was enough to set a man's nerves on high alert.

"Standby for your contact, Agent Fox, keep your phone in secure mode, speak slowly and ensure the connection is cleanly severed at the end of the call. If you understand these instructions, please respond to me in the native tongue with a yes."

"Enee," Chandler said.

Upon receiving his answer, the phone automatically started dialing another secure and unrelated phone number.

The lean voice of Stone came on the line, somewhat squabbled by the secure acoustics of the classified phone. Chandler stumbled over his response to Stone's greeting, the mental strain getting the better of him. Regaining his composure, he launched into his request. "I need a mass communique sent out worldwide, Stone, to see if anyone can give us information about this perp. We are at a dead end here."

"You know what you are asking, agent?"

"Yes, revered leader, I do. Our situation is that desperate. The killer has eluded us." Chandler added this last bit embarrassingly. "He has now openly threatened to destroy the Death Dog and his Handler. He has declared the two of them as hostile enemies, and demands that justice will be sought if they continue to be involved. He states he will stop at nothing to ensure they both suffer in excessive pain over a lengthy period of time."

"You have tried to trace the communication, I suppose?"

"Yes," Chandler answered. "It was sent from a computer at a public library. The user utilized a fake I.D. to sign for use of the computer, and the library is one in a rural community that has no cameras installed. The librarian could give no description."

"What about any other leads?" Stone asked.

"Very few to go on. The spiral metal dog stakes he uses to tie them to have gotten us nowhere; no prints, no DNA, no store tracking. He is very careful despite the bloody work he does."

"I understand," Stone replied. "Use secure Fax code 291076 with an asterisk and an exclamation point at the end to send me the criteria you are seeking. I will seek counsel with the approving authority, and respond back to you within 3 hours with a simple yes or no in our language. Do you have any questions?"

"No, respected leader. I appreciate your intervention in this matter."

The call abruptly ended. The auto-dial button marked tribe popped out of its detent, returning to its normal position. Chandler brushed long bangs out of his eyes and relaxed the tension in his shoulders. Turning the key on the phone, he watched as the blue light extinguished. Pulling it from the slot, he opened his middle desk drawer and slid the key back into the hidden compartment in the tray. Leaning back in the chair, he closed his eyes, imagining the Chief's reaction when Stone approached him with his request. He wondered if he would have a job in 3 hours or if Quinton might be ordered to kill him. He laughed at the last thought. Even Bear-who-will-not-hibernate did not have that bad of a temper. His laughter faded after considering that he just might. Looking thoughtfully at the paper and pen, he knew he needed to be quick but clear about the information required. Bending to the task, he first described the acts that had taken place, and then asked for any information even remotely related to it. He added lastly for agents to go back as far as their data allowed them to. He placed the page in the secure fax. Punching in the code Stone had given him, he said a short prayer that this worked. He pressed the send button, waiting anxiously for the transmission to say completed before removing the page from the fax tray and running it through his finer-than-powder paper shredder. Now all he could do was wait.

Stone pulled the fax from the machine, read it, and prepared himself to go before Chief Spirit with the unprecedented request. He slowly took the path that led from the village administration office to Chief Spirit's compound. His denim jeans met his moccasin feet where flashes of blue, red, and yellow beadwork shimmered in the fading light. His doeskin shirt warmed him, the sheepskin padding soft against his bare skin. He was a tall man, an inch taller than the Chief himself; but being modestly configured with natural muscle on average bone, he could not compare to the man's huge build. However, women always told him he had a beautifully proportioned face, although he was never sure what that actually meant.

15

He looked up as he walked, his loose raven hair frisking across his face with a rush of cool evening air. The day was almost gone, but it was a time of day that he loved, when the birds swooped down to the gourd feeders to refuel for the night; preparing for the temperature drop that came with the birth of the moon. The high thick timber walls of the village limited the view from certain levels, but the birds were always in sight. The tops of the timbers were almost always lined with every possible breed and color of avian that the Kentucky winter provided a domicile.

He reached the limestone steps that led to the front door of the Chief's residence. Absentmindedly, he climbed them like he had a hundred times before, the smooth bottom of his moccasins sliding perfectly into worn impressions in the rock. He looked over the fax once more as he climbed, forming the words he would use to explain the necessity of such an action. Reaching the flat plateau before the great oak door, he grasped the brass knocker in the shape of a growling Bear head, and tapped it against the hardwood door to announce his presence. The elderly attendant named He-who-climbs-the-tree answered the door dressed only in a loin cloth of stressed deer hide. Stone watched the cold rush of air that plunged past the old man into the room. It did not appear to bother the old man in the least; his tough leather skin did not even bristle, he observed. The elder stepped aside, inclining his head just slightly to acknowledge Stone's rank. Even this small submission caused his thin ribs to look as though they doubled over each other. But as old and wiry as the man was, he was still quite nimble and effulgent of mind.

"I wish to see the Chief about an urgent transmission, elder." The old man said nothing, only nodded his head and paced off slowly on boney honey-colored legs toward the Chief's living quarters.

Mantled only in blue gym shorts and treading on bare feet, Chief Spirit strode into the room, wiping sweat from his smooth upper chest and arms with a towel. His hair was braided in one long braid down the middle of his back, and Stone watched as he moved across the floor like a fearsome cat. The man was simply powerful in every way.

"Welcome Stone. What brings you here this time of the day?" "Great Chief," Stone began, inclining his head and setting his eyes downward. "I bring an urgent and unprecedented request from Chandler."

The Chief rubbed the towel across his forehead then tossed it away, reaching for the paper in Stone's hand. Retrieving it, he read it to himself. Slapping the back of his right hand across the paper, he bellowed, "Is he out of his mind asking for this?"

Stone saw the color rush to the Chief's face. "Before you decide, great Chief, please know that Chandler has asked for this because he has run out of leads, and the situation has become… more desperate."

The Chief flipped the paper away from him. "What do you mean by more desperate, Stone? It has always been desperate; all of these situations reach a point of desperation until we catch the killer. Why has this particular case become more desperate?"

Stone shifted uneasily as he tried to stand rigid before the Chief. Chief Spirit circled his second like a predator sizing up his prey.

"What exactly does this transmission not say, Sikona?"

Stone knew he had to tread lightly. He also knew it might do no good. "Great Chief," he paused. "The killer has threatened Titan, and…."

Cutting him off, the Chief spouted, "I know that, Stone – that is why Sky is there now. Tell me something I don't know."

Stone blurted his response like a schoolboy frightened into revealing a sworn secret. "He has also threatened Shawnee." Stone stood straighter, as if it would help to make his point.

Chief Spirit intertwined his fingers, resting his hands palm-ward atop his head. He turned his back to Stone and remarked softly, "I expected that too. That is why Quinton was sent there as well." He drifted to the window overlooking the colossal horse barns and exercise yards. He braced a hand on each side of the frame, pressing his weight into it causing muscles to ripple across his back. His favorite Stallion danced pugnaciously in his corral, his long black main lifting upward in the brisk wind.

"Tell me, Stone, have I not done enough?"

The stallion turned rapidly on his rear hooves as if hearing the Chief's words. Looking up at the window where Chief Spirit stood, the stallion snorted white plumes from his nostrils, stomping his front hooves in fervor. Enthusiastically, he spun in the opposite direction, trotting off to impress a young white filly in an adjacent paddock.

Stone contemplated how to answer. "The killer has promised to make sure the Death Dog and his Handler suffer. He intends to target them both exclusively until they are a menace to him no more."

The Chief straightened, folding arms over his chest, twisting at the hips without unfolding his burly arms, he faced his second in command once again. "If I do this thing, will it be because it is warranted or will it be because she is my daughter?"

Without delay, Stone answered, "No matter the reason my Chief, it will save more lives from being brutally lost. Whether that life be, that of your daughter or someone else's, I think it matters little. It is time to end it."

Thoughtfully, Chief Spirit approached the man he had come to depend on over the years. Gripping Stone's shoulder, he squeezed it tightly. "Thank you, my friend. I appreciate your advice and your loyalty."

Stone lifted his eyes to meet those of his Chief's. "It is my honor to serve you and my people."

"I will approve the request. Notify Chandler of my decision. Within the hour, I will have the information distributed. I will give them one week to get the information, after one week we will terminate the assigned access code."

16

Sky dug in for the night. He had checked and double-checked around Shawnee's home for signs of human tracks; nothing out of the ordinary could be seen. Quinton was inside keeping watch, while Sky was pulling guard duty outside. His night vision was extraordinary for a human. He had been trained to focus his eyesight in a way that illuminated distracting shadows or casts of moonlight. Fifty feet ahead in the deepest dark, he could make out the sideways movement of a snake slinking uncharacteristically through the grass in the cold night after an unsuspecting mouse. Sky's supreme skill was tracking, but at the end of that trail was where he had been trained to apply his second skill of killing. Where his abilities and skills resided in knives, he considered, Quinton was a man to truly be reckoned with. Quinton needed nothing but his bare hands to rend a man's body useless, but was proficient with every weapon made. Sky turned his gaze upwards, pulling tightly at the scar across his face, the result of an immature mistake in his youth. There was little moon tonight, he noted.

The smell of damp hide caught in his nostrils. A small red deer stepped out of the trees only twenty feet to his left. The animal twitched its nose, its eyes widening a bit as if catching sense of Sky's presence. Recognizing the wind was wrong, he realized it could not be him the animal smelled. He looked past the animal into the direction of the wind. Focusing his vision between each tree trunk, he scanned ever so slowly from one to the next, but saw nothing that caused him concern. Scanning again in the reverse direction, he glimpsed it, a still figure crouched low behind a lump of dirt and leaves, which had been collected against a fallen tree by the winter winds. The figure's head hardly moved, but he picked it out.

Sky rolled silently onto his back. He wore his softest buckskin trousers and shirt with bead-less moccasins. The clothes were dyed black to blend in with the night. Knives were held securely to the web belt around his waist, and each finely crafted blade was sheathed in dark smooth leather. His attire was not a play on tradition, but rather a practical functionality of warmth, mobility, and an ensured silence against leaves and trees that might be brushed against in the night. He slid down a brief embankment; as expected, the dirt and leaves rolled gracefully off the stressed deer skin. Upon reaching the bottom, he unhurriedly came to his feet, methodically releasing a throwing knife from its sheath at his right hip. He wanted to be ready.

Inching his way through the woods, he made sure each step was secure and free of anything that could give him away. He heard the deer snort in fear as he made his way behind and past the animal. He crept on, stopping every few feet to listen for movement ahead. Hearing nothing, he continued on. A small tree branch broke in the distance, the deer bolted back into the woods. Sky heard a man curse a string of profanities, and then heard the appeal of apologies from another man. The distance and the trees obscured the voices, but Sky could almost make out an accent, though he could not determine what kind. So there were two of them, he considered, they were noisy this pair. He was surprised he had not heard them before now. He widened the angle at which he approached them. Now knowing their position, he wanted to draw nearer from a rearward avenue. Standing for a moment with his back to a small poplar tree, he craned his ear for further sound. Again, the argument began in hushed tones. Hispanic, he thought to himself, both accents are Hispanic. He moved out, this time more purposefully. These two were not going to notice a snapped twig or two; they were too busy berating each other's stupidity. Sky pulled another blade from his left hip, this one a weapon meant for ripping into a man's body at close range. He closed the distance in a long sure gait, his feet found footing with a mind-of-their-own. His eyes honed in on the men still quibbling in the darkness. He froze for a second, listening to the conversation. The men were less than thirty feet to his right.

"He say to keel the perro only, right, the woman she come later?"

"See. So?"

"What eef da woman she gets in da way?"

"Then we weel have to keel her too, he wants her dead any ways, so we jest do it all tonight. Maybe he will pay us again for it."

Realizing these men were hired killers, Sky decided to take one of them alive for questioning. He retained the throwing knife in his right hand, and sheathed the other blade at his left hip. More complicated but not a problem, he surmised.

Rolling around the tree trunk, he calculated the range, the wind, the temperature, and picked his target. The man was standing, preparing himself to step out of the trees and make his way across the open ground where the house was located. Sky chose him as the man to die. He drew his right arm back, holding the handle of the blade lightly in his palm but with a firm grip of his agile fingers. He released the blade with a force bred from years of accuracy. The blade sunk deeply in the man's temple with a hard thunk, then a sickening sucking sound. The man's body leaned slightly from the impact, yet remained standing. Without warning, the legs foundered and the man collapsed in a heap to the ground beneath him.

"Pedro!" The second man, astonished by his friend's sudden demise, bent down to shake him. Finding the handle of the blade sticking out from his friend's skull, he became terrified.

Sky smiled as his quarry ran clumsily towards him. He leaned back in darker shadow, waiting. As the fleeing assassin dashed past him, Sky wrapped a flowing arm around his neck; the momentum of his course caused the man to be jerked cleanly off his feet. Sky twisted, flinging him to the ground with vigor. All the air exited the man's lungs as his back impacted hard ground. Sky was on him instantly, a knee in his chest and a shin across his throat. The man tried desperately to wiggle out from under the beast atop him, but he could not breathe. Finally, the object across his throat released, and he instantly began to cough and heave for air. Gasping a few gulps, he fought to see in the dark, to catch a glimpse of what had killed his friend and now held him captive. He could see nothing, but only feel the pressure of the object on his chest.

"Who are you?" Sky demanded.

Relieved to find his captor was human, the man began jabbering in Spanish. A large hand pressed hotly across his mouth. "English! I know you speak it." The hand popped from his mouth.

"I yam - I yam Juan."

"Why are you here? Speak plainly and do not waste my time!"

"I, I, I, was weeth my friend, we, we were to keel the perro….the dawg."

"For whom, who hired you to do this thing?"

"I don't know, señor, we are poor peoples, we do some leetle crimes, we go to jail sometimes, we, we get a letter in da jail from another preezner. Da letter it sez to keel the perro and not yet the girl. Da letter it haz five hundred dinero in it and dis address."

"I heard you say *he* when you were talking to your friend. How do you know the person who sent you is a man?"

"Who else would want to keel a dawg and a girl, señor? We don't think a woman does this thing?"

Sky studied the man, and then stood. Leaning over, he grasped the man by the shirt collar, hoisting him to his feet. He was short, barely reaching Sky's chest. "Turn around and walk toward the house. Do not think about running. I will kill you before you get two steps."

Frightened, Juan cautiously turned toward the house. On shaking legs, he began to walk... ever so slowly.

Quinton came out of the room, lips tight with anger. "He knows nothing more. He is a frightened illegal immigrant, who gave into what he felt was a vast amount of money with a promise for more later once Shawnee was dead."

Quinton looked at her sitting on the couch, sipping hot chocolate from a mug that read "I'm a dog person." She had no discernible expression on her face that he could read. "Does all this not frighten you, woman?" Quinton's tone was trembling with fury.

Shawnee flicked long lashes upward over the top of her mug.

Taking a sip, she set the mug against her thigh. "It is not like we did not expect it, Quinton. Why else were you sitting in a dark corner of the living room all night and Sky out in the woods?"

Quinton clenched his jaws.

Titan snored as he slept on his back in a corner of the kitchen. Suddenly smelling the turkey bacon Sky was frying; he rolled over on his stomach and stretched.

Quinton remarked while watching the dog, "You two have got to start taking this more seriously."

Titan watched him, wondering what he had missed.

Norm pulled his police cruiser into the driveway, his deputy following behind him in a separate vehicle. Chandler stepped off the porch, approaching the Chief's driver side window with haste. Chief Wiley rolled down the window, and reached a meaty hand out to Chandler. "Good to see you again, Chandler."

"You too, Norm, how have you been?"

"Oh, fair-ta-middlin, you know how it is."

"I am not even sure I know what that means, Norm, but I will take your word for it."

The big man chuckled.

Chandler rested both palms on the window sill. Leaning in toward the open window, he said, "Listen, I really appreciate you helping us out, we can't spare anybody to transport this guy right now."

"Always at you boys' disposal. You and your people have helped us out enough; it's nice to be able to return the favor for once. Still can't tell me what it's all about, huh?"

"No, afraid not, wish I could."

"Any need for us to keep a closer eye on Shawnee out here?"

"Yes." Raising an eyebrow, he added, "but I think we have it covered"

Quinton swung open the front door of the house, stepping out heavily onto the porch, dragging a fearful-eyed illegal alien by the elbow. The man's hands were zip-tied behind his back.

Norm let his eyes cast a look over the small framed despot. "He looks harmless enough."

"Perhaps," Chandler offered, straightening. "But his intentions were not."

Norm's attention drifted back to Chandler. He saw concern in the creases forming near his eyes and in the manner that he held himself; tight shoulders, clenched fists. The Chief ground out a knowing question. "Do I need to make sure this fella never has a second chance at those... intentions?"

Chandler looked down at the big man in the car, reading the meaning in the tone. "No," he said almost sadly. "I don't think this one is actually bad at the core, just momentarily misguided by the promise of money. For someone as poor as he is, it was too easy an opportunity to pass up. Or so he thought."

Norm nodded understanding. Chandler had already relayed to him on the phone that the FBI would be transporting a casualty across county lines – whether belonging to them or this fella here, he did not ask. He never asked, having learned long ago to involve himself only as much as he was requested to be.

Quinton pulled the man up against the hood of the Chief's car.

"Chief, this is Quinton. Quinton, this is Chief Wiley."

Quinton leaned in front of Chandler, reaching his free hand through the window, holding onto his prisoner with the other. Norm met his grip, shook it gladly, and remarked, "Always glad to meet friends of Chandler's and Shawnee's." Quinton nodded his appreciation without losing any of the tension in his jaw muscles.

To Chandler, he said, "Where do you want this creep?"

Chandler turned to the Police Chief for an answer. The Chief tossed his right thumb over his shoulder and responded, "Put him in the back of Olan's cruiser, he's the one gonna drive the boy down there."

Jerking the frightened man's arm toward the deputy's police car, Quinton walked briskly to the back door and tossed him in. He stomped past Chandler and the Chief, finding his way back into the house, letting the front door slam behind him.

"Don't appear that young man is too happy 'bout all this uproar," the Chief hummed.

Chandler seemed on the verge of smiling. "Let's just say he has his own intentions towards the subject of this uproar."

Chief Wiley blew out a long whistle from between a gap in his front teeth. Rebounding the heel of his left hand off the window frame, he cajoled, "And you ain't hauling two body bags outta here? I'm impressed, Mr. FBI, I am indeed." He laughed heartily, his chest bouncing.

Chandler did smile then.

After thanking the Police Chief and sending him on his way, Chandler spoke to the prisoner. "This deputy will be driving you to the border. You will speak of this to no one; if you do, I will know. You will never, ever cross back into this country. If you do, I will know, and one of those two young men in that house will be sent to kill you. Do you understand?"

The man swallowed a hard lump in his throat, answering with a hoarse whisper, "See señor, I do."

Chandler stared earnestly at the man, assessing the honesty of his answer. Satisfied, he inclined his head toward the deputy in the driver's seat. "Olan, be safe." He offered his hand to the deputy, who took it and replied, "Got a girl down that way Mr. Fox, thought I would stop on the way back and spend a day or two."

"Good, happy to hear it won't be all business for you." Patting the roof of the car, he added, "Get out of here, and don't speed." The young deputy spouted yee-haa as he sped out onto the Farm Road, kicking up dust and gravel behind the cruiser.

17

He knocked on Lizzey's door with a single loud rap. Strolling in shyly, he displayed his journalist notepad and credentials in a way that was sure to catch her eye; he had many duplicates with various names on them.

"Ma'am."

Lizzey turned her head toward the voice, fretting surprise at seeing a stranger enter her room. Noticing the Press ID dangling from the cord around his neck, she replied, "If you weren't so handsome, I would call for the nurse. Truth is I am so freaking bored that I am even glad to see one of you guys."

Corin smiled with a big broad grin; it was warm and inviting. "I am glad," he said, approaching her bed.

Lizzey took in the sight of him; chest muscles thick enough to stir any woman's blood sought refuge from the buttons that contained them within the shirt tucked inside tight jeans. He obviously dresses to show off his body, she beamed with delight. His brown locks flopped carelessly in his eyes, the need for a haircut making him all the more appealing to her. His blue eyes caught the light from the fluorescent tubes overhead. She found herself drooling.

Corin extended a hand to her in greeting. "I really am sorry to bother you ma'am. I told my boss it wasn't polite, but he insisted he would fire me if I didn't try to talk to you."

"You know," she replied, "had you bothered me a week ago, I would have screamed at you. Today, however, I could use the company. I have exhausted all my magazines, movies and television shows. Now I have started counting the lint on my blanket. Lots of fun times here, as you can tell." She swept her hand around the small hospital room, emphasizing her point.

He laughed, batting what many women had told him were beautifully long eyelashes for a man. He checked to see if she had noticed, she had. He interrupted her mesmerized gaze by clearing his throat.

She awoke from her dreamy trance, replying, "So what is it you think I can help you with, Mr....?"

"Oh, sorry, my name is Niroc Retsew."

"What kind of name is that?" Lizzey asked, shocked that a fine American-looking and sounding man would have such a foreign name.

"My mother had a thing for a famous Iranian actor named Niroc. Retsew is actually a Slavic name that was once too long to pronounce, so it was cut in half. My family has been in this country for several generations, though."

"I see."

He observed the natural brunette of her hair, peering through what was left of the blonde hair dye; he had guessed correctly. He moved closer until his hands were resting on her bed rail. She wasn't at all concerned, he noticed, she had become completely at ease with him. "Some cop," he snorted under his breath.

"What?" she asked.

"I was just wondering how your leg was feeling?"

"Oh, that thing," she pursed her lips in disgust. "Sometimes, I wish they would just take the thing and saw it off for good. But then I remind myself about all those excellent pairs of shoes I have waiting at home for me."

"It really is too bad that I could not have helped you out with the loss of the leg, but I am afraid your predicament here has thwarted my original plans for you."

"Excuse me," she issued, confused by what she thought she heard.

He reached in his right pants pocket, pulling out a length of the braided hay-twine. She stared as he let the loose end fall to the floor, unsure of what he was doing. She shook her head a little; her medication must be getting to her.

His tone became harsher. "You see, Lizzey, I had plans for you all along. Who knew you would step into my trap, literally? I thought you cops would have your head out of your behinds enough to be looking for those types of things. It was the stupid dog I was after." He shrugged. "How was I supposed to know you were as dumb as that dog should be?" He cocked his head to the side. "Are you sure you weren't born a blonde?" Corin laughed hard, bringing tears to his eyes.

Sudden realization lit her face. In two quick motions, he had pressed his left hand over her mouth while slamming his right fist into her temple. Both eyes rolled upward as her body went limp.

Moving to the door, he checked the hallway for anyone nearby. It was quiet, no one was in sight. He retrieved the hay twine where it had fallen to the floor. Tying it around her neck, wrapping it the traditional twenty times then ran it underneath one of the loops, leaving the remainder of the twine hanging down the side of the bed. Pulling another braided strand from his pocket, he wrapped her ankles and tied it off. His eyes searched above the bed; there was nothing to tie it to. He looked around the room, eyes resting on the bathroom door. Quickly throwing off the blankets, he reached beneath her, hefting her upward until he could lift her over the bed rails and into his arms; he had molded his body just for this purpose. Wedging his left toe in the opening, he pushed the bathroom door open, carrying her inside. He was pleased to see a walk-in shower. Setting her in the floor beneath the shower head, he pulled more twine out of his other pocket and began wrapping her wrists. Pulling a wet wash cloth off of the side of the sink, he stuffed it in her mouth in case she awoke while he was busy with his work. Her eyes fluttered but did not open.

Wrapping his left arm around her waist, he lifted her to her feet. Holding her there, he used his right hand to grasp the twine hanging from her neck and tossed it over the shower head and pipe. Grabbing the end, he pulled it, lifting her higher while supporting her weight. Carefully, he wrapped the twine firmly around the pipe, creating enough friction to hold it tightly; the shower head would stop it from sliding over, he surmised. When her toes barely touched the tile he grabbed the twine wrapped around her ankles, pulling her feet up behind her back. The pipe creaked from the weight, but the friction from the twine increased on the pipe, holding it fixed. He watched as the twine tightened around her neck, constricting her throat more and more. It wasn't as thrilling as how he normally crafted his work, and he had to abandon his desire to hang her by her feet, but it was satisfying nonetheless.

Her lids flew open, the bulbous portions of her eyes extending well beyond the rims. Unable to breathe, she struggled against her bonds, twisting feebly. Tiring of not being able to see the contortion of her entire face, he pulled her feet up further behind her back until her heels were touching her butt. With an extra length of his favorite fiber, he tied her feet to the twine hanging down from the showerhead. Now, he thought, I can truly watch the show. With the shower pipe creaking from the full weight of her body, he stepped back in order to watch her final demise.

"If mother could only see me now," he muttered.

"What!" Shawn shouted into the receiver.

The nurse on the other end was stuttering. "It is like nothing I have ever seen... it, it, it was… horrible."

Shawn slammed down the phone with a resounding bang. Laura swung in the doorway as he was trying to exit.

"What happened?"

"Lizzey is dead." Shawn pushed past her, stomping toward his Captain's office. Without bothering to knock, he interrupted a meeting. "Where was the guard that was supposed to be posted at her door?" Shawn demanded.

Pointing at the short, dark haired man seated opposite of him, the Captain proclaimed, "Shawn, the Deputy Chief and I were just going over the details, I uh…."

"I didn't ask you what you were discussing. I asked where the guard was, he was supposed to be stationed outside her door."

The Deputy Chief stood, his abridged stature making him seem all the shorter to Shawn's tall Irish lineage. "I think you are getting a bit out of line there, detective."

Shawn turned on him, "Out of line? My partner has just been hung in her hospital shower by that unhinged Bastard that I can't seem to catch. She was supposed to have a guard." Turning back to the Captain, he grated out, "Where was he?" Shawn's accent was getting thicker.

The Captain leaned back in his chair, still seated securely behind his desk. "We pulled him off two weeks ago. We did not think her in danger any longer, and patrol was short of patrolmen on the streets."

Shawn stared harshly at the sandy haired man. "Well, I guess that turned out to be one colossal mistake, didn't it now? Too bad Lizzey can't say thank you!"

Neither officer looked him in the eye. He pounded out of the meeting without apology. Listening outside the doorway, Laura marched in step as he defected from the Captain's office. "They could have your ass for that, you know."

"Like I care," he responded. "I hope the hundred dollars they saved not hiring a security guard was worth it to them."

"What can you tell me?"

Chandler could hear the exasperation in Shawn's voice over the phone line. "Different mode of ops entirely," Chandler answered. Continuing, he said, "Seems to be full of surprises this one. He went in there late evening just before visiting hours were over. Not too many people around at that time. The nurses did stop him, so we have a description at last, and they even had him sign in. Of course, it's a given that is a fictional name. I ran the name and came up empty; a Niroc Retsew. In all probability, he was wearing a disguise as well. But the race, Caucasian, and the build they described might be a good clue; seems he looks to be a bit of a muscle guy with kind of unshorn brown hair."

"Chandler, we…."

"I know, Shawn, we have to catch him. He is far more dangerous than I ever anticipated." Silence settled in. "Shawn?"

"Yea?"

"I am going to make a call. I want you and Laura to start working out of Shawnee's house. You can use the R.V with me; we kind of have the rooms occupied in her house right now. It would be better if we were all together from now on."

"I will have to get it cleared," Shawn sounded despondent.

"Don't worry about that, I will take care of it. Go home, get your gear, and meet me at Shawnee's place tonight at eight for dinner. I will send you the directions."

"Yea, OK."

"Laura too," Chandler reminded him.

"Yea, OK. Yea, I will tell her."

"Eight o'clock, I don't want to have to come looking for you."

"No, I got it, we will be there."

"Good, see you then. Sky is cooking, so be prepared for hot and spicy food. He never knows when enough is enough." The two men hung up their phones.

That evening was quiet at Shawnee's house; business was strictly not open for discussion, according to her. Titan managed to mooch something off of every person's plate before eating a full portion of his own dog food. Quinton eyed the two newcomers with suspicion, while Chandler amused himself with a psychology book on the subject of evil. Sky cleaned the kitchen as Shawnee watched a television show called the First 48, while wrapped in a fleece robe curled up on the couch.

"Everything was good, Sky," Laura offered, breaking the silence.

"Niyaawe, thank you. It was my pleasure, I enjoy cooking!"

Titan belched. Everyone looked over at him and was laughing within seconds, everyone but Shawn.

"It is the spice," Sky announced, pleased.

"Speaking of that spice, whew, is it some Native American mix?" Laura probed.

"Nah, a friend of mine named Aiman gets it from India for me. It is tasty, isn't it?" Again, everyone laughed except Shawn.

Chandler peered over the edge of his book, stealing a peek at the man slumped in his chair. The Irish gent had hardly touched his food during dinner, failing miserably to engage in any meaningful conversation. Even now with the looming calm upended, he was still receded inward.

Chandler set his book aside, stood slowly, and stretched. Approaching the despondent detective, he placed a hand on top of his head, receiving little if any reaction. "Sky, help me with him."

Sky, drying dishes in the kitchen, studied the beaten man seated loosely at the kitchen table. "What do you think, Grandmother Spirit's brew for depression and sleep?"

Without removing his gaze from Shawn's face, Chandler answered, "Yes, I think that will do the trick."

"OK, mind-man, you are the one who called it. I will have it whipped up in a second or two." Sky began opening cabinets and pulling spices and herbs from the shelves.

Laura watched in astonishment as he flitted around the cabinets like a young man bent on becoming a world class chef, but was about to brew some heart pounding concoction to bring the dead to life. "Is there something I can do?" she asked.

Sky, sojourned in his revelry long enough to think, said, "Sure, boil me some water!"

18

Three days later, Shawn awoke in the back bedroom of the RV. Sitting up he looked around the room in a state of Déjà vu. "Man, it seems like I have been here and done this before," he said, scratching his lightly whiskered face and scrubbing his head. He felt well rested, sublime even. Unsure how long he had been sleeping, he found his folded clothes, socks and shoes, and made his way out of the room into the parlor of the RV. Laura lay snoozing on the couch, the television playing a re-run of Cops.

"What day is it?" he asked, rubbing his eyes.

Hearing his voice, she rolled over. "I don't know; but man, I like working for the FBI."

"Seriously," he voiced with annoyance.

She sat up, pulling her robe tighter around her. "If what you are really asking is, how long have you been out, it has been three days. How do you feel?"

"I feel good. I…it was Chandler wasn't it?" he suddenly concluded.

"Uh, yea, but he had help," she supplied meekly.

"You too?"

"Yes, but I was not the only helper. You needed the rest and the….help."

"I will never trust anything that man hands me to drink again. I swear that's twice he has put my lights out."

"Really?" she quizzed. "You mean he has drugged you before and you, the profound detective that you are, let him get away with it again? Tsk, tsk."

Shawn shot her a look that said, *Don't push it!* Laura grinned sheepishly, enjoying having him at a disadvantage.

"So where are my sneaky Native American friends?" he prodded.

"Not sure, all I know is I was ordered on Shawn watch, and they have been gone since the morning after you went night, night. I think there is some secret council or something going on. Boy, that Quinton fella is a scary dude, he doesn't seem to much like us gringos invading his space."

"Chandler gave me the 411 on him. He is a bit smitten with Shawnee, and does not approve of involving us *gringos* in tribal business. Apparently, it is forbidden and Quinton is fond of the rules."

Raising her eyebrows, she remarked, "That explains it."

"Anything to eat around here?" he asked.

"Well certainly, my King, let me get right on that."

"I didn't mean for..."

"Shut up and sit down; it is part of my *Shawn duties,* or so I am told. But after today, you are on your own."

A helicopter whirled above the RV. Shawn and Laura left their half-eaten meal to press their faces to the kitchen window. An entourage of olive-skinned mercenary types clad in brown BDUs and boots hopped swiftly from the cargo bay as the helicopter landed with a pounce.

"That's not Chandler and group," Shawn tossed over the noise.

"I see that," Laura returned.

"Get a look at that guy," she said, pressing the tip of an index finger to the glass.

Shawn viewed the man through the dirty window pane. Even through the thin layer of dirt, he could see the man was formidable, built well, and from the staunchness of his advance he obviously meant business.

"Go see who he is." Laura jerked on his shirt sleeve.

"I am not going out there," he responded. "You go see who he is."

Bear-who-will-not-hibernate stepped soundly from the MH-47 Special Operations Chinook to the hard Texas soil. He was instantly surrounded by six armed guards; two in back, two in front, and one on each side. Despite the cold, he wore no shirt; he marched solidly towards the house where his daughter lived. He was use to the Kentucky winters, this Texas climate felt too warm to him. His tan leather brogans hit the yard with intended steps, arms swinging stiffly as each bicep bunched with the front and back flow; his fists were clenched. The wind whipped through his loose black hair, picking it up to trail behind him like his favorite stallion's tail. Powerful legs swelled in the denim jeans with every stroke of muscle.

"He is….gorgeous," Laura confessed as he drew closer.

Shawn looked at her, shocked she could think such a thing when they were surely about to die. "Have you thought what they might do when they find us here? That gorgeous man out there might just have us cut into little pieces and dropped in the Guadalupe River to feed the fish. If you have not forgotten, Chandler is not here to explain our presence, and we are *forbidden.*"

She looked him in the eye. "Perhaps he might just like us. You are so suspicious of people, Shawn, really one would think you were a cop," she countered, following up with a flip of her blonde hair.

A sudden pounding on the door yanked them both from their flouted argument. Each stood still and straight, as the man who was certainly in charge stepped up into the RV. In perfect English, he announced himself. "I am Shawnee's father."

Laura relaxed. Shawn threw up his breakfast.

Bear stepped gingerly around the contents of Shawn's stomach. "You are Laura," he announced with a nod.

Laura's eyes were transfixed on his tan pectoral muscles.

Looking at Shawn, he said, "And you are the Irishman that Chandler speaks so fondly of."

Shawn wiped a hand-towel across his mouth. Sweat was beginning to bead on his forehead.

"Where is my daughter and her Wisi?"

"Her wha.."

Laura cut Shawn off. "Titan is with her, your highness, uh, ….sir.

But we really don't know where they have gone. It is a private meeting, I think." Laura looked away, embarrassed at stumbling over her words.

Bear grunted in acknowledgment.

Stone ascended the steps into the vehicle. "Great Chief."

Without turning away from the pair, Bear answered. "Yes, Stone."

Stone inclined his head. "The Pilot wishes to know if he stays or goes."

Bear thought a moment. "Tell him stay. We all stay." He turned thick neck muscles to face his second in command, looking for any sign of objection in his down-turned face.

"As you wish, great Chief." Stone backed down the steps with deference, trotting off quickly to tell the pilot to shut the bird down.

Laura stared at the chiseled jawline, admiring the respect he so noticeably commanded.

Bear faced them once again. "You will stay in this vehicle until my daughter returns." He did not wait for a response; turning deftly, he exited the RV, and was gone from sight.

Laura sighed in grief for the missing picture of the perfect male body. Shawn tossed his stomach again.

Titan stood to bellow out a tribal howl. Shawnee, Sky, Chandler, and Quinton lifted weary eyes inside the old sweat lodge. Listening, they heard the second howl as Titan appeared just inside the flap opening. All eyes attempted to focus on his black and tan muzzle. He took one step further; assaulted by the suffocating steam from the hot rocks, he halted. Narrowing his vision, he used the subdued light from the open door flap to make out the figure of his mistress sitting to the right near the back wall of elk hide. He barked harshly several times. Shawnee rested her head on pulled-up knees. Sweat ran from her body at every crevice. Three days, they had fasted and remained entombed in the heat of the sacred sweat lodge, a caretaker regularly bringing them water and hot rocks.

She weakly opened the link to Titan's mind. *"What is it, my heart?"*

"It is Nime'soomtha (my grandfather)," he replied.

She lifted her head with energy she did not have. *"Is something wrong?"*

"He is well, but... he is here."

"What do you mean, here?"

"He is in my heart, I feel him near," was all Titan could explain. Shawnee broke the link.

Peering around the lodge, she could tell everyone was waiting for an explanation. Finally, she said, "I think we have a problem."

Pulling into the driveway of her rented property, Shawnee could see the stationary helicopter parked ominously in the open field beside her house. Hidden within the woods, she knew, were several groups of armed men keenly bent on killing anyone not authorized to be there. On the front porch sat her father, leaning back against the wall of the house with the two front chair legs pitched up in the air. He was using a long-bladed knife to slice slivers of wood from a piece of Silver Maple he had found nearby. He watched sublimely as the vehicles pulled in front of the house. Slowly, he grounded the front chair legs, stood, and set the knife and branch on the table beside him. In the woods surrounding three sides of the house, composite bows were tightly drawn.

Shawnee and Quinton stepped from the lead vehicle, exhaustion evident in their steps. Chandler exited the second vehicle. Sky stopped the third SUV, placing it slowly in park. He studied the Chief's body posture and face. "He gives nothing away. He has a poker face from hell."

Titan whined at Sky's assessment. They both eyed each other. "Well," Sky said. "I guess we just have to face the flute player. Whatever tune it turns out to be," he muttered.

Sky opened the driver's door of the black Toyota F.J. Cruiser. Titan bounced out behind him. No one seemed to be in a hurry to reach the front porch first, so Titan decided to be the brave one. Trotting past Shawnee and Quinton, he climbed the steps, pointedly reaching the feet of his honored grandfather, and promptly sat.

Bear looked down at the massive dog. "What is this? Normally, you would have tried to knock me over with exuberance. Could it be you have matured into this fine stout Wisi before me now, or are you an imposter?" Bear smiled broadly, and set heavy hands firmly against his hips.

Titan jumped from his hind paws, planting front pads upon the brusque chest of his beloved grandfather and Chief. Bear pulled him tightly to him. The dog's head perched beneath his own chin, he rubbed him gruffly with his knuckles.

Shawnee breathed a sigh of relief to see her father in a good mood. She approached him with respect, and hugged him affectionately. He kissed her softly on the cheek, brushing aside her still wet hair from a recent shower.

He pushed her lightly to arms-length, holding her softly by the shoulders. "Let me look at you, daughter." He swept his eyes from her beautiful face to her strong shoulders, then down to her feet. He smiled warmly. "A bit too skinny; but knowing where you have been the last few days, I would expect that." He tucked her tightly under his left shoulder.

Quinton approached his Chief, inclined his head, and remained silent.

Bear lifted his right arm; opening his palm, he wiggled his fingers. "Come here boy. How have you been?" In an unprecedented exchange of fondness, the two men embraced like father and son. Bear clapped him on the back, and then called to Chandler and Sky, greeting each one with a wave of the hand to come in the house; like he had lived there all his life.

Late that night: "Father, there is no need for you to be here."

"I will decide when I want to visit my only daughter, my only child."

She leaned back in the chair in her home office. Facing her father, she stared at his keen dark green eyes. "You know as well as I do, Father, that is not what this is about, a visit. How did you get past Mother with this, anyway?"

Bear grinned. "She thinks I am still in Montana meeting with our sect stationed there."

"Explains why you only brought one helicopter full of Bows, Arrows, and handguns. You would not have been able to fool her if you had loaded a second one with your stallion."

He chuckled at her comment. "You are so like her, you know. Not just in looks, but personality."

"Funny," Shawnee sighed, "she tells me the same thing about you and I. So Father, what are you really up to?"

Bear stood, sliding fingers into the back pockets of his jeans. "I want this to end," he said.

Responding with a bit of defiance, she commented, "We all want it to end. This killer is sadistic, the worst I have ever had to deal with."

"Exactly," her father countered.

Suspecting where this was leading, she announced, "You cannot run to my aid every time you think me threatened. You sent Sky, you sent Quinton, and now you are here. Do you not trust us?"

"I do trust you. I trust all of you. But, this is getting too dangerous… for all of you. We need a consolidated effort to catch this man."

He faced her. "I will not allow the future of the Death Dogs to be so blatantly threatened, nor will I stand by while the future of the tribe is put in question."

Shawnee gripped the chair's arm handles. "What do you mean, the future of the tribe?"

Bear remained silent.

"You expect me to marry Quinton, don't you? You have this all planned and arranged already, don't you? Is Quinton in on this too?" she fumed.

Calmly, he bent down in front of her, seated in the chair. Taking her hands in his, he pulled them to his lips, kissing them tenderly. "Hear me now, child. Just as Titan was prophesied to become the future of the Death Dogs, it was also prophesied that his bonded handler would become the future mother of the Maykujay secret sect. We really don't know in the latter case what that entails. The ancient stories only say the one named for her people and bonded to the future of the Death Dogs will secure the future of the tribe."

Shawnee stared over him, lost in the meaning.

Bear continued. "We know that Quinton is to be your husband; because other stories say that a Beaver in the clan will excel at the weapons of man and be the protector of the future mother of the tribe.

We have stood by for these many years, watching and waiting to see who from the Beaver clan would be this man. We felt sure the first time Quinton laid eyes on you as children, that it would be him. But we were not positive until he showed such promise at weapons. We even kept him away from you, sending him off to far away positions to make sure we were not influencing the natural course. But there is no doubt he is drawn to you as a moth to the fire."

Shawnee looked her father fully in the face. "Does he know all of this?"

"No. Only myself, Stone, the Council, and the tribal Story Tellers know – and now you."

"And why do you tell me this now?"

"So that you understand why I do now what I must."

Shawnee stiffened. "I will not abandon this case; do not even think of asking it."

"I do not ask, daughter. You and Titan will accompany me and Stone back to Moluntha Village along with Quinton. My security team will stay here with Sky and Chandler to finish the job."

Abruptly standing, her chair crashed to the floor. Immediately, the office door flew open, a tribesman fanning the room with a drawn handgun.

Bear straightened. "It is fine, Raven Claw, there is no problem. Close the door." The guard did so without question.

Clenching her teeth, Shawnee seethed venom at her father. "You cannot expect this. Whatever your ancient stories may say, they do not say that you must hide this mother of the tribe away – or her Death Dog, or her future husband – do they?"

Her father hesitated. "No," he answered.

"Then how do you know, great Chief, that you are not unduly *influencing* the prophecy now?"

"I do not, but it is a chance I am willing to take."

"Well, I am not, and I am willing to bet that the result of an appeal to the council will be in my favor. I am further willing to bet that an appeal to my mother will yield a result even more favorable to me!"

Bear took a step back, his tan face turning red with anger. "You are as stubborn as a badger; I can see you were named improperly."

"Try me, Father."

The guard knocked once on the door, cracking it open only slightly. Titan burst in, causing the guard to grab the door before it flung completely open. He closed it quickly, trying to escape his Chief's wrath. Titan stood between the two feuding relatives, looking from one to the other.

"Do not!" she warned him."

Titan whined.

"No," she confirmed, "this does not concern you, I will not open the bond."

Folding her arms across her chest, she turned angry eyes back to her father. "Well?"

Bear tossed his hands in the air. "So be it."

"And you?" she pushed on.

"I will go, Shawnee, but I will leave four braves here to guard the house." Seeing her intent to protest his demand, he waved his hands in an outward arc. "No negotiating."

She considered whether to challenge him further. Deciding he had given in all he was willing to, she conceded.

The helicopter containing her father and most of his entourage took off at a quarter past dawn, long before the forest creatures of the day were stirring. Shawnee watched from her bedroom window as the loosest tree leaves thrust awkwardly up, swirling frantically for a new perch.

Quinton knocked on the door.

"Come in," she said in response.

He stuck his head in through the opening, "Everything alright?"

She turned, forced a smile, and replied evenly, "Sure, everything is fine. Father just needed to get back to the village."

"Uh huh," he pried.

She shot him a look he knew well.

"OK, OK, if you say so. Breakfast is in 30, we are out the door in 45." He closed the door.

Striding down the hallway, he met Sky exiting the bathroom, chewing on his toothbrush, and naked as a Jay-bird. Quinton stopped in front of him, staring in disbelief.

"What? No one is ever up before me," he justified.

Quinton shook his head from side to side, leaving Sky to examine the 'ever' part of his statement.

19

Corin reached for the folded page of newspaper he had laid on the passenger side of his truck seat. He noted again the ad he had circled: SWF 22, looking for roommate AGAR for 3/2/2. "Any Gender, any Race," he said un-abbreviating the acronym. Setting the paper down once again, he again watched the house. It was a brown brick one story with a double car garage and a perfectly manicured lawn, like every other house on that block. He was parked along the curb on the opposite side of the street, tucked neatly amid other vehicles.

He checked his watch, it was 3:30 pm. Forty Five-minutes later, a bright blue Ford Focus zipped quickly by grinding the loose gravel on the road underneath as it abruptly turned into the driveway of the house he was watching. A slightly thin female in her early twenties practically skipped to the front door, unlocked it, and slammed the door shut as she went inside. Corin could not help but be pleased with himself. He knew since it was Friday afternoon, most twenty-two year olds were not going to spend five minutes longer than they had to alone in a house. They would be looking to get home, get changed, and get out to party. He beamed; she probably had not even locked the door behind her. It would be easy to take her by surprise while she showered, and kill her right then and there. But he longed for his old routine; and although this part of his plan was not his old haunt of a convenience store, he had every intention of taking her back to his farmhouse, where he enjoyed the feel of his concrete basement, metal gurney, and favorite rubber mallet.

Little more than an hour had passed before the same spry girl bounced back out the front door, dressed in straight leg pants zippered at the ankles, accommodated by heels way too tall for her already exceeding height. Her shoulder length brown hair flapped behind her as a brisk wind kicked up, showing off her fur lined jacket collar. Tries to look older than she is, he observed. Little does she know it does just the opposite, her youth is painfully evident; he sniffed in response to his own thoughts. The girl backed out of the driveway in as much of a hurry as she had displayed when she made her entrance. The gravel underneath the tires once again crunched and groaned as she turned the wheels sharply, then sped off at an accelerated speed. She gave little thought to the large pick-up behind her; she had other things on her mind at the moment, like getting out of the subdivision.

Corin followed, but did not try to stay too close. In his elevated viewing, he could see her wherever she went. After a few miles on the main thoroughfare, she whipped into the parking lot of a dance club called the Dirty Jersey. He knew it from a story he had written about the rave scene three or four years back. Metal Heads with an appetite for the drug scene made the place their hangout.

He checked his watch, then stopped along the curb, far enough away not to be noticed, but close enough to see what she was doing at a place that did not open for another hour. In his side view mirror, he saw a dingy brown Cutlass approaching. As it passed by him, he caught a glimpse of a butter colored black male at the wheel. The Cutlass turned into the empty parking lot, and stopped alongside the girl's vehicle. The heavyset driver cracked open the driver door, which groaned from years of abuse as he swung it wide with his foot. He took the few steps to the open passenger window of the Ford Focus. Reaching a folded meaty hand inside the car, he opened his palm and dropped something small into her grasp. She looked down at it, retrieved some folded bills from her lap, and handed them to the dealer. Within seconds, the fat-man was back in his car and pulling onto the main road. The girl also pulled out of the parking lot and back onto the main road heading out of town. It was now all but dark, the winter hour blocking out the sun early. Corin knew it would probably be late before he had the opportunity to grab her, but that was no problem; he told himself it would give him time to think about what he was going to do. Finding his own musings humorous, he laughed garishly. He was going to do the same thing he always did: Kill her, kill her dead.

He tucked his truck in between a couple of cars a quarter of a mile back from the girl's blue Focus. The road was not heavily traveled, but it was busy enough to keep him from being noticed by her. After about twenty miles, she turned off the main road onto an access road and traveled down it for another two miles before exiting onto a two-lane side street and heading south.

He slapped the steering wheel with excitement. "She is getting into my neck of the woods now!"

With no other vehicles on the road, he hung back further, keeping his lights on dim. He knew in another three miles they would pass a truly rural south Texas convenience store with a lime-rock parking lot. They sold only beer, ice, milk, and cigarettes. Corin felt a tingle of anticipation in the pit of his stomach. It would be sheer glee if she stopped at the store. It would be just as if he had planned to stalk the store and selected her from right there. To his amazement, her brake lights lit up just as she approached the parking lot of the store. He banged on the steering wheel again, and began laughing with giddiness. He laughed so hard that his eyes began to water and he couldn't see to drive. Rubbing furiously at the moisture to clear his vision, he passed up the store. "That's OK," he giggled as he slowed the truck down, "I need to give her a few minutes, anyway." He guided the right wheels onto the shoulder. Checking both directions, he cautiously made a U-turn and headed back to the store.

Pulling off the road onto the dirt entrance of a pasture, he made sure he could see her car parked in front of the store, and killed his lights. The girl exited the store carrying a 24-pack carton of beer. He cranked his truck, but left the lights off. The girl, true to fashion, started her car and backed out far too fast and in too much of a hurry. She gunned the car onto the road, driving back the way she had come. He pulled onto the road slowly, leaving his lights off for another quarter of a mile. As soon as she was far enough ahead of him, he switched the lights on and pressed the accelerator. As she crested a small hill, he lost sight of her taillights. When he caught up to where she had been, he found she was nowhere in sight.

"No, No, No!" he yelled.

He passed one dirt road, then the next. Just when he was about to boil over with rage, he caught a flash of dim red light through a haze of swirling dirt. Reclaiming his usual calm, he turned onto the unpaved road. Her car was sideways across the narrow lane, the front end dipping into the side ditch. She had tried to back it out but the wheels had churned in the deep sand and were now stuck. Pulling his truck to a stop, he blocked her passenger door. He stepped around the trunk of her car. The girl was perched, with one heeled foot out the driver's door and a cell phone in her left hand extended skyward.

"Get anybody?" he asked politely.

The girl peeked around the frame of the car. "No. I can't believe there is no phone service in this God-forsaken part of the state.

"City girl, I take it?" He smiled wide, hoping she could see his white teeth in the glow of the taillights.

"How did you guess?" she responded rhetorically. She tossed the phone onto her backseat. "I wasn't even going that fast," she said convincingly.

He was pretty sure she believed it. "Well, I don't have a tow rope on me. But if I can get you somewhere, I will be glad to give you a lift." He could tell he had poured on just the right amount of country charm.

"I was going to an all-night party just up the road here at a friend's house," she offered. "Could you take me there?"

"Sure," he answered with a bit of dripping honey. "What's your friend's name?"

"It's Mike, he builds motorcycles."

"Ah heck, I know Mike. I may just join you!"

20

Nearby Canyon Lake boasted three thousand square feet of shoreline and was surrounded by much sought-after hill country. The water was something between brackish and dark green, something fish seemed to desire. Bass were abundant, and it was a favorite for water skiers. The weather was still too cold, however, for the thin-skinned Texans to be venturing out, so the lone boat adrift on the lake in the very early dawn hours immediately caught the attention of the Game Warden on patrol. Marcus tossed the tie-down rope into the bow of his boat and hopped onto the platform; settling in behind the steering wheel, he turned the Johnson motor over with a twist of the key. It was slow to respond, complaining no doubt of being put to use on such a chilly morning. Finally, the propeller spun, churning up the water as the motor spat out a trail of smoke from the oil mixed fuel. Marcus eyed the lone craft while he let the motor warm up.

A brisk wind blew around his ears. He pulled his collared uniform jacket up, trying to ward off the elements. His short-cropped gray hair did nothing to protect his exposed lobes. Removing his brimmed straw hat, he stuffed it in a cubby and pulled a knit cap out of his pocket and over his head.

"Texans aren't made for this kind of whether," he mumbled.

With the motor finally warm, it growled that it was ready. Pushing the lever down in reverse, he slowly backed the boat away from the small dock it had been tied to, then shoving the gearshift into forward; headed for the drifting boat. The moon was still out, and the sun had not yet begun to peek over the horizon. He kept his speed moderate. He did not want to run into anything else out there adrift.

Freezing cold water sprayed his face, chasing any trace of morning fog from his mind. Thirty years as a Game Warden, he thought to himself, and here I am still writing boat owners tickets for not securing their water vehicles. They will never learn.

Slowing as he got within fifty feet of the Sea Ray 175 Sport, he noted the name on the side of the small craft and the silhouetted Hull Identification Number. He jerked a waterproof pad out of his back pocket, and began jotting down the number and the name. Throttling the boat lever forward again, he circled around, checking the outside for damage. He had never seen the boat before, but that was not unusual: The Lake's population had sky-rocketed in recent years. Finding no sign of obvious damage, he pulled up close and peered over the edge. No one was laid out drunk or dead inside that he could see.

He looked toward the still murky sky wishing he had not forgotten his flashlight. He never had much need for it, since he was not usually out on the lake until the sun was bright in the sky and he had drunk at least two cups of coffee. Flipping up the lid on his storage compartment, he removed a tow rope. Fastening it tightly to the driverless boat's bow hook, he gently inched his craft away until the rope was taut. Giving the motor more fuel, he increased the speed slightly, towing the homeless vehicle to shore. Back at the dock, he maneuvered the flow of the boat to have it drift harmlessly beside his own while he tied off his line to the dock. Untying the tow rope from his stern, he hopped the short railing of the unmoored boat, landing soundlessly on a cushioned bench seat. Grabbing the line tied to the bow hook, he slid off the platform into the water, knee-high rubber boots kept the shallow water out, but he could still feel the cold seep into his feet and calves. Heaving heavily, he managed to ground the front, which allowed him the time he needed to reach a secured mooring post on the shore to tie the rope to. He thanked no one in particular that the rope actually reached. After stomping the water and mud off his boots, he trudged slowly up the incline to the station shack to retrieve a flood light.

Making his way back to the shoreline, he pulled himself aboard vacant boat. He swept the big lens back and forth along the bulkheads and the general interior, but found nothing suspicious.

"Just one more inattentive owner," he griped.

Returning to the shack, he poured himself a cup of coffee and checked the time, only six fifteen. Martha won't be on dispatch until six-thirty, he noted. Powering on the television, he sat down to watch the news and warm his hands on his coffee mug. The newscaster reported, "....The FBI is not giving out much information on their search for this elusive serial killer...." Thank goodness we don't have the problems San Antonio does, he thought.

At six thirty sharp, he picked up his radio and called the dispatch office. "Martha you in, this is Marcus."

Martha's voice came back in response. "Of course I am in, Marcus, but you could give me two minutes to get settled in before you start to calling me."

"Sorry Darling, just wanted to get these numbers in to you so you can run them down for me soon as you get a chance." A moment passed, so Marcus assumed she was scrambling for pen and paper.

"Go on ahead."

"XDG 62600 1211. The name of the craft is Justinia."

"I don't have to look that one up, Marcus, it belongs to a little rich girl, just moved in here last month. Know it 'cause she only got it registered a couple weeks ago. Glenn gave her a ticket the first week she was here 'cause she was boating around unlicensed."

"Can you give me her contact info, I found her boat drifting on the lake this morning."

"She seemed like a bit of a partier from what Glenn told me, she probably swam home and left it afloat," she snapped.

There was silence again. Marcus was about to prompt her for the information when she responded.

"Here it is. Justinia Duncan, she lives on the north side of the lake at 124 Deer Trail."

"Thank you Darling," he replied.

"No problem. Now don't be radioing me again till I have a cup of joe, hear?"

"I hear ya' loud and clear, out." He pulled a map of the surrounding lake out of his top right desk drawer. Flipping it open, he traced the lines representing street names until he located Deer Trail.

Coming across #124, he exclaimed, "Gotcha! Lakeside and easy access!" Refolding the map, he tossed it back in his desk drawer, scooped up the keys to his boat, and headed out the door.

Climbing the incline of stone laid steps, Marcus let out a whistle at the size of the new house at 124 Deer Trail. Having its own dock, he had no trouble getting to it from the lake. Reaching the back porch, he transcended the few wood steps that would allow him to knock on the sliding glass doors. But as he curled his fingers preparing to rap on the spotless glass, he saw something that froze him in place. In plain sight hanging in the middle of the living room was a bruised and beaten woman. Instinctively he reached for his gun while backing away, never letting his eyes leave the woman's battered face. He stumbled backward down the wooden steps into the yard.

Pulling his radio from its holder, he hit the dispatch button. In a hushed but nervous voice, he expelled, "Martha." There was no response. He tried again, louder. "Martha." This time he got a response.

"Marcus, if she is drunk and disorderly just deal with it. Ain't nobody else on duty till 0800."

He gritted his teeth, and hit the radio button again. "Martha, she ain't drunk, she's dead! I need some help out here."

"Oh shit, now that's a quandary. Did she O.D. or drink herself to death?" she asked with curiosity.

"Neither," he replied rapidly. "She looks like she had a little help getting dead. I need the city patrol out here, homicide and FBI to boot."

"You serious?"

"I ain't been so serious about anything in my life. That girl is so beaten dead she could'a been run thru a meat grinder." He waited for her to continue her usual diatribe.

"Marcus honey, you just sit tight. I'm gonna get you some help over there. You sit tight, Marcus, you sit tight."

He thanked her wearily. Sitting down on his haunches, he kept his radio and gun in hand. His blood felt exceedingly cold, like he had just been dowsed with a bucket of ice. Shivering, he stood up. "Dammit, I guess I should have a look around, make sure this murdering bastard is gone."

Carefully, he picked his way around the left side of the house, peering through each window. At the front of the house, he noticed all the shades were drawn. These windows, he thought to himself, probably all look into the living room from the street. Pulling leather gloves out of his coat pocket he put them on. Surprisingly he found the front door unlocked. With a disappointed sigh, he pushed the door open, sucking in a breath.

"Mother of God."

The view from inside the front door lacked the security that peering through the glass doors had provided. Here he was face to face with the remains of the victim. He could smell the slight odor of death, mixed with pungent cleaners; it caused his gut to churn. Her body twisted with the slight imbalance of the house, making it appear like she had just been hung there. He slipped his radio back in its case. Folding two hands around the grip of his 40 caliber, he raised the weapon and stepped inside. He checked the carpet for footprints. He did not want to disturb any evidence, but knew he should make absolutely sure the girl was deceased. Scanning the spacious living room, he fanned the weapon wherever his eyes went. He checked the adjacent kitchen observing the pots and pans; which usually hung above the center island, were now scattered all over the floor. Backing his way to the girl, he kept blue eyes on the hallway. Out of the corner of his eye, he could see her just behind him. Using his teeth, he slowly removed the glove from his right hand; and reaching up placed the tips of two fingers on the artery in her neck, feeling for a pulse – but she was cold and getting stiff. He shivered again. Circling around behind her, gun held low, he looked up. The rope creaked as she twisted to where he was staring at her face.

"What the hell!" he breathed aloud and instantly was chastising himself for speaking out-loud. He knew the perp could still be in the house and overhear him. As hard as he was breathing, he was surprised the entire neighborhood couldn't hear him.

It was her head that had startled him. What he had thought to be a crop of short dark hair was actually a crudely trimmed mop drenched in the pooling of leaked blood beneath the battered scalp. Stuffing the glove into his coat pocket, he leveled the handgun to shoulder height as he approached the hallway. Clearing the first small room, he proceeded to the next, and the next, and the next, until he had cleared every potentially occupied space on both floors of the house. Realizing he was the only living thing in the residence, he relaxed his weapon but did not holster it. Breathing more steadily, he took one last look at the dead girl, and then quickly exited through the front door to wait for the experts.

Chandler, Shawn, Shawnee, Titan, and Quinton, arrived at the scene in the middle of a media frenzy. They parked a few blocks away to avoid getting trapped, and walked cautiously through the crowd that had gathered. Local policemen held the reporters at bay, and warned the locals to stay back. The girl's parents had just arrived from San Antonio, and were being consoled by neighbors. Chandler flashed his I.D. at a patrolman standing watch behind the rope. He leaned in to the man to explain that the others were with him. The patrolman waved them through while the reporters clamored for details. In the midst of the melee, Shawnee heard someone yell her name.

"Shawnee, Shawnee!" She turned to see a muscularly built man about her age waving his hand. "Remember me? I interviewed you after Patrice was found in La Vernia!" Shawnee acknowledged the man with a nod. Before Corin could ask for another opportunity to interview her, Quinton's back blocked his view. Quinton's jaws pulsed as he took her by the elbow, leading her away from the crowd. Corin spat obscenities under his breath then saw the dog and withdrew into the depths of his fellow reporters.

Titan paused, his hackles extended involuntarily, and he felt the urge to be on guard although he knew not why. He rumbled a low growl of confusion as a warning of caution trickled down the length of his spine. Shawnee turned, making eye contact with him as he shook off the gloom. He proceeded to follow her and Quinton through the plastic tarp that had been erected to keep prying eyes from seeing into the house.

Chandler approached Steve. "Good to see you, ole boy, just wish it was for better reasons."

"Humph," was all Steve managed, busy examining the girl twisting in the air in the middle of the living room. Her hands were bound behind her back, but her busted ankles had been left to dangle. The bruises and swelling managed to detract from her natural beauty, but the broken bones were what caused her to look shockingly like a wooden puppet on a string, limbs oddly jointed.

"It's him, all right," Steve expelled finally.

"Yea, I can see that," Chandler added. "This is the second time he has altered his normal pattern of hanging them upside down. I guess hanging them where they reside presents obstacles in that regard."

"He is not your usual serial killer, is he?" Steve said, straightening to look at him.

"No, I am afraid not, old man. He is far more complex than anything we have ever studied in the FBI."

Titan circled the girl, sniffing the long delicate piano fingers with perfect fake nails. Like all the others, she had been scrubbed clean, even though some blood had still trickled in thin lines as she had hung there; an obvious sign she was still somewhat alive for a while. The smell of alcohol was pungent, but Titan could smell the remnants of the cleaned-up blood that lay stagnant deep within the pours of her skin, where no human could detect it or clean it away.

"Hey, who let that mutt in here to contaminate my crime scene?" A short, squatty detective stepped out of the kitchen, pointing his pen at the furry beast to which he was referring. Everyone fell silent, glaring at the man. "I said, who…?"

"Excuse me detective," Chandler interrupted, pressing a firm hand against Quinton's forearm. "I am Agent Fox from the FBI, and I am afraid this is now my crime scene. As far as the uh…dog, I let him in." Titan cocked his head, amused at the dumbfounded expression on the man's face. "Any further questions detective?"

"Uh, no, yea, I mean, I will have to clear this with my boss."

"You go ahead and do that. In the meantime, I suggest you address him by his name." Chandler watched the man's features for any sign of understanding.

The detective responded with a frown, "Address who by his name?"

"The dog," Chandler said, "I suggest you call him by his name, it's Titan."

The detective jostled as if to laugh, but seeing the bleak faces staring back at him replied, "Yea, yea I will... do that... next time, excuse me." He swung on heavy heels, stomping outside through the sliding glass doors onto the back porch, disappearing from sight.

Titan was so amused he almost dropped to the floor to rub his back on the carpet, but then he saw the light floating nervously in the corner of the high ceiling. He watched for a moment as her essence drifted, uncertain of the activity going on around her. *"Come to me, dear one,"* Titan expressed the thought.

Her light flickered, trying to place the request into perspective in her limited view and cognition. He reached out again, projecting friendliness. *"I am Titan, and I can help you seek the road ahead. Follow me, sweet one, let us go where there is less noise."*

Shawnee and Quinton watched as Titan padded through the same open doors the squatty detective had departed through. "Should we follow him?" Quinton asked.

"No," she responded sadly, "he has work to do, let us not disturb him."

Corin stood in the dark beneath a Mountain Loral tree budding with a few fragrant flowers. He watched the dog in the backyard of the girl he had killed the night before, seething with resentment at the intrusion of the animal. It was as if the beast sensed him, which irked him interminably. Looking around, he reminded himself that he had to be careful. Moments before, a disheveled local detective nearly caught him off guard when he exited the house in a huff. The idiot had passed within two feet of his hiding spot, never even noticing him. Finding no one watching, he moved a step away from the shelter of the tree's canopy. Instinctively, he reached in his pocket for a length of twine: If he could only get close enough to the dog, he thought... The dog, which had been facing away from him, suddenly turned its face upward, releasing a lonesome howl. Instantly, the man he had seen earlier with

Shawnee bounded protectively onto the back porch. Corin stepped back into the embrace of the shadows beneath the tree; in mere minutes, there would be too much daylight to hide any longer.

The dog turned its head in his direction, its black lips curled back revealing a pink gum line, and the dog growled deeply. Before he could slink away, the large man on the back porch jumped the railing, bursting into the obscurity, tackling Corin like a Pro-Linebacker.

"Hey, what's your problem, man?" Corin complained to his attacker.

Quinton thrust the man upright, wrapping one large hand around both wrists behind the back of the peeping intruder. Roughly with one move, he tilted Corin's shoulders toward the ground and his wrists upward.

Corin flinched, the man was powerful.

"Who are you?" Quinton demanded.

"I am a reporter, who do you think? I have credentials," he gasped, "around my neck."

Quinton snapped the lanyard downward, breaking the clasp. Inspecting the tags, he sneered, "So Wester, what are you doing back here? The media is supposed to be behind the rope in the front yard."

"What do you think I am doing back here?" Corin quipped. "I am trying to get the lead on this story!"

Quinton tossed the man away from him. "You are lucky that I don't kick your sorry ass all the way to the front yard." Pitching the man's credentials to him he added, "I suggest you start running before I change my mind though."

Corin made a show of stumbling and falling in his effort to get away from the big bad man threatening him. When he was once again behind the media rope, he bent hands to knees like he was trying to catch his breath. In reality, he was laughing, exhilarated by the closeness of his almost certain apprehension. Yet, it was so easy to fool these fools.

Cameras began clicking off as reporters pushed and shoved each other to get an interview or the award winning photo that would catch their editor's eye. Corin stood at the commotion. Contractors for the city wheeled the gurney out the front door and through the plastic sheeting, blocking the interior from view. The body, zipped tightly inside a dark body bag, jostled just slightly as a wheel rolled over a wayward rock from the adjacent landscaping. Corin embraced a slight smile, proud of his accomplishments. She had begged for her life, he recalled, like they all do; but she in particular had promised him things no one else ever had. She could not know he had no interest in such things; rather, it was the thrill of her death that excited him, not her female anatomy. Too bad for her, he mused.

He reminisced a moment, remembering how he had seen her at a party; unusual to his normal mode of doing things, he had thrown caution to the wind, recklessly deciding she was the perfect victim. Even though he followed her home and gained entry to her house with a ruse of needing to use her phone for a tow truck, he felt a certain loss at not going through the planned paces of lurking in the dark, and savoring the passion of the hunt. But it would give the investigators a little twist to figure out, he smirked. He laughed out loud at the prospect of throwing them yet another curve. Luckily, he had all the tools he needed to do the job in her house, even though he had to settle for a few unorthodox things like a pair of scissors to cut her hair; he had missed the feel of pulling the electric shears through her scalp. It had been a pleasure, though, developing a new method of abuse as he used them. A few reporters turned to see what was funny, but paid him no real attention, their focus quickly diverted by the sounds of the body being loaded into a city van. The drivers hopped inside and steered the van slowly onto the crowded road. A State Trooper pulled his vehicle in front of the van, escorting it through the throng of gathered gawkers and journalists. With the show over, he decided to leave. He had parked his truck far down the road, knowing the scene would become popular in this upscale life-scape. Once again he had outsmarted the smart people. As he began the walk to his vehicle, he gleefully swung his arms and whistled a tune from a country song he had heard called *"I'm gonna miss you."*

Inside, Chandler and Quinton inspected the interior of the house. Chandler stopped to watch the Evidence Technicians, busy collecting forensic samples from the bathtub and sink in the downstairs lavatory. Wade directed them like a conductor in a finely tuned orchestra.

Spotting Chandler leaning on the door frame, Wade motioned to him to step inside. The lavatory was large and roomy, but with all the activity and buzz it had gotten somewhat crowded.

"I didn't want to get in your way," Chandler voiced as he stepped up next to Wade.

"We are wrapping it up, anyway. Looks like the bathtub was used to contain her while he beat her then cleaned her up. Not much forensically. We have the obvious cast-off blood on the ceiling and walls from him wailing on her. He did leave the hammer behind that he used." Wade held a hand up to cut Chandler off… "We dusted it."

Nothing. I am sure he wore gloves as usual. He must have brought a gallon of alcohol with him to wash her off; he poured bleach down the drains." Wade pointed at the discarded bottles in the corner.

"Yea, I can smell it," Chandler wrinkled his nose.

"No prints on those either," Wade added unnecessarily. "We did find something special, though," he said smiling broadly.

Chandler's forehead creased, showing his intrigue.

"Jonathan, hand me sample #5."

The youth reached a gloved hand into a brown paper sack, and rifled through the plastic baggies. Pulling out a clear bag with the #5 written on it, he stretched a hairless arm out to Wade.

"What are you, twelve?" Chandler joked.

The young man turned red with embarrassment.

"Jonathan is part of a high school Vo-tech program for forensics. He is interning with us for a quarter as part of his curriculum."

Chandler gave Wade a worried look.

"Don't worry; we keep a wary eye on him." Wade winked at the boy. Handing him the baggie, Wade watched as Chandler held it up to the overhead light.

Tapping it with his index finger, he salivated as the strand of mid-length brown hair jumped lightly from the jarring. Briskly, he turned to Wade. "Has it got a follicle, are you sure it's not hers?"

Wade could not contain his enthusiasm, "Yes it does, and yes I am!"

Gripping Wade's forearm, Chandler displayed a wide grin. "We might have him yet!"

Chandler hung up the phone in frustration.

"What is it?" demanded Quinton.

"The hair DNA comes back to a female, and it does not belong to the dead girl in the house; Justinia Duncan."

Quinton sighed, "Can't seem to get a break, can we? So who does it belong to?"

Chandler thought for a moment before answering. "What it could be or what my thoughts are?" He cocked an eyebrow.

"I would rather hear what you think about it; I trust that more than simple possibilities," Quinton decided.

"It was planted; it belongs to the next victim."

"Then we have a lead," Quinton offered.

"No, not exactly. There is no match in the databases for the DNA profile. It doesn't help us in the least." He ran his fingers through the mop of soft black hair, rubbing his head roughly with both hands. "I swear I have never had an opponent like this, he defies all the rules, like, like, he knows our every move." Chandler looked up suddenly. "Dammit Quinton, that's it!"

Quinton shook his head, "What is it?"

"Where has my brain been all this time?" Chandler paced around the living room of Shawnee's house, waving his hands in sheer astonishment at his incompetence. "He is in law enforcement, or works closely with law enforcement. I thought maybe he had an insider feeding him information, but that's not it: He is the insider."

"What are you saying that this guy is a cop?"

"Yes. No. Well maybe."

"Which is it?" Quinton grated, trying to hide his lack of patience.

"I don't know, but he is no run of the mill farm boy, he is close - closer than we ever thought. Where are Shawn, Laura, and the rest?"

"Weapons training at the private compound in Boerne."

Chandler sighed, "I can't tell you how tired I am of this mess."

Titan moaned.

"What's he making noise about," Shawn asked.

Sky and Shawnee smiled at the tall man they had grown so fond of. Sky answered, "It is hard to say sometimes, but we know he often conspires with the Great Mystery through his dreams."

Shawn smirked lightly. "You are kidding, right?" He looked at both of his companions before answering his own question. "I guess not, as usual."

Sky and Shawnee both laughed. Shawnee grabbed up her bow and quiver, "Come, I need practice."

Sky slung his quiver over one naked shoulder and his bow over the other. "Coming?" He asked before taking off after Shawnee.

"I will catch up to you in a bit," Shawn called after him.

Sky grinned, and then took off at top speed trying to catch up with his younger cousin. The tiny bells on the fringe of his quiver danced out a song of joy as he ran.

Shawn sat down on the ground with his back against the small trunk of a Black Jack Oak, and rested his handgun in his lap. The wind kicked up briskly, swirling dried leaves around him, he closed his eyes to seal out the flying dirt. When he opened them, he found himself on a hillside filled with lush grasses and Indian Paint-Brushes. He reached down to pick one of the yellow flowers, when a Red-Tailed Hawk dove past his hand with a screech admonishing Shawn's audacity to defile the Great Mysteries painting.

Titan appeared at his side just as he pulled fingertips back from the edge of the bird's beak. *Not smart, Irishman,* " Titan chided.

Shawn looked at the dog, wondering if he had truly heard him speak.

"What, you think I can't talk?"

Shawn answered shakily, *"I hear you, but your lips do not move."*

"Yes, well, I only speak your language telepathically and normally only with my Mistress. But, things work differently here. They work however my father wishes them to." Titan cocked his head to the side. *"In fact, white man, he must like you a lot, because he does not usually consort with your kind here."*

Examining his surroundings with apprehension he patted himself, *"where is....here, am I dead?"* Shawn asked.

"I am not entirely sure; about where we are, that is, I only know that in my dream-space, my father often speaks with me. Usually, it is because I am in trouble, but sometimes he just talks to me, tells me things I need to know, and offers me advice that I usually do not take."

"I am guessing that is why you are in trouble," Shawn responded.

In his own way, Titan grinned.

The Red-Tailed Hawk circled above them, screeching a warning now and then to respect the landscape.

"So what is his story?" Shawn pointed toward the bird.

"Don't mind him," Titan scowled. *"I got stuck with him in some failing attempt to control me, but that bug-eater is not smarter than me despite what his pea-brain tells him."*

Shawn leaned closer to Titan and whispered, *"I can see why you stay in trouble."*

Titan straightened. *"Really, why?"*

Shawn stared at the dog trying to decide if he was joking.

Answering, he said, *"Because if some spiritual entity had assigned a... creature to watch me, I think I would heed the... creature's warnings. Otherwise, I would expect to be in trouble a lot."*

Titan stared at the lanky man blankly. Seeing the bewildered look on the dog's face, he shook his head. *"You really don't get it do you?"* Shawn was about to try and explain further when the hawk landed on his knee, compelling him to stiffen in fear. His eyes moved to his lap, where the handgun lay. The bird leaned in closer, narrowing intense eyes in threat.

Titan felt a calm abiding presence surround him. In response, he respectfully touched all four elbows to the Earth.

"Young one, we meet again."

"Yes Father, I am in your wondrous presence, a place I cherish."

Titan felt rather than heard the joy of laughter.

"Do not placate me; you cherish little except your own musings."

Titan bowed his head in accepted truth. *"Why did you allow the white man Shawn to come here, Father?"* Titan asked with curiosity.

The billowy voice boomed, yet it comforted like a cloud of cotton. *"He is not of your people, true, but he has the heart of your kind. I allowed him this moment to feel the energy of the purpose he serves. He has been deeply vexed by all these happenings of late, I offer him only some moments of peace and solace. Perhaps he will carry it away with him, and it will give him rest within. Even now he drifts off to deep sleep, though your keeper the hawk eyes him worriedly."*

"Does that thing have a name?"

"Your keeper's name, if I can truly expect you to have a keeper, is Nenemki (Thunder). You have long outgrown the Seraphs, and I must say they were pleased to pass you along to another."

"I am sorry, Father, that I am so difficult."

"Ah, young one, you do not know the love I have for you. Trouble you may be, but I relish in your conviction for your people, the exuberance of your commitment to your service, and the way you simply take on the world. What worries me about you is all of those things. Your abilities have only begun to develop, yet sometimes I hold them back."

Titan's head shot up. *"Why, Father?"*

"Because you lack discipline. Because you try even my patience, because you are you."

"Then why did you choose me?"

"Exactly because you are you. Hear me now. The pestilence you and your people have been tracking is growing impatient and bored. He is becoming more impulsive and taking more chances. The time is near for an opportunity to stop him. You know that I do not interfere in the world in a way that tips the hour glass. I seek only balance between the light and the dark. That is why you and your sect exist, have always existed. That is why I tell you no more than I do. I warn you only to listen closely, follow tightly, lead confidently, and kill mercilessly those who choose the dark."

The trees above him swayed wildly back and forth, the fondness of the spiritual presence receded. Titan relaxed. Sitting up, he eyed the man before him; leaning against a tree trunk, peacefully asleep with a slight streak of dribble running down his chin.

The sounds of gunfire woke them both. Shawn bounded to his feet, his weapon already trained on anything he could reasonably see with sleep-filled eyes. Titan, undisturbed by the practice session, only yawned in his boredom.

Shawn stared down at the dog, trying to rationalize the protruding memory of having a conversation with the canine. "I must be losing it," he muttered as he dropped his gun hand and swiped a dry hand across his lips.

A voice on his radio startled him. Snatching it off his belt, he answered, "This is Shawn, go ahead."

Shawnee's voice returned. "You and Titan about ready?"

Shawn peered at the dog, wondering again if he had dreamed the conversation. "Yea, we are ready."

21

The secure fax began beeping uncontrollably. Chandler rolled off the bed in the R.V Lab, and strolled tiredly to the machine. Retrieving the key from his desk drawer, he slid it into the slot, then entered the receive code. Instantly, the papers began flowing.

Laura stumbled into the room. "What is all the racket?"

"Sorry. It is a secure fax from our Command Post."

Suppressing a strained yawn, she responded, "Oh, I will leave you to it, then."

Chandler read through each page....Massachusetts no findings, Oklahoma no findings, Virginia no findings. He continued reading, tossing each response away as he scanned the data and the final conclusion for each state. Balling up his fists as he read the last page, he clenched his jaws in pure frustration.

He fell on his bed, fists against his forehead. "What am I missing?" he mumbled inaudibly.

Suddenly, the fax began singing again. He jumped up, stubbing his big toe on the floor, and hopped the next few steps to the machine. The key still in the slot, he punched the receive code. The papers began to slip out: Croatia no findings, England no findings, Russia no findings, Afghanistan no findings. Again, he read through each page, all stating the same... no findings. The final page spewed out and read: "All inquiries are in except for Germany, waiting on response." So, it comes down to one last lifeline, he contemplated. He was doubtful Germany would have any better news. He scratched his chin hostilely, the pain felt good.

"Ah, hell," he seethed. "Will we ever get a break?"

Shawn strolled by the lab door, muttering as he went. "I don't know, but if you keep waking me up at 2 A.M., I am going to break something."

Chandler chuckled despite his frustration; Shawn's accent at two in the morning was thick as molasses. Mood lightened, he proceeded to the kitchen where he knew Shawn would be making coffee. Laura appeared soon after, setting her compass west in a direct route to the refrigerator; to start breakfast.

"Might as well," she murmured as she reached for the eggs. "Doesn't look like we are going to get any sleep." Just as she finished her sentence, the fax alarm cried out again. "See what I mean!" she said, pitching a shoulder toward the noise.

Chandler sighed. What's the use, he conceded in a bow of his head, they all say the same thing! Slowly, he made his way to the lab and entered the code, waiting for the last page of bad news to be printed out. Retrieving the page, he read the first line: "Germany reports apologies for the delay. The following information is provided in hopes that it helps your investigation." Chandler continued reading. In disbelief, he read it again.

Bursting into the kitchen, he waved the piece of paper in Shawn's face, unable to speak in words. Pressing palms to cheeks, he kissed Laura hard on the lips, and then bounded out the RV door on bare feet, donning only a pair of blue flannel pajamas. Banging loudly on the front door, he waited. With no response, he began pounding away again, and was caught off guard when a large arm wrapped viciously around his throat, slamming him bodily onto his back, a broad hand pressed into his throat. Quinton stared down at the wide-eyed Chandler, still holding fast to the fax page.

"Who is it?" Sky called from the corner knife blade pulled back with a bent elbow.

"What the hell, Chandler?" Quinton rebuffed, removing his hand from his neck.

"Chandler?" Sky questioned. "What the heck?"

Sitting up on the cold front porch, Chandler coughed profusely, his eyes squinting as Sky approached. Hoarsely, he asked, "Are you naked?"

Sky looked down as if to make sure. "It appears like it," he said smiling brightly.

Quinton rolled his eyes. "What is going on, Chandler?"

"Yea, what is going on?" Sky repeated.

"What are you, a parrot?" Quinton rebuffed.

Shawnee opened the front door. Titan leaped out, licking Chandler on the face, making sure he was well. "You three mind coming inside before all of you catch pneumonia? Sky, are you naked?"

"That's it," Quinton tossed. He had all he could take. Pointing at Sky, he said, "You get dressed. Waving his hand in the air, he shouted, "All of you inside! And you," he said fixed on Chandler, "start explaining yourself."

Chandler nodded. Gathering his legs beneath him, he accepted a nudge on his cold feet from Titan, who prodded him towards the warmth of the open door. Shawnee stepped aside, allowing Chandler and the rest to move by. A hand gripped the edge of the door as she began to close it; Shawn's thin face slipped through the opening. "Mind if we join you? This has to be an interesting story."

She smiled crookedly, releasing the door.

Shawn and Laura bundled in slippers and coats, found the group huddled in the kitchen around the page from the fax machine. "Well, what does it say?" Laura blurted.

Chandler read the communique. "Germany responds… a Corin Jordan attended the Henri Nannen School in Hamburg Germany. Was suspect in death of girlfriend… never charged, due to lack of evidence. Held dual citizenship… USA/Germany…. No record of Corin Jordan leaving Germany." A groan escaped the room.

"You woke us all up for yet one more disappointment?" Quinton chastised.

"No, wait for the rest," Chandler offered.

"Go on, finish it," Shawnee encouraged.

"When all court records had been checked… located a name change for Corin Jordan authorized by a German Magistrate one year after Jordan's graduation… name now Wester… left Germany six months after name change processed… destination, San Antonio Texas… has not returned to Germany… major was in Journalism."

Quinton ground his teeth. "He was there."

At once, everyone turned to face him.

"Who was where?" Shawnee asked, puzzled.

"Wester, I had him in my hands." Quinton looked down at his turned-up palms. "I could have killed him right then and there."

"Quinton!" Chandler shouted.

Quinton snapped his eyes up. "Wester. I had Wester at the House at Canyon Lake," he explained. "He was lurking in the backyard, he had reporter credentials, and he was… watching Titan." Quinton looked over at the dog listening to the conversation. "I am sorry, Death Dog, I nearly let him get to you."

Titan turned his eyes to Shawnee, who nodded and closed her eyes in concentration. The mark on the backs off their tongues warmed with the coldness of a winter bone.

Shawn opened his mouth to speak. Chandler held up his hand, shaking his head no. Shawn acquiesced.

"Do not allow him to feel responsible for me, mistress. I knew the man was there; I would have taken care of him if I needed to. I am to blame as well for his departure; for though I sensed a cold heart, I did not know it was the evil one."

"It will do no good Titan. Sky and Quinton were sent here to see to our safety, they take it personally. They both love you very much."

"Still, I ask that you say to him what I spoke."

"As you wish, dear one." She broke the link and repeated Titan's request. Quinton nodded respectfully in Titan's direction, but did not go so far as to say he accepted relief from his responsibilities.

Suddenly, Chandler snatched a pen off the table and began scribbling on the fax page. "I can't believe it."

"What?" Shawn interrupted.

Chandler turned the page around where they all could read it. Scribbled at the top, it read "Niroc Retsew," and beneath it in reverse order, "Corin Wester."

Chandler, Shawn, and Laura were downtown working overtime, searching court records and databases for any properties belonging to a Corin Wester. Back at Shawnee's house, Quinton was practicing barehanded killing skills on a sand-filled dummy, while Sky trimmed the edges on his blades.

Shawnee and Titan sat in silent discussion in the living room. *"So what will happen, Mistress?"*

"As soon as we get information on his whereabouts, we will go after him. Shawn already checked with the Newspaper; they have not seen him in days. Apparently, he free-lances a lot, uh.... works when he wants to, and shows up when he feels like it. We now know what he does the rest of the time."

"What if there are many places to check?"

"Well, then we will probably split up into teams. That would be my guess. We have to find him as soon as we can before he can hurt anyone else."

Titan flopped his left paw on top of his right, licking the fur like a cat. *"Will our great Chief come here, too?"*

"Oh, I think you would have to lock him in a concrete cell in a faraway land to stop him." Shawnee chuckled out loud, and then added, *"I cannot say that I look forward to it. His coming here will mean more guns, more men, and more testosterone than I care to deal with."*

He stopped grooming to stare at her with a puzzled expression. *"What is this testrone?"*

"Testosterone," she corrected. Realizing her mistake, she added, *"And I have no intention of having that discussion with you. Ask Sky – no, forget I said that! If you must know, ask Quinton, who I am sure will interject far more respect into the conversation. No more talk, you need to rest while you can, you may not get another chance."*

Titan whined, but she returned a stern look that told him she would not concede in deferring the answer to his question. Relenting, he plopped down unceremoniously on his side and stretched out his legs;

in moments, he was drifting into slumber. He found he was in a dark forest so dim he could not see. He tried shifting the elemental fragments within his pupils, but succeeded little in fracturing the darkness; there was no heat signature, no living faction to view. Above him, he could barely hear a high-pitched cry. He concentrated, pressing ear canals inward, narrowing the tubular path the sound carried through. Again, the sound came, the pitch higher and louder. In a flash of recognition, he yelped a call for help. The Red-Tailed Hawk dropped from the heavens into the black of the night sky onto the decayed wet sod of the terrain. He landed gracefully before the dog, cocking one dignified eye at his charge. The bird shrieked at the big dog as if to confirm that all he had heard about him had been true; trouble. Titan shook off the despair of the ink surrounding him, and waited for the bird to make the next move. Suddenly, the avian lifted up, flapping its spread wings, disappearing in seconds into the void. Titan's heart sank, then came the bird's call again. He moved carefully in the direction of the sound, which was all that he had to go by. With each step, he used his nose to find the fallen log or wayward crevice, but increasingly the severe decay of the forest floor dulled his senses.

He stumbled once or twice, only to be chastised by the percussion of the bird's admonishment. Titan felt humiliated to be so dependent on the creature. Silence ensued, he froze. Thunder landed three strides in front of him, tossed his head and screeched, looked back at Titan, and repeated the demand. Titan took the several strides forward to meet up with the bird. He looked down into the bleakness of a drawl, and tried once again to adjust his eyesight. He focused, but still he could factor no heat signature with which to define any real shapes. Thunder screeched again, pecking the dog on a back paw. Titan whipped around, attempting to snap at the bird, but the bird had backed into the deeper bog around them where his presence was undetectable. Fuming with indignity, he forced the gels and fluids within his eyes to blend in ways he had not attempted before. Suddenly, a beam of bone white light shot across his vision, and he could see. Once he held the configuration within his eyes, allowing it to settle, the picture became clearer in moments. The hawk's silhouette came into view only paces in front of him. Titan leapt, the bird took instant flight, the wind from

Thunder's wings battering his face. With the bird gone, he took in the scene around him, death was all about. No tree, bush, blade of grass, leaf, lizard, ant or frog lived. All was dead and rotten.

He turned back to the drawl the hawk had led him to. Upon scanning it with his new vision, he saw it was not a drawl but yet another dry creek bed, for no living waters would dwell within it. Extending his claws, he slid carefully down the dirt wall to the base. The earth changed from decay to dust in the bed; it choked his lungs as he breathed in his surroundings. Satisfied he was meant to follow the creek bed, he trotted along its bottom, kicking up dust in his wake. He was the only thing stirring in this death trap, he thought. After traveling what seemed like an hour, he saw ahead a broadening sphere of light; within it, the familiar wood porch of his home. With a gladdened heart, he picked up his pace, meeting the front door with a jarring pounce. Shawnee opened the door for him.

"Titan, Titan, Titan wake up!" Shawnee grasped the powerful shoulder, squeezing it gently, shaking him lightly at first, then more aggressively. "Titan!" she conveyed louder.

Startled, Titan flung open his eyelids, he was confused. How had he gotten from the front porch to being asleep on the living room floor?

"You were dreaming, I had to wake you, we have news."

Sitting, he shook himself several times to clear his mind and to release the static buildup from his dream.

"We have leads; we have to get our gear loaded and get out of here."

Sky paced by with a big green duffel bag tossed over one shoulder, his usual smile beamed across his scarred face. "Come on, Titan, I will make you comfortable in my truck; the fun ride." He smiled wider, stretching the limits of the scar.

Titan, infected with Sky's endorphin personality, hopped up instantly, forgetting the woes of his despairing time in the dark of the forest, and bounced out the open front door ahead of the man.

Shawnee shook her head. "And I was worried he would grow up too fast, no fear of that happening around Sky," she laughed.

"What is funny?" Quinton questioned, heading out the door with hands full of weapons.

"My Cousin and our Death Dog, I swear they are just alike."

"Oh, don't put Titan in that class, please, he has far more self-respect."

The pair chuckled, and went back to gathering bags to load into the vehicles.

"So where are we meeting Chandler?" Shawnee asked.

Sky, behind the wheel, responded, "He will be with Shawn and Laura at the Japan Cup on San Pedro; it's a tea house. From there, Quinton and I will reconnaissance the apartment complex and enter at will."

"Is Chandler calling in any other FBI agents?"

Sky looked over at her in the passenger seat. "No, your father said this was to remain a private operation."

She met his gaze. "We both know what that means," she remarked.

"Yea," Sky responded, looking back to the road. "This guy has been deemed so dangerous that civilian law enforcement will not be involved. It's just us ducks." Sky displayed his usual smile with a quack.

"Not just us. Like you said, Shawn and Laura will be helping," Shawnee added.

"Ah heck, those two are as much us as us now. I don't consider them local law enforcement anymore," Sky responded with guff.

True enough, she thought. The pair had been integrated in an unprecedented way. Lately, it appeared as though that move was not only right, but permanent. Times are changing, she decided.

Parking the SUV next to Chandler's vehicle in the parking lot of the Tea House, Sky ran the right side windows down on the vehicle as Chandler did the same with his left. Titan, feeling the gush of cold air popped up from his rest on the backseat, sticking his huge head into the space between the vehicles. Shawn reached a long, pale arm across the gap and patted him on the head.

"I think I am getting used to you, you big oaf." Titan licked his hand, and retreated back inside.

Quinton parked his SUV to the left of Sky's. He moved cat-like to the driver's window, tapping on it for Sky to roll it down. Sky pressed the button a fraction at a time while Quinton offered him a look of petulance.

"You are such a child," he told the bubbly Sky.

"It is what keeps me young, my brother in arms. You should try not being so serious all of the time; you will get old too fast."

"Are you ready or not?" Quinton asked with a frown.

"I am always ready. I just have to grab my belt and change my boots."

"Then you are not ready."

"Ready enough, I...."

"Stop!" Shawnee said, motioning her surrender. "I cannot take any more of you two, you feed off each other."

The two men tried in vain to restrain themselves from displaying joy at their success in irritating her. She looked across to Chandler behind the other truck wheel, asking for help with the pair.

"Don't look at me," Chandler flicked a hand. "I have learned it is best to just ignore them." Exiting the driver's seat, Chandler added, "No lights, we cannot afford to warn him if he is in there, and we can't afford to warn him off if he is nearby. Go in quietly; and above all, don't get each other killed with your bickering."

"How do we take him?" Sky asked.

Quinton answered for Chandler, "We eradicate him here and now." Quinton looked from Sky to Chandler.

Chandler nodded. "That's our orders. We take no chances with this slaughterer, we take him out. If he is not there, search the apartment for any obvious clues. If you find none, get back here quick. We are waiting on another call to come in. The Chief has his best researchers looking at the public records for the entire county. He thinks he may have another lead."

Shawnee approached the group, now huddled at the rear of the trucks. "My father is here?"

"He is now," Chandler responded ominously. Everyone breathed deeply.

Laura broke the ice. "Good grief! Why are all of you so scared of that beautiful hunk of man?"

Shawn rolled his eyes. Tossing his head back, he sighed. "Here we go again."

"What? All I am saying is that something so handsome cannot be that dangerous!"

All eyes turned to Laura. Her blonde hair shimmered in the lamplight of the parking lot.

Dumbfounded by their expressions, she voiced, "What did I say?"

Sky and Quinton slunk through the murky dawn across the apartment compound and up the stairwells to Corin's apartment door.

Quinton pointed at the number sixty-six painted on the outside. Sky confirmed the number was correct by nodding affirmation. Quinton softly pressed an ear to the door and tried the knob. He shook his head to convey it was not unlocked. Reaching in the small leather pouch on his belt, he extracted a palm sized set of tools. Selecting two of the smallest, he inserted them quietly into the key slot. The resulting click was scarcely audible. Sky drew a twelve inch blade from the right side of his belt. Meeting Quinton's gaze, he signaled for him to open the door, but Quinton slowly released the tension on the knob and waved a negative response to Sky. Sky returned a puzzled gaze; but trusting his friend, he waited.

Swinging the small pack on his back around to his chest, he reached in for a bottle of oil. Squeezing out some of the contents on the upper hinge, he did the same for the lower one, watching as the thin lubricant coated the metal pin. Securing the bottle and pack, he gripped the doorknob, turning it gently until it reached its stop. The door was eased open a couple of inches as they listened for any movement. Satisfied, Quinton pushed the door another few feet until Sky could slip in unmolested. With Quinton on his heels, Sky moved silently into the living room. The pre-dawn illumination of the moon afforded just enough light to make out the room's contents. Empty. Sky straightened, Quinton copied his movement. Using a hand signal, he sent Sky toward the kitchen while he headed down the short hall to the only bedroom, where he found an air mattress, a few pairs of jeans, shirts in the closet, and no furniture at all. The bathroom was as empty as the rest of the apartment. Sky looked for trash cans to rifle through, but found only one, and it was empty. Both men sauntered into the living room, dropping their air of defense.

"Obvious he is not living here," Sky announced.

"Indeed," returned Quinton. Swinging the pack off his back, he said, "Let us secure our weapons before we head back outside. Too much light now to go unnoticed and we don't want to freak out the civilians. "

"Good idea," Sky acknowledged cheerfully.

Arriving back at the vehicles, they debriefed Chandler and the rest. As they wrapped up the discussion, Chandler's phone rang. Answering, he responded, "Yes sir...yes sir...yes sir, yes my Chief."

He clicked the end button on the phone, and eyed the waiting group.

"Well?" Laura blurted impatiently.

"As I feared, there is another missing girl."

Quinton smoldered in exasperation. "I hope I get to kill this ingrate myself," he spat.

Shawnee reached for him, grasping his left hand. He turned to look down at her, his temper cooling instantly.

"The good news is, the Chief has a lead on a location for Mr. Wester, who it appears owns property in the southernmost portion of the county. We missed it because it is not registered under Wester, but Jordan." Chandler looked to Shawnee, "That's what your father has had Stone working on."

Quinton met the stare of each team member. Seeing they all shared his same resolve, he gritted his teeth and growled, "Let us go and send this evil on its way to hell."

Frozen silence followed while each person compartmentalized their own personal anger and frustration, preparing for the hunt and fight ahead. Titan entered the circle, sat promptly lifting his head toward the morning haze, and loosed a howl of challenge.

"I think that about says it all," Shawnee committed.

"Let's do this," Chandler voiced, "load up and follow me."

The drive south of Bexar County seemed an eternity. Shawn broke the solemn mood with an old Irish joke his elderly fermented grandmother use to tell. It was so out of place and out of character for the thin man that Quinton and Laura enjoyed the moment. Silence quickly took over again, the whine of the tires on the coarse asphalt the only sound.

In the lead vehicle, Titan perked up his ears. Sky, sitting beside him, asked, "What is it?"

"I hear it," Shawnee responded from the front passenger seat, "listen."

Seeing her point toward the roof, Chandler shifted his gaze up, keeping one eye on the road ahead. The whirl of the helicopter blades split the air above them, passing ever so close to the vehicle itself. The big bird spat past the convoy, the outline of a black stallion clearly visible on its side door.

In the second vehicle, Quinton leaned over the steering wheel to get a better look. "Great Mystery help him now," he said.

"Help who?" Shawn asked from the passenger seat.

"Always slow on the uptake, aren't you Shawn. That's the big man himself who nearly ran us off the pavement, or didn't you notice?"

Shawn twisted his head around to stare at his blonde headed partner in the backseat. Laura made bug-eyes at him. Quinton, watching her in the rear-view mirror, grinned in response.

"I am so glad I can entertain you two," Shawn decried, looking from one to the other.

"Uh Oh, Quinton, watch out! His accent is getting thicker."

Turning to Shawn, Quinton offered an apology. "Sorry ole boy, we can't help it, you are just such an easy mark."

The phone in Chandler's breast pocket began vibrating. Snatching it up, he hit the talk button and answered, "Yes, my Chief! Yes, yes, I understand. Yes, I have it." The call ended quickly.

To Shawnee and Sky, he said, "We have the coordinates." Instantly, he began punching them into the GPS affixed to the dashboard. "We will meet him in a field two miles south of the location. It has a wooded barrier securing it from sight of any public road. We wait till dark to go in."

"Is it wise to wait? He could be killing that girl right now," Shawnee despaired.

"No way to help it. We need the elemental surprise darkness will afford us."

Corin was busy all day preparing the ingredients to his favorite chili. He was nearly ready to place it all in the crockpot his grandmother had left him, when the girl tied to the kitchen chair started thrashing about again. He had decided not to kill her right away; a good chili should be shared with others. "Now, now. Is that any way for a pretty young lady to act at the dinner table?"

She eyed him coldly; gagged and bound, she was unable to do much else.

"Just wait until you get a taste of this chili. It is my grandmother's recipe, a brilliant cook that woman was, let me tell you." Picking up a knife from the counter, he pointed it at the girl. "You know, you should be grateful that I am giving you the honor of having dinner with me. This is a first."

She doubled her efforts towards loosening her bindings.

"Daughter. A word." Shawnee followed her father until he stopped short of a skinny Mesquite tree. She faced him. Bear smiled. "This night will be fraught with danger. I will only ask rather than demand that you stay behind."

"Father, I love you, but you already know my answer."

"Your mother said you would say that."

"As wise a woman as you are stubborn, my Chief."

Bear eyed his dark haired offspring. Breaking a small smile, he pulled her close. "Stay close to Titan. Keep that thick head of his from getting him into trouble. Above all, stay out of harm's way, both of you."

Shawnee embraced her father with real affection. Standing on tip-toes, she kissed him on the cheek and turned to go. She stopped after only a few steps, faced her father once again, and said, "Notha, Niila Tapalot Kiila."

Bear bowed his head in respect, unexpectedly kissing the tips of his fingers, projecting it towards her. She smiled glowingly, turning abruptly she departed.

As blue cloudy skies gave way to gray split by horizontal streaks of orange and pink, Stone gathered his troops. Thirty warriors clad in tan and black BDUs stood rigid awaiting their orders. Ten carried Compound Bows slung from left shoulder to right hip, and a deerskin quiver full of metal-tipped arrows was strapped securely to the middle of their backs. The next group of ten held firmly in their grip a burnished AR-57, unlocked and loaded. The last group of ten rested a hand solidly on the heel of .40 caliber handguns planted in leg holsters at their thigh, a pair of night goggles hanging delicately around their neck ready for reconnaissance. Each and every warrior donned an eight inch blade on their belt loop. Their long black hair, normally free flowing, was held fast with a leather headband. Their ominous faces showed the determination bred from training and the birthright of the clan. Their loyalty to their Chief was unquestionable, love for their people undying, and service to the Great Mystery unending. Stone briefed the protocol. The formations were to merge, ensuring a complement of each weapon type and skill was available at every turn. On Stone's signal, the three teams moved out, creeping slowly toward the Jordan property. Once there, they would form an impenetrable barrier around the innermost interior of the large expanse of land, and await the entry team. Nothing was to get through… alive that is.

Sky ran a thumb over the edge of each of his custom blades. Quinton watched as the blood dripped to the ground, becoming lost in the fading light. Titan appeared, his nose glued to the ground where the blood drops had fallen.

Sky looked down at the wide black back of the Dog. "It's just me checking my weapons, nothing to worry about."

Titan stared up at Sky.

"That's him asking if you are stupid," mocked Quinton.

Shawnee, walking past, quipped, "Titan come with me before the two of them rub off on you." Titan bounced away after her.

"Not fair," yelled Quinton after the pair.

"What is not fair?" asked Sky, looking confused, still checking his weapons.

With a baffled expression, Quinton asked, "Are you sure you are related to her?" Sky started to answer, but Quinton held up a large palm to stop him. "No need," he responded, looking away while shaking his head. Sky shrugged indifference and continued to inspect his blades.

Gathering at the Rendezvous point, Quinton, Sky, Shawnee, Titan, Shawn, and Laura readied themselves to make entry. Chandler appeared fresh from a briefing from Stone. "Stone says his teams have seen zero movement on the property or in the residence, but report they have limited visibility into the house. They have cleared all out-buildings, and have located no security systems on the property. Knowing our young friend's affinity for booby-traps, I for one find that part surprising. Unless he is just that sure he is not exposed here."

Darkness was omnipresent on this piece of land. Shawnee shivered from the cold night air, but felt a far deeper sense of dread pulling the heat from her body. She slithered like a Rattlesnake after an unsuspecting meal toward the front of the homestead, a knife perched at the back of her waist. Sky closed in behind her, belly crawling on the naked skin of his upper torso. Beside him, Quinton moved cautiously, smearing dirt on his face as he inched forward. Titan deemed it undignified, and stood erect on all fours at the heels of the pair of warriors, his black and tan fur concealing him naturally. Progress was excruciatingly slow, but they had to take the time to be sure the killer inside did not suspect an invasion. The Red-Tailed Hawk swept low in front of Shawnee, halting her progress. All came to a stop behind her and waited.

Thunder lifted high in the air, then came spiraling downward, catching a rare vortex and slipping sideways across the front yard. Instantly, a motion sensor set off a flurry of floodlights. Just beyond the edge of the lights' boundary, the entry team froze, even Titan dropped cautiously to the ground. Shawn, lying still beside Laura, silently thanked the stars for no longer having the placid obstructive view of Titan's rump. The front door cracked open an inch, then two; the hawk swooped fluidly through the beams of light, showing off the red flare of his tail. Corin flung open the door and the team tensed in the darkness. With shotgun in hand, he took aim at the bird, but the hawk jetted upward and was gone from sight. Frowning with disappointment, he stepped back inside, shutting the door hard and locking it.

Sky, reminded of how much Titan disliked his keeper, looked aft and furrowed an eyebrow at the dog. Titan looked away, unwilling to accept the carrion had a true purpose.

"Now what?" Shawnee whispered back to Quinton.

Before Quinton could answer, the hawk set its feet soundly in the dirt before them. It eyed each of them with a keen eye; suddenly the hawk took flight again. Once again, it flew through the path of the sensor lighting up the dark yard. The team lay glued to their positions. Corin stepped back out into the front yard, shotgun poised for action. Once again, Thunder swept swiftly past, screeching as he went by. Corin rotated the weapon at his shoulder, trying to catch another glimpse of the bird, but all too soon it had disappeared. Maddened by defeat, he kicked at a small cactus, sending it flying into the darkness. He turned on an exaggerated heel, reentering the house, slamming the door behind him.

The cactus hit Sky in the head with a thump, the pin like needles set barbed ends firmly into the flesh of his scalp. Quinton's eyes flashed surprise as Sky winced yet made not a sound. Quinton shimmied gracefully to his side, pulling a Leatherman from his side pants pocket. None too carefully, he plucked each barbed end from its birth, taking humorous pleasure in the effort. With an unseen grin, he patted Sky on the back, returning to his place in the convoy of bodies. Shawn looked to Laura for an explanation of what was happening. Laura ignored his hand signals, focusing instead on the ground yet to be covered. Shawnee waited for the hawk to return, but the night was void of the feathered vanguard; and thus she crawled forward, extending her hand up for the rest to stay put. Quinton shook his head to say no, and started after her; Sky grabbed his ankle, twisting it to keep him in place.

As expected, Shawnee's small frame intersected the sensor's beam, her petite size the reason she had been on point in the first place. The lights lit up the yard and her with it. Sky bent his right elbow, reaching slowly for his best throwing blade, but did not unsheathe it. They waited, but no curtain shifted, nor did the door open again.

"Well done, hawk," she breathed. She continued her crawl forward. Finding no other intrigues, she waived the others onward.

With the expectation that Corin was done with the bird hunt, the others leapt to their feet in a crouching run, eating away at yards of dirt until they were all propped with their backs against the front of the house. Flattened against the mixture of stone and brick-work, they waited for the lights to flick back off. In the dark once more, Quinton and Sky took the lead, working their way to the front door. Quinton softly turned the old bronze-colored knob; it was locked.

Shawn and Laura crouched below the window sill, trying to find a sliver of visibility into what was happening inside. Shawn motioned for her to look from his vantage point. Laura moved closer, leaning into his chest to see what he had discovered. He breathed in the scent of her shampoo, wondering why she had bothered with such a thing as clean hair on a night like this; but then again, he was a guy, what did he know? She squinted, peeking through the hardly visible crack between the thick curtain and the window frame. At first, she saw nothing but the edge of a kitchen table; then he walked briskly past, causing her to catch her breath.

Shawn eased the handgun from his chest holster; Laura leaned away at the awareness of him pulling the gun for the ready. She did the same, quietly pulling back the mechanism, loading one deadly bullet into the chamber. Sky and Quinton caught sight of the pair. Shawn motioned that the perp was just inside. Making the peace sign, Sky pointed at his eyes, then at Shawn while curling in one finger; signaling to keep an eye on the man.

Quinton removed lock picking tools from his hip pouch, easing the middle stocks from their slot. Carefully, he slipped the thin pieces of metal into the key slot, but stopped suddenly. He steadied a trained eye on the mating surface of the frame to the door; a tiny safety wire was serving as a grounding wire… to what? He released the tools, allowing them to stay inserted in the key slot. Pressing his eye to the crack, he observed the wire ran vertically along the frame to the bottom of the door. On his hands and knees, he inspected the threshold, discovering a metal box to the right of the door with a lock protruding through a clasp. He picked the lock cautiously, opening the small six inch door. He sat straight up. Sky stepped around him, resting his hand on Quinton's shoulder so he was aware of his movements. Peering inside, he could make out enough detail to determine the box was packed with C4 explosive material. Quinton chanced the green glow of his pen light to get a better look. The wires were pretty basic; nothing he had not seen before, and certainly far less sophisticated than he had been trained to disarm. This guy might fancy himself a predator, but a bomb maker he is not, he thought.

He pulled the Leatherman from his pocket and went to work. Gripping the pen light in his teeth, he cut the farthest wire in the rear of the box. The white wire was the tricky one, it had to be cut next, but it was braided into the two black wires and the black wires must remain intact. He breathed in tranquilly and held his breath. Reaching for the wire to pull it away was not possible; he could only fit one set of fingers in the opening. He trained the pen light on the wire; slipping the end of the knife blade neatly between the wires, he cut the white wire in one swift motion. Pleased, he folded the tool. Dropping it in his pocket, he went back to work on the front door lock. Just as he was about to unlatch the lock, he heard the heaviness of footfalls and the muffled sounds of someone gagged trying to scream. Sky held up his fist in an effort to keep everyone calm. Shawn gazed through the crack in the curtain, witnessing Corin drag a petite young girl by her hair past the window. He jerked away just as the man trudged by. From the sound, it seemed the pair disappeared down a set of steps, going lower into the residence even though the team had thought they stood at the ground level. Few if any homes in south central Texas had basements; the ground was just not conducive to digging; too many rocks and too much clay. Shawn wondered what other surprises this killer had in store. But Sky and Quinton knew it was a stroke of luck. They might not have found the staircase right away or known where to locate the man at the moment they made entry. Now they knew exactly where he was and how he got there.

Quinton turned the tools half a click until he felt the soft catch of the notch that would unlock the door latch. Methodically, he turned the knob, bracing one hand against the door to prevent it from opening too much at a time; dim light spilled thru the opening. With the precision of one trained through many grueling hours of practice and implementation, Quinton slid through the door and flattened himself to the floor as unnoticeable in the dimness as the rough rug beneath him. Sky scurried by in a slouch, passing Quinton, and taking an erect position in a dark corner of a wall. Laura and Shawn entered next, less concerned with concealment and more concerned with training their weapons against any possible threat. The combination of all their skills was critical and lethal.

Shawnee appeared in the doorway, bent low, validating every team member's position. She opened the bond; the familiar burn produced itself. *"Come Death Dog."* Titan stepped one heavy paw after another through the doorway and into the entry parlor of the house. His heart pounded, yet he felt a strange and bewildering calm. The muscles in his back contracted with the tension of waiting for the moment this evil would present itself to him. All eyes were on him.

Sky quietly slid a honed dagger in between his teeth, still gripping fast to the large blade in his right hand. He fixed his attention on Quinton, who returned the nod of anticipation. Quinton looked sideways to Shawnee, who also nodded in acknowledgment. Shawn and Laura finished scanning the visible passageways, also returning a ready signal. Quinton pushed himself to his elbows and knees, pressing one hand down heavily for every shift in weight he made. If the wood floor made no sound, he continued. Reaching the landing providing access to the first step, he inspected the stairwell as best he could in the minimal light. The stairway was far from the low light source of the parlor, which offered little assistance as it was, but was still not dark enough to use the night vision tools they brought with them. Finding no wires or electronic beams, he waved for Sky to make his way to him.

Titan nudged Quinton's combat boot with his nose. Turning, Quinton looked from Titan to Shawnee for an explanation. Shifting her eyes to Quinton, she whispered, "He smells much old blood coming from the basement, but nothing fresh, nothing within recent hours."

Quinton nodded, comprehending: The girl was not yet being tortured.

Shawnee continued. "He wants to inspect the house, make sure the man cannot retreat from another place... He says it is something he dreamed about." Shawnee shrugged at Quinton's questioning expression.

He turned from her to stare upon Titan's maturing face. Pursing his lips, he pointed sharply with his chin, indicating for Titan to do as he felt he needed. He would not question the logic of one chosen to converse with the Great Mystery.

Titan turned away, padding slowly from the group, with Shawnee as always following close behind. Shawn, seeing the pair exit, exchanged looks with Laura; instinctively, both stepped off quickly after them. Sky reached Quinton's side, asking why he let them go. Quinton placed his palm over Sky's heart, and then pointed upward. It was a sign that the Great Mystery would take them or watch over them, it was not for him or Sky to decide. Sky's face fell, he was sad to be separated from their charge to keep Titan safe. They both knew the time would come when duty would require the big dog to travel purposefully into harm's way without them to protect him, but it was too soon for Sky. Before Quinton could traverse the first step, Sky, seeking separation from his emotions, took up the lead position. Pressing himself to the left wall, he climbed softly down the set of 20 steps. Quinton caught up to him soon after. It was a perilous position to be in; trapped in a stairwell. They did not want to be there for very long. Quinton felt for the lock on the thick metal door at the bottom of the stairs. It was a bunker type door, and bore not a key lock but a digital keypad. Frustrated, he rolled his eyes and let out an exasperated breath. Swiftly swinging the pack in front of him, he reached where he knew the handheld password cracker would be. Pulling it from the pocket, he flipped up the satellite antenna and waited for the connection. The soundless piece of equipment began running the cryptographic algorithms, displaying one series of numbers after another. The keyless entry on the door was a fairly low-tech security system, from what he could tell. He did not expect it to take very long to break the code, but every second was excruciating.

22

Titan did not know exactly where he was going, only that he needed to be elsewhere. Waiting impatiently at the rear door, he paced in circles until Shawnee gently unlocked and opened the door. Titan burst through the opening with the finesse of a bulldozer, pounding down the concrete steps into the yard. His sudden escape drew the attention of the warriors hidden around farm equipment and inside barns and buildings. Instantly, their weapons were raised to fire, only to be held in place once again by Stone's command.

Reminding himself about the sensors in the front yard, Titan assumed the backyard was the same and hugged himself closer to the house. His nose caught no familiar odor of death or the fluids of the dying, so he trekked on. Reaching the corner of the home he stopped soundly. Sliding around Shawnee, Shawn reached a hand to Titan's rump, maneuvering himself in front of the dog. Raising two fingertips to his eyes then pointing outward, he signaled that he would clear that side of the house. Laura took a rear position behind Shawnee, preventing any surprises from popping up. Shawn held his semi-automatic with both hands as he turned the corner, stretching out each long leg in methodical motion. Half way down the outside wall, he stopped, turned, and signaled for the others to follow. Titan reached him first, and Shawn peered down at the dog, meeting his gaze.

Parting his lips slightly, he whispered, "Go ahead." He didn't like it, but felt more than knew that the dog was trying to find a secret way into the house. For that to work, he would have to let the dog be in front as much as possible.

Titan trotted ahead, slowly testing the air. A burst of cool night wind kicked up swirling dust from several yards away into their faces. The powdering of microscopic debris plunged into the lining of his delicate nose, his memory flashing back to the dry creek bed in his dream. Suddenly, he realized he had to find that creek bed. The problem was the motion sensors on the yard lights. He cleared his mind, and established the link with Shawnee.

She answered him. *"Yes, Nitehi?"*

"I know where we need to go, Mistress; but the lights that will come on when we cross the yard, what are we to do?"

Shawnee turned to Shawn and Laura. "He needs for us to go across the yard, but the lights will come on. Any ideas?"

Laura piped up. "I think the hawk already fixed that problem for us; I say we just run for it."

Shawn voiced agreement.

"Titan are you ready?"

With a low whine, he darted across the yard to the tree line, with all three of his team following closely behind. Before they had traveled six feet from the structure, the sensors picked up their movement, causing several flood lights to flash on. They were illuminated like thousands of fireflies on a night with absolutely no moon, but they all kept running. Making it through the barrage of light back into the shadows, all four of the escapees breathed at last, but kept running.

A winter cloud vacated its resting spot overhead, allowing the soft radiance of moonlight to drift into the trees, showing the group how far they had yet to travel. Titan was the first to speed in between the living vertical beams, followed by Shawnee, Shawn and then Laura. Laura and Shawn had not holstered their weapons the entire time; even now they leveled their guns in all directions, stopping at last they dropped hands to knees and gasped for air, their chests heaving from the exertion. The cold air chilled their lungs even as sweat broke out on their foreheads. Shawnee and Titan waited for them to recover.

"OK," Shawn puffed, "I officially admit it: I am way out of shape."

Laura stood erect, breathing with almost as much difficulty – said, "Let's go."

With an awkward start, Shawn once again was off at a trot; keeping pace with the team, but running in the rear. Titan didn't run very fast, since the woods were dark and he couldn't see as well as he would like. He knew the humans could see even less. Above him, a silhouette floated back and forth almost in a circle; it was the hawk. In a moment of clarity, he remembered his dream. He slowed, coming to a stop. Shawnee felt him beside her, and stopped as well. Shawn, lacking the grace of the others, slid into Laura, tumbling them both to the ground.

Wasting no time, Titan concentrated on moving the liquids within his eyes like he recalled doing in his dream. Opening his eyes, he checked the progress, but his vision was blurry. He tried again, keeping his eyes open this time. He felt the fluid in his pupils, and mixed it cautiously with that beneath his cornea, all the while watching how the contrast of the tree trunks moved in and out of a pristine picture. Once the flash of light shot across his sight, he knew he had the right formula. It was like seeing in the daytime, only with more limited depth. Shawnee felt the tension leave him. Knowing he was practicing some skill or focusing on some aspect of his mission, she had left him alone. Ready to begin, he whined then pounced off. Even though he could see things the others could not, he maintained a brisk but calm pace.

The walking trail they were on came to an abrupt end. Titan had not noticed the drop-off in time, and scrambled down the slight embankment into the dry creek-bed. Shawnee, who had been holding his tail, felt him drop suddenly downward; she scrambled haphazardly after him. Having completely lost sight of the pair, Laura found her way only by staying on the steadiness of the thin trail, but now tumbled headlong down the creek wall, landing face first in the dry bottom with Shawn falling solidly on top of her. The impact drove the air from her lungs.

Shawn stood, "Sorry about that luv, I did not mean to crush you; thanks for breaking my fall, though." He dusted himself off and reached a hand down to her, floating it there while she continued gasping.

Regaining the rhythm in her breathing, she tried to slap his hand away, but missed it entirely in the dim moonlight; making her even madder. "I lost my gun," she coughed, "you think you can be a smidgen useful and find it, luv!"

"Sure, I'll just flick on my headlamp, or maybe I should start shouting for Mr. Wester to come help us?"

Titan, listening to the bickering detectives, looked about. His new night vision was a marvelous improvement. Spotting the handgun just several feet from Laura's head, he tramped lightly over to the gun. Notching strong fangs about the body of the barrel, he carried it to where she lay sprawled on her back.

Taking the gun from his mouth, she asked, "Is there anything you don't do?" He licked her across the eye; he liked her. "I probably could have done without that," she commented while wiping her eye with a dusty hand. "But thank you still." She had long come to realize the dog was able to understand her words.

Titan turned east into the creek bed. He maneuvered his entourage around boulders, scrubby shrubs, and dead branches; all the time keeping a steady pace. He did not know exactly what he was looking for, only that he would find it in due time.

Quinton watched the numbers flash across the dim screen of the device until finally it began flashing a steady brilliance of a constant set of numbers. Staring at Sky, he jerked his head toward the door, and asked with a silent expression whether he was ready. Sky reached his empty hand behind him, removing a long slashing blade from its holder. Quinton took that as a yes. Pressing the enter button on the piece of equipment, he was rewarded by a pop from the door. He dropped the device back in his bag, zipped it closed, slung it onto his back, and pulled a semi-automatic from the webbing on his thigh. Pulling the door slightly toward him he blinked as bright light spilled through the opening. He could hear some kind of electric buzzing noise; then suddenly the light vanished, and the room was cast in utter darkness. He flung the door wide, slipping quickly into the basement room from a crouch. He maneuvered to the right, giving Sky ample space to slip in behind him. Both men sat on their haunches, backs against the wall, twitching their noses from the smells that inundated their senses. Sky unzipped the pack on Quinton's back retrieving two small sets of night vision goggles. Handing one to Quinton, Sky pulled the head-harness onto his scalp in one motion, never setting down the blade. He yanked the goggle left and right until he had a good fit, then felt for the ribbed switch and turned it on. The room lit up in a green glow. Searching the room with his eyes, he began to take inventory of their surroundings. To the right was a couch, television, coffee table, and recliner. To the left was a standing shower, tub, huge metal sink and a long counter. In front of them was a large metal table and what appeared to be a hospital gurney. Sky tapped Quinton on the shoulder, both eased themselves up the wall to a standing position. Sky was the first to see that the gurney contained the body of a girl.

Quinton pointed his weapon at shoulder height, sweeping the room in cop-like fashion, clearing every obstacle that could hide this master monster. Sky ran directly for the girl, pressing two strong fingertips into her neck to check for a pulse. He was caught off guard when she began thrashing on the table. Quinton swung his head in the direction of the commotion, but kept his gun pointed down the concrete hallway connected to the room. Sky sheathed his long blade, and pressed a warm palm onto the girl's forehead to hold her head still. Bending down, he whispered to her that they were there to help her. His voice was soothing like coconut crème, and the girl, recognizing it was not the voice of her tormentor, settled down but continued shaking violently. He kept his hand on her forehead, not only to still her but to ease her anxiety; he knew she could see nothing of what was going on in this dark room. He looked her over; she had duct tape over her mouth, straps were cinched around her body and the gurney. Her arms were behind her back, so he surmised that her wrists were bound like her ankles. He slid his hand down her face to her shoulder, then her forearm, as he walked about the gurney. He wanted her to know that he was not leaving her. She was naked, and the act could have been considered suggestive in another setting; but he hoped she understood he was only trying to sooth her fear. He trailed his fingers down her bare leg, feeling the violent tremors of her frightened nerves. Then he bent low, searching beneath the gurney for any wires or items of any kind that did not belong. He searched the opposite side, and found no surprises, all the while keeping his hand pressed to the girl's flesh. She shook less, he noticed, and that made him feel better.

At her left shoulder, he placed his palm atop her head and felt no hair; the girl flinched with pain. Removing his hand, he could see the bloody lacerations in the scalp where Wester had begun the insane process of shaving her hair off. Sky seethed with resentment.

He bent to her ear, and whispered in a voice filled with sympathy, "I am going to cut your bonds. If the cold of my blade touches you, do not fear it, I will cause you no harm. Shake your head if you understand."

She must have thought him strange, asking her to shake her head in the dark – like he would see if she did or not! But trusting in this bit of hope that had happened upon her, she shook her head vigorously. Sky patted her shoulder while slipping his short blade under the strap around her upper torso. He pressed the thin razor edge of the blade under the fabric of the strap. Pulling it upward, using the thick strap's own tension against it. The strap gave way in a fury, separating like butter on a hot knife. He did the same with the second strap, acquiring a duplicate effect.

She bent her knees, pulling her heels to her rump, ecstatic to be free from the confines of the table. Throwing legs over the side of the gurney, she prepared to spring to the cement with her ankles and wrists still bound. Sky reached for her, grabbing her by a bicep, holding her in place until he had maneuvered around to stand before her. He whispered to her to wait until he freed her wrists and ankles. He pulled her into his bare chest, and wrapped his arms behind her. She melted into him. He bent his head awkwardly to ensure a good sighting through the goggles, and determined he needed a different blade. Keeping her pulled tightly into his chest, he set the short blade on the gurney and extracted a cutting knife from his belt. Normally he always returned a cutting instrument to its sheath, but he was apprehensive about releasing the girl in any way at the moment to do so. Gingerly, he slid the small metal edge over each twist of twine; watching as each popped away, exposing the next one. He knew there would be twenty strands. Returning the knife to its proper place on his waist, he gathered up the short blade, and – pushing her gently away – crouched down to where the girl's calves were dangling freely from the gurney. He set the short blade next to his left boot. Again extracting the cutting knife, he slid the sharp edge through twenty strands of the dreaded hay-twine. With hands unbound and ankles free, she leapt from the gurney, intent on a panic stricken run to possible safety. Sky jumped up quickly to catch her before she could knock them both to the floor, exposing them to attack. The girl was frantically clawing at the tape over her mouth, but was unable to lift an edge to tear it away. He took hold of both her wrists, and held them tightly until she stopped the terrified behavior.

Bending to her ear again, "I want you to keep it on, so you don't give us away if something scares you, understand?" He pulled back to see if she shook her head. The girl responded with a defeated nod. Squeezing her wrists, he let them go, but held onto one hand, wrapping it softly into the fold of his own.

Sweeping the floor, he spotted his short blade and bent slightly to pick it up. It felt good to have it in his hand again. He looked to Quinton, who was staring robotically down the hallway, ready for anything that exposed itself. He made a soft chirping sound. Quinton looked to his friend, understanding Sky was asking whether they should go on with the girl or get her out of there. Quinton, who had already observed the heavy dark stains on the floor, walls and ceiling, knew the girl would be killed if they were caught off guard and succumbed. He made the decision quickly: They would get the girl to safety. He tossed his head back toward the bunker door. Sky acknowledged the decision by backing toward it, pulling the staggering girl along with him. Quinton, too, walked backwards, keeping his eyes on the hall, knowing the evil they sought had gone that way to escape them.

Reaching the door, Sky pulled the girl down, pressing her to the wall next to the door frame. Quinton too pressed his back to the wall, while Sky shuffled in front of him. "The girl's legs are weak, I will have to carry her," he whispered.

Quinton nodded acceptance. He alone would bear the burden of protecting himself, his friend, and now this frightened girl. Holstering his handgun, he palmed the automatic weapon under his arm. Sky sheathed the short blade to free his hands. Placing palms on the girl's shoulders, he felt her flinch, but she settled quickly. Pulling her to her feet, he turned her so her left shoulder pressed into his chest, then folded his right arm around her and squeezed his fingers into her right shoulder. With his left hand, he reached up and removed his night vision goggles, extending them to where he knew Quinton stood. There would be too much light in the upper house and outside with the motion lights to use the goggles, and with his hands occupied he would be unable to remove them. Quinton took one last look toward the hallway, and then pulled his goggles off, tossing both pairs in his pack. Securing the pack, he reached for Sky, pushing him back so he could take the lead. He was concerned Wester might have made his way out and around to the basement entrance and was waiting for them. Easing his head around the heavy doorframe he cast a look up the stairwell, the way was clear. He ran at a crouch, taking two steps at a time. Sky curved, reaching under the girl's knees, he swooped her up into his arms for safe-keeping. The muscles of his upper torso constricted slightly to support his charge, but she was light and it took little effort. She folded herself into him, grasping his neck with shaking hands. He followed Quinton through the door; but just as he placed his left boot solidly onto the first step, a powerful electric jolt shot through his body. He was nearly paralyzed by the effect, his left foot slipped awkwardly from the step. He struggled to stay upright but his legs faltered, causing him to fall to his knees, dropping the girl to his thighs. Through it all, he held fast to her.

Hearing the loud static of the Taser against Sky's bare back, Quinton swung toward the sound, firing three quick bursts past the head of his partner toward the silhouette of the perpetrator. But the bunker door was already slamming shut, the bullets caught solidly in the steel of the door. Quinton dashed back down the steps to Sky, who was rigid and stiff; the shock of the electricity riveted his body, singeing every nerve. The girl tried to leave his grasp to stand, but he tightened his grip on her.

"Alright?" Quinton asked.

Sky managed a breathy, "Yes."

Quinton climbed upward, trusting in his friend's judgment and training. Sky clenched his jaws, tightened his abdominal muscles, and willed his leg muscles to obey him. Shoving himself upright, he put a well-placed boot back on the first step, and lifted himself and the girl atop it. He felt pain throughout his body, like all the fibers within his nerves were arguing with each other, but he pushed on. He took each step carefully, making sure he held fast to the suffering creature in his arms. Finally at the top of the stairs, Sky stepped past Quinton, who was standing guard and leaned himself and the girl heavily against the china cabinet near the front entrance of the house.

Quinton made his way to stand next to Sky. Peeking through the open door into the front yard, he began clucking like a chicken. Sky looked at him, stricken.

Quinton shrugged. "Chandler said it would be unmistakable, that no chickens would be awake this time of night. I thought it stupid, too, so don't look at me like that."

He held his place for just a moment, exposing his entire body. He let go of his weapon, allowing it to swing loosely under his arm: clipped securely to a shoulder harness. He stared into the darkness, knowing full well there would be numerous sets of eyes on him from afar. He held up three fingers, for three persons; then thrust them away from him, for coming out. Waiting for a response, he got one in the loud chatter of a desert chipmunk, which did not reside in this part of the country. Even under the circumstances, he could not help but grin slightly. It was comforting knowing his brothers were out there to protect them. He looked to his right. Sky stared straight ahead; the girl was folded into a ball in his arms, hugging him tightly. He placed a large hand on Sky's forearm. Sky turned his face to him.

"Ready?"

His much steadier voice answered, "Ready."

Quinton looked left, then right before running straight into the darkness of the yard. Instantly, the floodlights flashed on. Despite the weight in his arms and the pain in his muscles, Sky stayed in Quinton's wake as he ran. Soon, they were past the boundary of the front lights and once again in the security of the dark. Before they had made it six feet into the blackness, they were surrounded by dark clad warriors. A warrior named Pelawi Hanikwa (summer squirrel) slung his bow onto his shoulder, reaching for the girl in Sky's arms.

She pressed closer to Sky, and began snatching at the tape on her mouth. Sky, whom she could now see by the brace of moonlight, whispered, "Not yet."

Her face hardened in defiance. "We know not where he is. You may give my brothers away without meaning to, be patient?" She glared at him then like she had done before, nodded yes. "Go with Summer Squirrel; he is stronger than I and will not drop you, I promise." She looked from Sky to the young warrior, slowly moving her hands toward his neck in a conciliatory tone. In purposeful fashion, a breeze whipped by, wrapping his black hair around her face. Summer Squirrel folded her into his arms without a second thought or any real effort. Instantly, four warriors surrounded them, and together they vanished into the thick woods without disturbing even the air. Sky dropped to one knee and took a deep breath.

A winter chill swept through the creek bed, throwing pebbles and dust into their faces. Instinctively, Titan slid a thick membrane across his eyeballs to protect them from the debris, and was astonished that he could still see in spite of his sight being minimized. Thunder screeched somewhere above him, jarring him into the realization that he had just performed a skill he never knew he had! When the wind stopped, he slid the membrane away, returning his eyes to the night vision he had enjoyed moments before. Hopping atop a large lime- rock precipice, he drew upon all his olfactory senses, processing the particles and rafts the wind had displaced. As his brain identified the microscopic flecks of dried human blood, he flung open his eyes, jumping consecutively to the ground, taking off at a run. He knew the path now and that the trail was ahead. He was close, so very close!

Pain seared through his brain as the mark burned in his mouth like white hot embers.

Sliding to an abrupt halt, he kicked up rocks and accumulated leaves, and shook the pain from his head as he reluctantly opened the bond. He complained to her about the sudden connection.

She closed the connection just as abruptly. "Yea well, it doesn't feel any better to my head," Shawnee quietly flung at him as she and Shawn gained on his position. Laura came hopping up behind, cupping her right shin and cussing under her breath.

"See. Go slowly, we must stay together," Shawnee scolded.

He followed the scent his nose had discovered. It took him up the embankment, climbing further and further up a steep slope, until at last his front claws gripped the edge of a flat plane. He heaved himself onto it with a compressed lurch of leg and flank muscles. The tunnel ahead was not within range of his night vision, but he knew it was there and there was no mistaking the odor that exuded from its long contained depths. Fingers scraped at the earth behind him. Turning, he gripped Shawnee's wrist, pressing strong fangs into the leather band she wore for that purpose. Pulling, he helped her breach the edge. In turn, she helped Laura up as Shawn boosted her from below; something was said about the precarious placement of his hands, but Shawn never responded to the accusation, boosting himself up with long high jump-like legs and puffing his chest out at his manly ability. No one except him seemed to be impressed.

"Where to?" Laura puffed.

Observing everyone was present, Titan inched his way toward the tunnel. He was processing the odors, categorizing them, trying to understand what awaited... *brain fluid, blood – old and some fairly new; no dead are buried in there, but much evil has been done.* Another familiar odor caught his attention. He processed it, analyzed it, and then understood: The man beneath the tree at the girl's house next to the water, it was him, he was there, somewhere within the depths of the tunnel. As they entered the tunnel opening with Titan in front, Shawnee calmly opened the bond between them.

Instantly, without ceasing in his methodical movement forward, he responded. *"Yes Mistress?"*

"There is no moonlight in here, my heart. Can Shawn turn on his headlamp?"

"It is not wise," he replied.

"OK, stop a moment then."

He did as she asked, she closed the channel of communication. Looking back, he watched to see what she had in mind.

"Shawn," she whispered.

"Here," he said, acknowledging her.

"Loop the rope you brought through your belt, pass it to Laura. Laura, do the same; then hand it to me, and I will hold onto it and to Titan's tail. He does not want us to use lights just yet."

Shawn nodded his head, but realized no one could see him in this blackness. "Got it," he replied. Pulling the loop of rope from a keeper on his belt, he tied one end around his belt loop, and then pressed the remainder of the rope into Laura's hand. She, in turn, repeated the steps, handing the rope off to Shawnee, who clenched it in her left hand, wrapping her right hand lightly around Titan's thick tail.

"Ready," she said in little more than a soft acknowledgment. Titan took one pronounced step after another until each team member was moving rhythmically. His night eyes were brilliant in this closed environment; he could see clearly at least ten feet ahead of him. There were no obstacles, no unpredictable terrain. The walk space was at least a man high with an arched ceiling, and two people wide. The dirt floor was smooth, well worn, the smell of the bricked side walls was very old like it had been used by the man's ancestors, and had been built well enough to withstand time. Ahead, Titan could see an intersecting opening to his right. He came to a smooth halt; the others to his rear felt the shift in momentum and adjusted. As he took two steps forward, the air from the intersecting tunnel hit him in the face. He tested it, noting the familiar smells of a household kitchen. Turning to Shawnee, he opened the link.

Again, she felt the familiar burn, and repeated the act. *"I felt the rush of air, Titan, does the tunnel split?"*

"Yes, Mistress. What do you wish to do?"

She considered the options. Pressing her portion of the rope into Shawn's hand, she said, "We have two paths to cover. Titan and I will maintain this course, you and Laura follow the new tunnel."

"Is it wise to split up?" Laura asked.

"No," Shawnee responded, "but it is probably the only way to make sure he does not get past us."

Laura considered the statement and realized the truth in it. "Agreed," she said simply.

Shawn, barely able to overhear the exchange, pushed into the two. "Are we splitting?"

"Yes," Laura said flatly, annoyed he was not paying closer attention. The tension was building, the closer they came to their goal.

Turning back to Titan, Shawnee replied through the still-open bond, *"They have no choice, now they will have to use the headlamp."*

"If it must be...," he stated simply. Shawnee closed the bond; keeping it open too long would only mean a massive headache later.

She huddled around Laura and Shawn. "Time for the lamp, Shawn, no other choice now. As soon as we reach the new opening, Titan will smell for any detectable danger. If there is none, we go straight, you and Laura take the new route. Follow it as far as it takes you. If it is a dead end, come back this way and follow behind us. If it continues, take it where it leads you."

Laura responded first, "Got it."

Shawn reached up and pushed the switch on his headlamp. Titan yelped in pain as the glow of light penetrated the darkness, mixing with the light he used in his adjusted night vision. It took several moments for the pain to pass; he kept his eyes squeezed shut until it subsided. Shawnee asked if he was OK. He concentrated on the forward darkness as he adjusted his vision. Instead of trying to block the light from Shawn's headlamp, he filtered it, allowing it to blend with the shadows of his night sight. He did not attempt to re-mix the fluid within his eyes, knowing that all too soon Shawn would go in a different direction and the light from his headlamp would disappear completely. He stepped out, covering the short distance to the intersection while breathing in short, choppy breaths through his nose. He detected no smells of danger, no smells of death, only those of food and appliances. Waiting for Shawn and Laura to approach, he watched as they descended into the new tunnel with guns drawn and instincts on high alert.

With the glow from the headlamp gone and Shawnee once again holding onto his tail, he focused on the dark before him and began filtering the fluids in his eyes, until he had achieved the best genetic composition he could contrive with his limited experience. Ready at last, he moved onward.

The tunnel continued for another hundred feet, twisting in half circles, donning cubbies and burrowed out rooms all along the way. The dilapidated wooden boxes scattered throughout each small cave told the story of a prohibition hideout and delivery route; the tunnel leading from the house to the once-flowing creek was no innocent access. But now it was a perfect escape route for their serial killer. The tunnel came to a sudden and unexpected end. To the right was one last room-like cave. Titan searched the room. Finding a smaller tunnel connected inside, he pressed ahead, peering down the length of it for any sign of the killer. Finding no clear danger, he stepped slowly inside. Shawnee felt the tunnel close in around her; reaching up, she pressed palms to the side walls – it was only a couple feet wide, she surmised.

She opened the bond. *"We are close to the house,"* she said with certainty.

"Yes Mistress, we are very close."

"Do you smell him?"

"Yes Mistress, I smell him and the death he has caused."

"Leave the bond open from now on, my heart, this is what we have been saving it for."

Shawn and Laura reached the end of their tunnel. Along the way, the ceiling had gotten progressively lower until Shawn bumped his head. Now having reached their destination, they searched for another route or opening. Above them, Laura spotted the makings of a hidden wood hatch. Shawn turned off the lamp, and looked for any protruding light from above. Dim light eventually eked its way thru thin gaps in the slats of wood. He reached out in the dark, and gripped Laura's bicep. She jumped at the touch, slapping his hand away, chiding him for unnerving her. He almost laughed but caught himself, remembering where they were and what they faced. He reached for her again, this time gently tapping her forearm. She responded by stepping up close to him.

He leaned over her. Pressing his cheek into hers, he whispered, "I am going to feel for a latch or a handle; and if I find one, I am going to try and open this thing very slowly. Cover me."

"OK," she replied, practically inaudible.

He found the hatch again by the dim light protruding through it.

Flattening his hands against it, he felt for a way to get it open. Finally, his fingers caught the lip of a recessed aperture just large enough for his hand. Inside, he grasped a small wooden bar. Turning it clockwise, he felt gravity take over as the heavy wood hatch tried to drop. He caught it before it had a chance to fall more than a few inches. More soft light spilled down toward them. Laura maneuvered around the orifice, where she could point her gun with line of sight precision. Shawn ever so slowly allowed the hatch to drop a little at a time, trying to keep the wood and hinges from creaking, giving them away. As the hatch hinges swung backwards, the hatch traveled its path to hang completely straight down. He noticed a rope extended downward with the door, and remained attached to the locking bar. With the hatch hanging all the way down, he located a small wood ladder bolted to the interior side of it. No wonder it was so heavy, he thought. He fiddled with the ladder in the gloominess, trying to figure out how to release it. Laura, seeing his clumsy attempts, brushed by him and pointed toward the opening. Flustered, he pulled his weapon from its holster and took up the cover position. Quickly, she found the two side clasps that held the ladder. She released them while holding onto it so it would not free-fall to the tunnel floor. Bit by bit, she lowered the extending legs until the feet pressed the dirt floor firmly but quietly. Without hesitation, she began climbing the few rungs. Poking her head through, she saw only a familiar kitchen with the same dirty pots and pans and an unclear table from tonight's intended meal. Otherwise, by all appearances she judged the place to be clean and tidy.

Heaving herself over the edge onto the kitchen's wood floor, she once again pulled her weapon from its resting place. Shawn climbed up, gun still in hand. Despite the dreariness he felt in the house, he was glad to be out of the tunnel. Feeling around the floor, he found a hole just like the one he discovered from below. Reaching inside, he felt the knotted end of the rope and pulled the heavy door using a great deal of effort to bring it up to mate against the surface. Gripping the rope hard with both hands and using his weight to hold the hatch up, he growled at Laura to reach in the recess and turn the locking bar. With the bar secured, he released the rope, and was relieved when it held.

"I see why Mr. Wester is built like a blasted Ox. He has to be to close this thing by himself," he blew through joined teeth.

Laura did not respond, she was busy keeping watch.

Shawnee heard the noise ahead of them even before Titan terminated his progression. He churned a low growl in his chest and throat, but did not vocalize it; he did not want to give away their presence. *"He is ahead, Mistress,"* he said through the still open bond.

"I know," she responded. Reaching behind herself, she pulled the knife from the sheath at her back. She was not the practiced artisan that Sky was, but she was deadly with it nonetheless.

Titan scanned ahead. He saw nothing of the man. Either he was in a side chamber, or they were not yet close enough for his night vision to make him out. *"We need to proceed, Mistress, I cannot yet see the man."*

"Go, Death Dog!" She said, acknowledging his duty and his ability. *"I will follow. And when you have him at your advantage, I will use my headlamp and be at your side in but a moment."*

Titan turned, rubbing his cheek across her shin in a sign of affection. He quickly departed.

Shawnee reached in her side pouch. Pulling out the lamp, she fitted it on her scalp, careful to keep her fingers away from the switch. Titan became invigorated with each powerful lope. His muscles tensed with nervousness, but his mind was clear, his eyes focused. Saliva formed in his jowls at the anticipation of removing this Death Dealer from the world. Large bidding claws pierced the dirt floor beneath him, dust swirling in his slipstream as he navigated the tunnel. Oddly, the heel of a bent foot crept outward from a side opening. Titan pressed bulging muscle into bone, coming to an insonorous pause. The foot receded back into the bay, and the noise of items being packed for travel reached Titan's ears. Warningly, a bright light swung Titan's way. He froze at having been discovered, anger setting in. The light swept upward, disappearing into the space whence it came. Footfalls gave alarm that the man was escaping. Gathering his limbs, Titan thrust his body into motion, catching sight of the man turning into another berth. He ran swiftly with a small duffel bag strapped to his back. Titan took the turn, still able to see the man ahead of him running hard. He stretched his four legs out in a longer gait, expanding already restricted tendons. Elongating his head and muzzle, he became more aerodynamic than he had ever attempted before; willing his body to become one with his mind, unable to conceive of allowing this creature before him to escape. He gained on him with every snap of a paw, and then he was falling.

Corin ran as fast as he could. His muscles bunched and lungs throbbed, but he could not let the dog take him. Damn that animal, anyway! He had one chance to divert the dog, one chance to get away. Carefully, he observed the walls ahead, the flashlight bouncing up and down in his hand. He could hear the dog at his heals. Almost there, the thought clamored in his head. He saw the marker and the protruding brick. Without slowing, he slammed his right fist into the brick, causing it to recede and to match the flatness of the other bricks in the wall. He had passed over the trapdoor even as he released the lever that secured it. He was taking a colossal chance that his weight would be off the door before the lever released its hold on the hatch. Seconds after he traversed it, he heard the door swing downward with the dog on it. He was elated it had worked, but had no time to revel in his joy. He had to keep running.

Shawnee sensed Titan's pursuit through the bond. She was already at a run when she switched the headlamp on. Finding the new opening, she turned, witnessing the end of his tail disappear as his body leaned into a new passage at an explosive run. She followed him, but could not keep up: He was running faster than she had ever seen before. She could perceive the shine of the man's flashlight ahead, bobbing up and down as he made an attempt at flight. Titan was close on his trail when he suddenly vanished from sight. With the bond still open, she felt him falling even as she heard his yelp of surprise, then the bond was closed.

She skidded to the opening he had fallen through, thwarting her own demise by gliding her hands along the walls of the passage to decrease her speed. Peering down into the abyss, she could barely distinguish his features. He lay still at the bottom some thirty feet below. She inspected her surroundings, noting there was nothing to lower herself with. She leaned as far into the opening as she could to centralize as much light on him as possible. She watched his ribs... they were moving, she sighed with relief. Looking back the way she came, she judged whether she should return to look for something that would help her get to him, but there was nothing of use back that way that she could recall. Perhaps she should go forward after the killer and see what she could find that direction. She turned once again to the opening. Studying the door, she decided that if she could climb down the door, she could subtract about eight feet from her fall. The length of her body combined with the length of the door would afford her that. Deciding to take the risk, she sheathed her knife. She straddled feet tightly on the edges of the hanging door, and then scrambled down, clutching the frame with her hands. An index finger brushed slightly across what felt like a knot on the backside.

Balancing with her feet and right hand, she felt around the rear until she located a rope that was looped and secured to the opposite side. Apparently, she surmised, this was not built as a trap, but a quick exit or entrance – but to where? Feeling for what secured the rope, she felt a strap and pulled on it. The rope dropped, but stayed knotted to the heavy door. Grasping the rope with both hands and swinging her feet onto it, she quickly climbed down to the bottom, dropping the last few feet to the floor. She smelled water before she saw it lapping lightly at a rock edge. She swept the lamp upward; some kind of natural cavern, she comprehended. Titan lifted his head, she sped to his side.

"You with me?"

He moved to his stomach, shaking his head lightly. Opening the link between them, he mumbled, *"What befell me?"*

"You," she said. She would have chuckled if she had not been so concerned; the thought of how thick his skull was did not correlate with it being able to be jarred.

He stood and came to his legs, wavering only a second as they became the usual columns beneath him. Dissipating the fuzziness in his mind, he willed his night vision into view, in what seemed a natural act to him now. *"There is water here,"* he mentioned.

"Yes," she replied.

He trudged toward it, Shawnee beside him. Her lamp caught sight of an object bucking in the pool. *"A boat,"* she pointed. Wading in the few feet to reach the wooden craft tied on a short line around an iron hook, she released it, pulling it to land.

"My head is hurting," Titan prompted.

"Let us close the bond," she offered. Looking over the old boat she voiced out loud, "Looks sound enough." Shining her lamp inside, she felt around for a paddle. Bumping one, she pulled it from its perch. "Worn, but serviceable."

Titan jumped inside. Seeing his impatience, she too climbed in, pushing away from the shore with the paddle. The cavern air was clean and crisp, unlike the more confined air of the tunnels. She paddled in easy strokes, unable to see very deeply into the shadows.

Corin was pleased with his accomplishment. With any luck, that beast had not survived the fall. The woman would not pursue him, he was sure of it; the dog would be her priority. Now all he had to do was make it to the next tunnel and find the hidden door to the outside. Once he gained access to the woods, he could make his way to the dry creek bed, where he would follow it to the old frontage road and his hunting lodge. At the lodge, he had a spare vehicle and all the provisions and money he would need to make a clean getaway; home free. Another fifty feet, he recalled, and he would see the next tunnel. He reached it, but came to an abrupt halt at hearing a rock clatter in the distance. He switched off the flashlight before hugging the corner to peer around it. Deep within the length of the corridor, he saw light. Damn them! He fumed at the knowledge that they had discovered the entrance. He flustered for a moment, pressing his back harshly to the wall, breathing in gulps of air. Calm yourself, think! He scolded. Obviously, he could not take the intersecting tunnel now that it was occupied. He looked left: He could go back to where he had left the dog, and hazard the woman still being there. He looked right: Or he could continue down this path, but he was not as familiar with its route or where it emerged. Every tunnel had a hidden entrance/exit – his grandfather had versed him in that knowledge, because Corin had loved to explore the expanses. They provided a much needed outlet to his urges. He had failed to ever take the route ahead, foregoing it for the intersecting passage that housed the decussate to the woods so near the creek bed. No choice, he decided, but to go on. He chanced a look around the corner. Noting the lights were still dim and too far away to capture him, he moved across the junction. The duffel bag shifted as he bounced down the tunnel. Reaching back, he palmed it; he had not been about to leave the tools of his trade behind, nor his trophy bag of hair. He kept running.

Twenty minutes went by. He was beginning to disparage, but then he eyed the end ahead of him. Now all he had to do was find the hidden door that would release him to the outside. He scanned the ceiling with the flashlight, the dust from his escape accumulating thickly in the beam. He spat dirt from his mouth, cursing his luck. Finally the dust dissipated. He twisted, searching the ceiling for the door, trying to fight off the fear creeping into his mind: The fear of being trapped with time running out. Gazing to the floor, he frantically swept aside dirt with one booted foot seeking a trap door. Suddenly, he berated himself. In his anxiety, he had forgotten to look for the marker or the protruding brick. Instead, here he was, just stirring up more dust, he swore. Walking a few feet back the way he had come, shining the light along the walls, he located the tell-tale sign, a small square chiseled into a brick that was larger than the rest. He ran the tip of a finger along the lines, marveling at how long ago it had been tooled there.

Again, the notion of time crept into his thoughts. Snapping back to the task, he backtracked toward the tunnel end. He knew the protruding brick would be only three feet past the marker; he counted it off with the dust still swirling about him. Stopping three feet away, he felt for the brick; it would be on the right side, it always was. Jamming fingers into its extended corporal, he would have cussed yet again, had he not been overjoyed at finding it. Coughing, he pressed himself to the wall and slammed the brick back flat. The heavy wood door swung open loudly, releasing several layers of caked earth from its surface to drop to the flowing water below. He hoped the noise had not reverberated down the tunnel. Bending downward, he felt behind the door for the heavy braided rope. Finding it, he jerked it free. He wasn't worried about it holding up, the rope was built to last, but he gave it a tug anyway; it was serried to the door. Satisfied, he swung down, descending into the immense cavern; the same cavern the dog had dropped into, he was reminded. Reaching the ledge below, he jumped down onto it.

He knew where he was now, having spent many hours in this grotto. It led directly into the Natural Bridge Caverns many miles away; something the caretakers of that place had not discovered in all these considerable years due to the narrow channel that led to it and how high within the cavern it resided. The caverns he stood within now were not known to anyone but his family, as the majority of what could be explored was contained beneath his land. He stood in cerebrate recalling a small but traversable den about half a mile away that opened into – of all places – his grandfather's crypt. The crypt was situated nicely within yards of his hunting lodge. He slapped his knee, giddy with how his luck was turning for the better. His feet consumed yards of the rock ledge with a certainty born from memory. He would make good time.

Shawn and Laura cleared the house and were certain no threat remained. Returning to the door in the kitchen, they hastily regained entry into the tunnel backtracking to the passage that Titan and Shawnee had taken. They were impatient to find the pair, worried about their safety. Both detectives cast a concentrated beam of light from the headlamps they wore. As they ran after the dog and handler, they almost missed the opening on the left. Coming to a stop at the entrance, they cast around, seeking any sign whether the duo had passed by or taken the new tunnel.

"There," Laura pointed.

Shawn followed the diagonal ray of light from her lamp. Leaning in, he detected the clear outline of Titan's massive paws. "Let's go," Shawn said, grabbing Laura by the shirt sleeve and pulling her with him.

Shawn's body reminisced teenage years spent in track as his long legs produced extrapolated strides. He threw dust up behind him, nearly blinding Laura's view. She yelled for him to slow down, but the response that came back in reply was a wail of surprise. She ground to a standstill, choking from the plowed soil. Waving a hand back and forth in front of her, she attempted to clear the air. It had little effect.

"Laura," he called, his voice sounding like he was in a box.

"Where are you?" she coughed.

"Get on your hands and knees, and be careful," he bellowed with difficulty. "I fell through an opening. I'm just barely hanging on here!"

She fell to the floor; feeling back and forth with her hands, she crawled onward. After about ten feet, she felt the edge of the opening. "Shawn?"

"I'm here," he gasped with effort. "I lost my headlamp, though."

"Wouldn't do you any good in this dust-up, anyway, I can't even see your face." Patting around the frame of the opening, she located one of his hands. Gripping him tightly she said, "Got you. Climb up."

Shawn divested one hand from its roost to find higher ground. Laura leaned back to take on the weight. With the delicacy of a mountain goat, he clamored over her and onto the packed earthen floor. "Thanks," he blurted out with sincerity.

"Don't mention it," she said, staring up through the thinning dust from the flat of her back. Standing, she trained her headlamp at the opening. "Too much dust to see what is down there right now, I suggest we keep moving." Shining the headlamp to the side, she indicated they could get by if they were careful. Tip-toeing to the other side, they both sighed with relief.

"I have the lead this time, track-star."

He made to argue when she held her hand up.

"I have the headlamp," she emphasized, placing the tip of her index finger against the device. "Plus, I pace myself slower, so I won't leave you behind; filling your lungs full of God only knows what."

Rebuked, he yielded. With that settled, she took off at a moderate pace, not wanting to befall the same fate as her partner.

The perimeter team, having located the hidden door in the woods, had guarded it until Sky and Quinton could arrive. Choosing flashlights over the night vision goggles, they hopped down into the tunnel. Sky checked for any passing tracks, but found none.

"He has not come this way."

The dyad took off in unison, heading in the only direction they could from their vantage point. Sky scanned the ground for tracks as they ran, stopping only when something caught his eye. Instantly, they would be encapsulated in flying dirt, but then be off again. Eventually, they came to a T-intersection; they could go left or go right. Sky bent to the floor trying to get a glimpse of the terrain, before being overtaken by the dust cloud following them. He saw it just in time: The distinct foot pattern of a booted man, who had stood in this spot for a moment before taking flight to their right. As he canted his chin toward Quinton to tell him in which direction to go, he saw the blur of another dust-filled light off to the left. Both men retreated, killing their flashlights. They waited for the light beam to spill into the space where they hid before grabbing the two intruders. With brute force, each slammed their prey to the floor, pressing a knee between their shoulder blades. Flicking on his flashlight, Sky lit up the blonde hair of his prize.

"Nikanuh! (my friend)," Sky voiced, jumping to his feet in embarrassment.

Quinton, realizing that Shawn lay beneath him, also jumped to his feet to let the tall man up.

"I hope that whatever you said means sorry," Laura spat dust with an infuriating demeanor. Flipping around onto her butt, she blew blonde strands from her face. "I swear if I get knocked down once more tonight, I am going to shoot somebody, and I don't care who." To punctuate her point, she snatched the loose weapon from the dirt at her feet.

Sky held up both hands, actually scared that she might use it.

"Care to help me up?"

Sky scrambled to be the gentleman, clutching her gently, pulling her to her feet. Quinton flicked on his flashlight, shining it toward her face. The ruined pieces of her headlamp dangled from the strap around her scalp. Her face was ashen with dust, and a slight trickle of blood made its way down her forehead, coagulating in the dirt at the bridge of her nose.

Shawn looked at Quinton. From the side of his mouth, he whispered, "Is best not to say anything just now, if you know what I mean."

Quinton coughed in answer, understanding that Laura was in a bit of a temper.

Sky, surveying her condition, made to point out the current characteristics of her face when Quinton slapped his hands together with a smack.

"So where were the two of you headed?" Quinton asked to change the subject.

"We were on the trail of our favorite dog and his handler, when Shawn here almost took a dive down a hole in the floor."

"Not a hole, really," Shawn added, "more of a trap door of some kind."

Sky and Quinton exchanged worried looks. "Did you see where the hole went?" Quinton asked.

"Couldn't see anything much from all the dirt swirling around in here," she spit out.

"Dammit," Quinton expelled.

"What?" she asked.

Sky responded, "If you were following our Death Dog and his Mistress, where are they?"

"Good question. Is there no sign of them coming this way?"

Sky shook his head. "I only see the boots of a man in this passageway."

"Perhaps they were ahead of Wester, and his tracks have erased theirs," Laura offered.

"My headlamp fell down there," Shawn chimed in. "I had a moment where I could see the bottom before the lamp hit. I did not see anything that would make me think they had fallen down there."

Sky turned to Quinton. "Your call, my brother."

Quinton bowed his head in thought. His insides were churning, his heart burning with emotional pain. Looking to Shawn once again, then to Sky, he nodded. "We track our killer. I pray to the Great Mystery that is what we find those two doing as well."

All four stepped off in the direction of the tracks. Sky stayed in the lead checking for further patterns of passage, there were plenty to follow. Soon enough, fresh air bounded toward them, and Sky held up a fist to slow the crew's advancement. Air rushed past, preventing the dust from settling around him. The big heavy door hung down with a knotted rope dangling to the depths. Sky shone the light to the bottom, noting a river of sorts with tall rock-sided walls. He checked for a byway they could use; the rope, he decided, had to lead to something besides the water. There, atop the naturally carved out barrier of rock, was a ledge approximately twelve inches wide running parallel with the water. It was wide enough to traverse. Looking up, a thought struck him. Flashing the light back inside their current tunnel, he bit his lip. It was a dead end. Where was Titan?

"He probably fell through the opening that Laura and Shawn found," said Quinton somberly, answering the question Sky had been unwilling to voice. "You know how he tends to get ahead of everybody."

Sky stood stiffly, "But Shawn saw nothing, brother. If he fell, Shawnee reached him, and they have gone this same way from below, still on the path of our madman."

Quinton tightly pressed his eyes shut. He checked his emotions, allowing hope to suppress his fears. "Let us do the same, then," he responded finally.

The Quad lowered themselves one by one to the ledge.

"Careful everybody," said Sky. "The way is slippery, and the water looks deep and fast."

He found the den with little effort, reaching it, barely out of breath. Lying oblate to climb inside, he wobbled his body through the stony entrance, gaining entry to the interior where it expanded into a more spacious ambit. Standing, he shone the flashlight, locating the passage that would take him to his grandfather's crypt. He sped toward it, adjusting his pack as he traveled. The tunnel was narrower than he recalled, and his shoulders brushed the sides, causing him to tuck them toward his chest. With the underpass leading upwards, his calves contracted with the feat, he reached the manhole-like-cover at last. Lifting it, he slid it sideways across the stone floor, and pulled himself up and through it. With legs dangling down, he lay back on his pack enjoying a moment of relief and exquisite excitement. Staring up at the moonlight streaming through the stained glass, he jumped to his feet.

"Perfect," he announced with glee. Moving to his grandfather's casket, he laid a hand upon it. Conflicted with a strange and sudden feelings of loss, he snatched it away, turning for the door.

He pressed outward on the portico cautiously, peeking out through the crack, completely missing the large padded paw prints and small booted feet that had crossed the same surface. The door creaked when he pushed it. Seeing nothing to fear Corin stepped out in the moonlight, breaking into a bent run, making for the hunting lodge, tripping twice from feet bound in tangled vine. Normally considering himself fairly stealthy, he presently felt like a bull in a china store. Picking himself up and brushing off more vine, he sought around for a better course; the glade he was in was too thick with foliage. If he was going to get to the trees and his lodge without getting caught, he had to move faster. Selecting an alternate route to his left but finding the going no easier, he chose to horse step through the glade, continuing in a straight line. It would be faster than trying to run through it. Eventually, he reached the trees and within them his lodge. Kissing the hood of his truck, he bounded for the front porch of the cabin.

The four team members ascended the passage in single file. Sky followed the man's track and that of Titan and Shawnee before him, easily locating the den and tunnel. Finding the opening above him, he hopped up into what he could guess was an above ground burial vault. The casket confirmed his suspicions. Reaching down, grasping Laura's wrist, Sky pulled her up, then Shawn after her. Quinton refused the assistance, pulling himself up through the hole.

Looking around, Laura exclaimed, "Creepy."

"This way," Sky moved toward the open door, moonlight filling the space unobstructed.

With care, he examined the perimeter. Finding nothing to detain them, he leaped clear of the vault and onto the ground, flattening himself. The others held their position inside, waiting for Sky's signal. Motioning for them to proceed, one by one each of them leaped to Sky's position on the ground.

"Anything?" Quinton asked.

"No," answered Sky.

"Which way?" Shawn intruded.

Sky pointed into the glade. "There. Our friend has left signs that even you could follow, Irishman." Sky grinned, his teeth luminous in the moonlight.

"Ha, ha," the tall man returned.

"Can we go now?" Laura rolled her eyes at the men.

Quinton could not help but chuckle.

"What?" she purposed.

He shook his head. "It's usually just myself and Sky that gets in trouble, I am just glad the wealth is getting spread around."

"Whatever. I am tired, hungry, thirsty, and I have to pee. I want to kill this guy and be done with this. So can we get a move on, please?" Sensing that her temper was flaring again, Sky got to his feet in a hurry, dashing for the trail the killer had left in the glade. Extending hands back, he extracted the two longest blades from his waist. In crisscross motions, he started chopping away vine and shrub without missing a step. The others ran quickly along the path he created. Before moments had ticked by, they were out of the glade and into the trees, where they halted long enough to determine where they were and which way to go. Sky found the pattern of paws, then a small boot print, followed by the track of a larger footed man.

"This way," he voiced, breaking into a trot. Spotting the truck, he halted. The others did the same.

"A cabin," Quinton acknowledged.

At that moment, a dim lantern flickered inside. Instinctively, the crew ducked further into the dark.

23

Using a Phillips head screwdriver he found on a table in the living room, Corin frantically pried the short boards up from the floor of the kitchen. One, two, and then three popped up; he yanked them back, breaking off the ends. No matter, he could get one hand in. Feeling for the stashed bundles of money, he removed each stack, stuffing them in his duffel bag. Suddenly, a board creaked behind him. Turning, he was met with the cold stare of the woman who was normally with the dog.

Looking about him, he asked, "Where is the mutt, did he not survive the fall?" Corin smiled at the prospect.

She twisted a grimace, "He survived well and good. If you like, say hello to him." She pointed away from her over Corin, who was still crouched on the floor. He spun around on his rump; the beast he had tried to eliminate was blocking his exit.

Titan growled deeply, the anger he felt inside rippling through his veins, crawling along his skin. He could scarcely contain himself. Corin sucked in a large gulp of air, scooting back on his haunches and dragging the duffel bag with him, until his back hit the kitchen cabinets. He could go no farther. Leaning into the cabinets for leverage, he brought himself to his feet. Shawnee turned sideways, readying herself for his lunge, hand clasped around the knife blade behind her back. Titan curled the tips of thick claws into the rough oak floor, preparing to leap. Corin assessed his situation, it was not good. With an unexpected quickness, he twisted at the hip, palming the sink lip and hopping upon the counter. He dove headlong through the thin window pane, all the while clinging tightly to the duffel bag.

He landed in a tumble outside.

Without hesitation, Titan jumped for the busted window, but was caught mid-air by Shawnee. Both fell hard to the floor.

"Can't risk the glass cutting your belly open," she shouted as she got to her feet. Snatching up the flashlight rolling on the floor, she scrambled for the door.

The group waiting in the woods was creeping for the house as soon as they heard the glass breaking on the other side of the cabin. As they reached the porch, Shawnee and Titan flew out the front door, hurdling over the railing and making for the opposite woods. They gathered their feet beneath them, intent on catching up to them. Sky let out a pack call that both Shawnee and Titan heard, although neither responded in their haste to catch the killer. Corin ran hard for the dry creek bed; he could make better time that way he thought. His arm was bleeding badly; the thin glass was easy to break, but a jagged piece had stayed in place, cutting his forearm as he dove through it. He held onto the wound, trying to stem the flow. Stumbling into the creek bed, he looked back to see if he was being pursued. It was too dark to tell, and he had dropped his flashlight at the lodge. At least he had his bag, he delighted. Again, he started running – he had to keep going!

Titan had no need for his night vision to find this fiend; he left a trail of blood for him to follow, and the moon had decided to grace his path. He rounded a turn at top speed, scratching furiously at the Earth, changing his direction. The evil thing he sought was headed for the gloom of the dry creek bed. Reaching its edge, he did not slow but jumped, becoming airborne and then landing in the creek bed with a thunderous impact. The hawk, joining the fray, screeched above him. Titan wasted no time acknowledging the bird; he continued the hunt. Shawnee jumped into the base of the creek bed after him. Sky, Quinton, Laura, and Shawn close behind also picked up the chase. Almost there, Corin gritted. He was trying to get to a hunting trail that would lead him to the main road, where he could hitch a ride on the premise of needing a doctor; which he actually might.

The fires flamed up across the creek bed in unison. Corin ceased advancing. Taking in the breadth of the bright orange fires, he was bewildered at this new development. He looked right, intending to jet up the embankment, but a line of Native American-looking soldiers notched arrows to bows as they stepped out of the dark to the edge of the non-existent creek. He swung to his left, but the same scene befell him there. Eyes darting back to the fires, he watched in near slow motion as a buckskin-clothed warrior stepped between two biers. The long fringe on his sleeves and pants legs swayed with each amelioration causing sparks to fly up from the fires as he passed by them.

Corin began to experience true fear. The warrior's menacing movement created the appearance of gliding toward him in dangerous and ominous tones. He squinted. His eyes must be deceiving him, for it seemed a blanket of tiny winged creatures flapped as thick as a cloud at the warrior's back, the illumination of the fire causing them to glow in a brilliant frosty white. If events could not be stranger, a large chocolate brown Red-Tailed Hawk swept down on a current, perching itself nimbly on the big man's left shoulder. The warrior never broke his rhythm as his mouth opened, releasing a roaring command, "Death Dog Cease!"

Corin rotated to his rear, ducking as the dog sailed over his head, touching down between him and the buckskin warrior. The warrior halted as the big dog spun on massive paws, claws raking half-moon patterns deep in the rocky dirt. The man's long black hair flowed fluidly around his shoulders from the sudden stop.

Addressing Corin, the warrior said, "He wishes your death, this one," casting his eyes down to Titan.

On his shoulder, Thunder screeched. The warrior lifted his head toward the bird, then back to Corin. "Apparently, so does his Keeper."

Corin was dumbfounded, wondering if he had bumped his head and was dreaming some drug-induced nightmare.

"Nice of you to join me, daughter, and you four as well," acknowledging the arrival of Quinton, Sky and the rest.

Corin faced Shawnee, realizing now how much trouble he was really in; *his daughter*, he vexed.

Quinton took several steps before Sky backhanded him hard against the chest to detain him.

Bear-who-will-not-hibernate continued. "You have a choice, Death-Dealer. You can cause your own demise this night, or we can assist you."

Blood ran down Corin's arm, dripping to the ground from the end of a fingertip. He clenched his fist despite the pain it caused.

"There are no other choices, Mr. Wester," Chandler added, stepping around his Chief, pausing at his right side.

The Chief's gaze never left his prey.

Corin stared at Chandler with hate. "I would rather go out my own way, thank you," Corin seethed.

"Very well. Sky!" Bear called.

"Yes, great Chief," Sky responded knowingly. He approached Corin, facing him sternly. Sheathing the long blade in his hand, he pulled a smaller thinner edged knife from his waist.

Corin tensed as Sky flipped the knife in his hand, offering him the handle. He hesitated, finally taking the weapon. He thought about gutting the fool for giving it to him, but decided against it for the moment. Sky backed away to his Chief's left side. Thunder jumped from Bear's shoulder to Sky's, his naked flesh twitching as the bird furled talons inward short of piercing the epidermis.

"It is for your own throat," Bear explained without emotion. Corin looked at the knife, and thought about what to do. Titan, observing the knife in the murderer's grasp, rolled gray-black lips away from pointed fangs, rumbling out a warning. He faced the dog, loathing consuming him as if the fires beyond were licking at his flesh. Clenching his jaws in decision, he burst toward the dog, elevating the knife with brutal intent. Chandler grabbed for the dog knowing that no command would halt him, but Titan was already contracting leg muscles to meet the man in transition. Instead, Chandler's momentum at missing the dog took him directly in the path of an arrow that skirted off a metal buckle on Corin's duffel bag strap and took Chandler in the side. A unisonous chorus of weapons headed for one target: Corin. Twenty elite guards surrounded Chief Spirit before the arrow that hit Chandler had even pierced his side. As Titan's body flew through the air to impact the evil he sought, Sky had sent two throwing knives toward the man; one headed for his throat, the other he had to deflect at the last minute to miss the Death Dog. Laura and Shawn both sent a bullet spiraling for a shoulder blade; they hit even as Quinton had seamlessly pulled a garrote from a leather band at his wrist, swinging it around Corin's neck. The appulse of Titan's paws against Corin's shoulders and waist sent the man over backwards; with Quinton affixed rearward, hands still twisting cable about his throat. The arrows protruding from Corin's back snapped as they impinged the ground, driving them deeper into already expiring organs. Titan stared into Corin's eyes as he stood atop the man, watching the life fade completely from the orbs; he felt no pity even as he watched the dark powdery ebb depart the body. Titan could feel the defilement of the essence, as if it were drenched in wickedness and absorbed with disease. He stepped away from it, watching as it flitted about confused, seeking a portal to anyplace where it could hide. The big dog shuddered from the elemental portrayal of rancor it exuded; eventually, it ceased to have even coagulation, disappearing into the dust of the night.

Quinton wiggled out from under the dead man, kicking at him to free his legs. Bear strode to the corpse, observing as Sky retrieved his blade from the damaged throat, wiping blood off on the dead man's shirt. Over-kill perhaps, Bear considered, but he had not been willing to take any chances with this one. He had decided mass force was necessary.

"Irishman," Bear said with finality.

The grounded tone created pavor down Shawn's spine. Nothing struck such anxiety in him as the Chief addressing him directly. "Ye...Yes, Sir?"

"You and Laura will take care of getting the trash taken out. Yes?"

"Of course we will," Laura piped in, unfazed by the persona of the Chief.

Bear nodded. To Stone, he asked, "Chandler?"

"He is on his way to the hospital. The wound does not look beyond repair."

Again, Bear nodded. He swept moccasin feet past the dead man, returning to his entourage manning the fires.

"I will take care of it," said Stone at his heels.

Chandler left the hospital a week later, returning to Shawnee's house. The arrow had slit several vessels that needed finite surgery by a specialist. It turned out to be a blessing in disguise, since upon performing surgery Doctors discovered Chandler's appendix was preparing to rupture. Sore from numerous sutures, he shuffled around the house, bored out of his mind but thankful the whole affair had ended.

Over midnight hot tea, Shawnee asked, "How did you not know you had appendicitis?"

"I don't know," he winced. "I guess I was just too busy to be in any pain. I am making up for it now."

"Better you than me, hoss," Quinton added. Maneuvering behind his friend, Quinton offered, "Let us get you in bed, you need your rest."

Chandler palmed the kitchen table, readying to stand.

Wrapping his hands under Chandler's armpits, Quinton prepared to assist him; but before the pair could follow through, a sleepwalking Sky cornered the hallway into the kitchen... stark naked.

Quinton straightened, "You have got to be kidding me."

All three watched as he opened the refrigerator door, selected absolutely nothing, then returned to the hall on his way to the room where he slept, closing the door behind him. Shawnee could not contain herself, and burst out in laughter bringing tears to her eyes. Chandler begged her to stop before he too began to chuckle, causing him more pain.

Quinton, exasperated by Sky's exhibitionism, slid hands beneath Chandler's armpits once again and complained, "If you two are done, I would like to get to bed myself. If I can, in fact, sleep after that picture has been imposed upon my mind."

Shawnee involuntarily expelled a mouth full of tea in a fit of humor at Quinton's expense. He eyed her despondently. He huffed, walking Chandler a bit too roughly to the room they were sharing during his convalescence.

Titan collapsed into sleeping bliss upon returning home. His grandfather Chief was already on his way back to Kentucky with his war-band; but before he left, he kissed Titan on the head, telling him, "Well done, Death Dog!" Titan's chest had swelled at the praise.

Now drifting in a dream state, he sat on a precipice overlooking a lapping ocean shore. There was a strange smell of salt and sea life on the wind. A Sea-Lion balked at Titan's elevated station on the escarpment. He peered down at the odd creature, thinking only about how peaceful it was here.

"You excelled in your task, young one."

Thinking back to the demise of the man in the gulley, he responded, *"Thank you, Father, but I was not the one to take the man to his end, there were many who did this."*

"I am pleased you are able to say it is so, it proves you are maturing."

"I am not in any trouble then?"

"No, though I am sure in time you will find some."

Titan, weary, laid his chest and belly against the cool earth beneath him. An accommodating breeze enveloped his mind, soothing his thoughts. Thunder swooped onto a boulder, warning the Sea-Lion to quiet its protests. *"Rest Titan. All too soon, you will be needed again. Regain strength in this place, for as much as light dwells in the world, so does the dark and the dust."* Titan rolled over on his side, and was instantly oblivious to the world; light or dark.

THE END

WORKS CONSULTED

Howard, James H. SHAWNEE: <u>The Ceremonialism of a Native American Tribe and its Cultural Background</u>. Athens: Ohio University Press, 1981.

Chrisley, Ronald L. <u>An Introduction to the Shawnee Language.</u> North Baltimore: R.L. Chrisley, 1992.

Ramsland, Katherine. <u>The Forensic Science of C.S.I.</u> New York: Berkley Publishing Group, 2001.

Holmes Ronald M., and Stephen T. Holmes. <u>Profiling Violent Crimes:</u> <u>An Investigative Tool</u>. 4th ed. California: SAGE Publications Ltd.

www.ingramcontent.com/pod-product-compliance
Lightning Source LLC
Chambersburg PA
CBHW070440120726
47910CB00003B/864